Aust

F/S

G000139772

SPINIFEX &
SUNFLOWERS

GUYRA SHIRE LIBRARY

G0000305111

Avan Stallard was born and raised in the south-west of Western Australia, where he was surrounded by countless books, animals and chainsaws, though which of those had the greatest influence is still up for debate.

As a child he harboured grand plans to become a barrister, and went on to complete a law degree at the University of Western Australia. However, the reality did not match the fantasy, and he never practised. Instead, he pursued an interest in history with a PhD at the University of Queensland where he taught Australian history, won the Dean's Award for Excellence and became a furniture removalist.

He returned to Western Australia and worked as a guard at an immigration detention centre, the experience of which inspired this novel.

He and his wife now live in the north of Spain where Avan has been known to take a long winter dip in the cold Atlantic, after which his words are always slurred, though only sometimes on the page.

Avan is the author of the history book *Antipodes: In Search of the Southern Continent*. He continues to write novels and works as an editor.

INCUBUS

It's early and I'm driving through the bush-covered hills of the Darling Range east of Perth. A hangover is coming on hard and fast, and I know exactly what it needs.

I pull into the car park of the Mundaring bakery. I kill the engine, swing a leg over my bike and begin what very nearly counts as a skip toward the bakery door, such is my lust for a pie. I stop when I hear a crashing sound.

I look around, but there are no cars backing into poles, only my motorbike on the ground. It doesn't make sense. There's nothing near it. I go back and pick the bastard up. It's a heavy machine — a tourer — not the sort of thing you want to be lifting in my state. Once I have it up, I lean it back over. It drops to the ground again.

That's when I realise the kickstand's not out. So I pick up the bike, which seems even harder the second time, and extend the kickstand, whereupon it leans gently to the side. I don't check for new dents or scratches.

I totter into the bakery. The lady at the counter says, "Are you ok?"

And I say, "I'll have a steak and kidney pie, please."

I get a carton of flavoured milk from the fridge — the green one catches my eye and I don't think twice. I sit down and eat and drink in a vacant stupor. Once finished, I lean back and take a breath and presume myself cured. But then, partially revived, a thought comes.

Normally mine is a good motorbike, the sort that does as told. So why would it do that—fall down—on such a morning as this when I'm clearly in no state to be picking up great pieces of unyielding steel?

The caffeine or sugar or God knows what else that's hidden in green milk suddenly kicks in and a wave of clarity sweeps my mind. The whole sorry bike-dropping affair becomes eminently explicable. Which is to say, I forgot to extend the kickstand because I'm still drunk. Drunk as a boiled owl.

Before anything worse can happen, I buy a custard tart for morning tea and drive the last forty-five minutes to the Northam Racecourse, park my bike with the use of the kickstand and head inside. A few people say hello. A few people mention that I don't look too good and ask if I'm sick. I say yeah, I might be a bit sick.

I could just as well mention that I'm drunk. None of this lot would care. I'm already assured of the job—in fact, I'm already on the payroll—so my presence at the training course, however shabby, will suffice.

RACECOURSE

It's at a racecourse — of all places, we're being taught how to be refugee-prison guards at a racecourse. I don't know why, and nor do they. That also happens to be the first lesson of training: nobody in this system knows the answer to any "why" question. Shit just is.

The second lesson is that I am the only one who calls refugee prison "refugee prison". And that's a big lesson. That lesson is retaught every day. Words matter. Not words like wanker, slut, poofter, whore: to be used at will and without discretion. No, we're talking the far more important words of bureaucrats. So a refugee prison is actually an "immigration detention centre", and the refugees are actually "clients".

I head around the back of the "training centre", looking for Alfred. I don't want to drive here drunk again. There are too many kangaroos on the roads between Northam and Perth. If I can be so drunk as to not know how to park my motorbike, I might not be up to dodging Skippy — who is, despite every TV series, documentary and tourism advertisement ever shown, a wilful idiot and inveterate cunt. And, while I appreciate this is verboten to say in Australia, I say it anyway because I know it for a plain and obvious truth.

Until a person has lived with roos they have no standing to speak on the topic. We took in a total of four joeys throughout my childhood in Manjimup, each orphaned after a car hit the mother. It's common for the young ones to survive — the roo pouch is like a protective airbag. Mum couldn't bring herself to drive past a fresh carcass and not check, digging her hand into the pouch to see if there was a scared sack of bone and fur hiding inside. She would put the young and unviable ones out of their misery, but if they were far enough along she brought them home.

Clem hated it. He'd rant and rave, but Mum was the boss when it came to those sorts of things. Shitter—so named for her habit of shitting all across the verandah every day of her life when there was a big yard and plenty of bush to crap in—was the best of them, and even she was a moody ingrate. She'd let you give her a quick scratch under the cheek or behind the ear, then she'd suddenly decide she'd had enough and lean back on her tail and take a swing. It wouldn't be a mischievous swing, either, like a playful kitten. It was the sort of swing that said, "When I'm big enough I will rip your guts out with my massive mono-claw, human scum, but until then I will shit on your verandah and eat your cat food as I please." Still, I was upset when a dog got her. Even Clem was, the unsentimental prick.

The point being, there are thousands of unreasonable roos to dodge on the roads. Of course, I could just resolve to not get drunk to the point where I'm still drunk in the morning. But it wouldn't be worth a damn. Sober and rational promises are wonderful while sober and rational; they're worth nothing in the heat of the moment. Like when your cock is hard, or you're having a brew and that pesky incubus says screw it, Nick, have another, have another ten. I know he'll get me, sooner or later—the incubus, Skippy, one of them.

I find Alfred out the back on the steeples, smoking a cigarette, looking at the only green grass for miles. He's one of the few people who drives to Northam with an empty car. I arrange for him to give me a lift from Perth each day and I agree to give him some money for petrol.

I get a cup of tea and head inside just as training begins. I

EXPERIMENT

Our principal trainer is named Warren. He's a big guy. Thick forearms. Fat head. He keeps breaking down the "complicated" bureaucrat rules about what us guards can do at refugee prison into simpler terms that are borderline retard-speak.

"Don't steal stuff."

"Don't have sex with clients."

I think Warren was really good at his former job, and is not so good at this job. He used to be a prison guard. A real one who got to call himself that because it was at an actual prison with murderers and rapists and expectorators. Warren keeps hinting about all the violence he saw, and the violence he dished out. Warren angry. Warren smash. Warren has never actually worked in a detention centre.

The training manual is a massive binder full of procedures, policies and rules. Warren explains that it has been adapted from the parent company's prison guard training manual. Where it said "prison" it now says "detention centre". Where it said "prisoner" or "inmate" it now says "client". Where it said "guard" or "correctional officer" it now says "client service officer". Of course, there are dozens of slippages where the manual talks about prison and guards and prisoners. Oops.

Warren trains us to do headcounts; there will be at least three per shift. He encourages us to recognise detainees by a number, not their name, because that's just how it's done in the centres. He teaches us radio protocols and the international system of code alerts: green for an escape attempt, black for officer needs assistance, red for fire, blue for medical emergencies.

We're given advice about not trusting our clients and all the horrible things we can expect. Warren shows instructional videos. There's one that shows a refugee casually escaping from a detention centre on Christmas Island by climbing over a fence while the guards look on. Scott is freaked out by this. He asks if the client is still roaming free, presumably living a Robinson Crusoe–like existence as the Christmas Island Yowie. No, he is not still roaming free, you fucking idiot.

We visit a medium security prison to receive first aid training. Our trainer for the day is a first aid–qualified prison guard. She gives lots of examples of things we might see and have to deal with, all of them drawn from her experience at the prison. She tells us that prisoners are generally unpleasant and sometimes deranged. It makes sense. I figure I might be deranged and unpleasant if I was locked up here. The complex is utterly devoid of signs of normal life. It's a massive square, enclosed by razor wire, surrounded by a barren security perimeter. Which is to say: looks like a prison, feels like a prison.

Throughout all this, my thoughts turn again and again to the research project of a goateed Stanford psychologist with the groovy name of Dr Zimbardo, which always reminds me of *Dr Zhivago*, a very fine film, two thumbs up. It came to be known as the Stanford Prison Experiment and, if it showed anything, it is that even the strongest characters will tend to act out the roles they are asked to perform, no matter how that clashes with their sensibilities and beliefs.

Four decades later, here we are, a bunch of average Australians about to be given a uniform and thrust into an institution bordered by fences and razor wire, saddled with a swag of rules and procedures that must be enforced and told that we are the enforcers. Oh, but fellers, ladies: you're not guards and it's not a prison. It's a detention centre filled with clients and you are client service officers.

Who do they think they're kidding? Well, Scott for one, the short fat bloke missing a front tooth who's still wondering about that escapee on Christmas Island. I think Scott might be a bit dumb.

ROY

We're sitting around going through the big folder of rules when Roy suddenly gets up and says, "Nah, can't do it, fuck it, I'm out, nah, not for me."

Old Cynthia, who is very sweet, goes to Roy and keeps asking what is wrong till Roy tells her he can't read so well. He's good with signs and labels, but sentences are difficult, though not impossible, unless they have big words, then they are impossible. A fair few of the sentences written by the white shirts do have big words.

Cynthia is nice and encouraging, and everyone else, too, because five minutes with Roy and you know he needs it. Fifty-nine, a bit thick, suffers from verbal diarrhoea, drives a 1987 Mitsubishi Triton, lives in a share house in a town in the dust-belt, been fired from more jobs than he's had, and speaks like John Jarratt in *Wolf Creek*. Where the hell is Roy going to go?

We plead with him to stay and he does; he says he'll stick the rest of the day out, see how it goes. After lunch, Roy seems a lot happier because Warren puts the folders away. He begins explaining "control techniques", then we pair up for some drills. Roy is a strong old bastard and mad as a cut snake. He completely ignores everything Warren says and just lays into the body pads with the sort of vigour Warren can't help but respect.

"Take that, you bastard!" Roy says after every blow. If you see and feel that sort of punch, as I do being Roy's partner, there are certain questions you've gotta ask.

"Roy, you get into many fights when you were younger?"

"Too right. I was a scrapper. Come from England when I was a little feller. Any bastard said something, *bam!* That fixed 'em."

The violence of punching and kicking pads is good for Roy. It's healing. It helps assuage his feelings of inadequacy after the episode this morning where Warren asked him to read out loud. Only problem is that Roy is starting to feel too comfortable. I can see why he's been fired from so many jobs. Now that we're up and about, a constant stream of shit flows from his mouth in a mixture of mumble and exclamation. "Fuck" and "shit" and "mate" are his punctuation.

Turns out Roy is an especially eager proponent of jokes involving rape, or violence, or rape and violence. Anytime another bloke is bent over, Roy is into him with a rape joke, or a spot of simulated fucking. I think it's funny. The sort of funny where someone is so irreverent and so clueless that you've just got to appreciate the utter absence of guile. He's like a twelve-year-old boy: spastic movements matched by boundless energy, thinks he knows everything, thinks he's hilarious, no conception of mental states that are not his own.

Roy wears on the other trainee guards. They wish he'd shut up. They wish Warren would ask him to read again. I wish he'd shut up. But I also hope he doesn't. Roy is an original. He isn't in the least average. He is so stupendously below average, he's precious. So, yeah, Roy and I are friends.

The next day's training is shifted from the racecourse without any racehorses to an office in the big city. I spent three years in Perth, so I know my way around. To Roy, though, Perth is a concrete labyrinth. He manages to find his way to the office, where he makes a farce of the computer-based training, then when it's quits he has to find his way to a mate's joint in Claremont. Roy asks Nige if he drove; give us a lift, will ya mate? Apparently he didn't drive. Roy asks Tom if he drove—just need a lift to Claremont. Oh, wrong direction. Roy asks Cynthia if she drove, but Cynthia is going in the wrong direction, too. The group is beginning to disperse and so Roy just starts asking the group as a whole, calling out, pleading with somebody, anybody, to give him a lift.

They walk off. To the last man and woman, they walk off. Because I'm a bona fide saint of a man, I bother to hang around long enough to see if Roy is going to get a lift. I can't give him a lift myself because I drive a motorbike and I've only got one helmet. With everyone else gone, Roy thinks he's stranded. I tell him not to worry. He can easily get a direct bus to where he's going if he just walks up the road; the bus stop he needs to wait at will say bus #102.

Roy is nervous as shit, so I accompany him up the street, find the stop, wait with him, then deposit him on the bus. Roy is effusive. He's floored that I bothered to stick around because, I realise, Roy isn't like that twelve-year-old kid. Roy knows he is annoying and a bit fucked in the head and he doesn't expect any help from anyone, ever, because that's what he's learned to expect in life. So I give him five minutes of my time and now we're mates forever. Seriously, Roy thinks I'm great.

I dunno what the point to that story is, but there is a point.

TITS

Chantal is small and cute. Cherubic face, nice tits. She's only eighteen, or maybe nineteen, but, whatever her age, she looks young and talks young and acts young. She's the best-looking female at training, so I try to flirt with her, but she is just so clueless that I literally cannot find anything to say to her that allows the spark of real conversation.

Chantal is very earnest about one topic: being raped. Marilyn the Polish emigrant is forty years older than Chantal and she doesn't want to get raped, either. I guess none of us want to get raped, but the rest of us are pretty blasé; it only really animates Chantal and Marilyn. They talk about it a lot. So Chantal asks Warren about getting raped in refugee prison.

Warren does nothing to allay her fears. Even though we are in Western Australia and have no prospect of being sent to New South Wales, Warren tells us about an infamous client he heard about in a little suburb of Sydney called Villawood.

This client is a bad man. An angry man. A very, very big man who doesn't speak great English, just enough to threaten to rape any female client service officer he comes into contact with. Sometimes he threatens to rape the male officers, too. Warren tells us that the man has in fact tried before and will try again if given half a chance.

So this is what Chantal takes away from today's training: a big, deranged, angry Middle Eastern man with a dirty boner wants to rape you. I think this might colour Chantal's impression of her "clients", and she hasn't even met one yet. I wonder if the refugees are having the same conversations about us.

I still haven't given up on flirting with Chantal, so the next day I sit at the same table as her for our lunch break. We're talking about nothing, because that is all Chantal can talk about. I guess I'm just happy enough to be at the table, sneaking furtive glances at her tits. Chantal tells us she's lived in Northam all her life. She says that she doesn't know much about "things" or "places". She's saying that she's not very worldly, which is actually the sort of self-aware comment that makes me think there may be more to her. Then she tells us that she's never met an Arab. Then she says, "I'm probably a bit racist."

"What do you mean?" I ask.

"You know, just calling them ragheads and camel fuckers, that sort of thing."

She giggles a bit. I bite down on my sandwich and go back to sneaking glances at her tits.

The next day, I don't bother sitting at Chantal's table for lunch. Talking to her is too hard. But I haven't given up on tits, so I sit at Meg's table, which is what we call her even though she introduced herself as Meghan, the version of Meghan with the stupid pronunciation that sounds like leggin', like when you're leggin' it after eggin' someone's Corolla.

Meg's by no means unattractive, but her face isn't as pretty as Chantal's. Still, she has nice eyes, and nice lips. Not a bad arse, too, ample and amply round—likewise her tits. Plus, she's talkative, the sort of talkative that drives itself without any outside stimulus, so it's easy to be in her presence and look at her tits without overly taxing one's brain. And I know that sounds terrible, like I'm a dirty lech, but it's not as though I'm doing anything evil. I'm being affable while I look at tits. And either Meg doesn't notice or she does notice and she doesn't mind, because she starts to seek me out during breaks and we become friends. Which, by default, means I become friendly with her buddy, Scott, the gap-toothed dwarf with a pot gut.

ROLES

The last day of training is underwhelming. We sign a bunch of forms and get our uniform. It's a blue polo shirt. I was expecting something more. Something prison-guardesque.

I have a chat with Roy. He's excited to finally get to bash some blokes and taser some blokes and rape some blokes. Thankfully, we aren't issued tasers.

Meg and Scott and pretty much all of us are excited about the money. It will be nice, there's no denying it. Something like two grand a week, maybe more with all the penalties and allowances. I don't think a single one of us here has ever seen that sort of moolah.

But there's also apprehension. None of us has ever met a refugee. We still don't know what to expect—anything from normal blokes to deranged fuckwits. Of everyone, I'm among the most sanguine. I've read a lot, travelled a lot, watched plenty of documentaries, so I know that, for the most part, refugees are just average people with middle-class aspirations who happen to come from another country. I have sympathy for what they've gone through and wish they had better lives, but at the same time I've seen how letting an unending tide of refugees into a country can lead to horrible societal rifts like in France or Britain. Compassion is great—I'm all for compassion—but not at any cost.

So, while I can't speak for my colleagues, I have a fairly strong sense of how the next few months are going to play out for me.

Basically, I'm going to go to my refugee prison in the middle of nowhere and try to be a nice guy because, even though I don't want to encourage an influx of asylum seekers, I know the refugees who have made it here don't want to be locked up and will probably be decent people. I don't want to add to their misery. If I can do something nice for them, I'll do something nice for them. But I'm not going to shed a tear, and I'm not seeking to change the world. I'm not Mother Conscience — I'm just trying to pay off an outstanding credit card balance from a trip to South America. Yeah, it's not even anything exciting like a drug debt or newborn bastard.

The fact is, I will become a guard. Regardless of what they call me, no matter how clever I am or how immune I think I am to societal rules and expectations, the moment I walk behind those fences I am a refugee-prison guard and I will become a refugee-prison guard. Even Dr Zimbardo got lost in the power trip and his performance as superintendent in the fake prison at Stanford. If I learned anything from reading his memoir, it's that we act out the roles we fill whether we intend to or not — and I've just graduated from trainee to guard. Simple as that.

WELCOME

We get off a tiny steel lozenge on a street known as Derby Airport. A moist fist punches me in the face before I realise it's actually a vicious flailing with a steamed lettuce before I realise it's just the wind. A hot, sticky, suffocating wind that has the ineffable quality of weighing on you from all sides.

It somehow manages to make my hangover worse and I silently curse Keely for forcing the last of his bottle of Johnnie Walker Black down my throat by telling me to not drink his fucking Johnnie Walker Black—and then promptly passing out. I take a swig of water from my bottle and breathe, deep as I can, as I gaze out upon a strange land.

I was born and raised in a farm and forestry town in the south-west. I haven't been back in five years, but it remains the lens through which I view the world. So when I see trees, I'm looking for the karri and jarrah giants of eucalypt forest. When I take in the sweep of an entire horizon of land, I'm comparing it to the hills and valleys of dairy farm and vineyard. And when I taste the air, I'm searching for the pollens and oils I know should be there.

Here, all I taste is dust. All I see is dust—that, and low-lying scrub, the colours monotonous silver or khaki. But the real gut punch is the land itself. The flatness. It's like old parchment laid over an earth-sized sphere. That may be great for attempts to break the land-speed record in jet engine dragsters; otherwise, it's just alien and hostile.

I climb down from the plane and collect my bag. A van is waiting to whisk us to the centre, which isn't in town—it's fifty kilometres south-east, even further into the dry, desolate interior.

The drive feels long. There is nothing to punctuate the view. I certainly don't see the picturesque white sands and cerulean waters that people visualise when thinking about this part of the world. That would be Broome, the Australia of postcards and promises, two hours to the south-west. But we're not in Broome. We're in the shire of Derby, which, I've decided, is a shithole.

Of course, these days, now that we've learned to cast off outmoded colonial ways of looking at the Australian strangeness and quit seeking reproductions of Europe, even places like Derby are meant to be unique and precious and hold their own special type of beauty.

Right—and while the shiteaters in the tourism bureaus keep telling gullible Japanese and German tourists that, the fact is, I've landed in a unique, special type of shithole. It's little wonder the white shirts decided to put a refugee prison out here. You get off that plane or bus and you don't even think you're in Australia. You think you're in Africa, and I don't mean the good bits.

We pull onto a side road and cross a fence-line, pass some checkpoints that remind us the detention centre is situated on air force land, pass another fence, then pull into a parking lot. There's a big sign that says "Welcome to Curtin".

I guess time is money, so, almost immediately, our induction begins. We're introduced to chief swinging-dick Benedict. He's one of the senior managers who spends time in the headquarters and around the grounds. He's a big bloke, broad and thickset, obviously a formidable man back in his prime. He's carrying a good few years on his face, and a slight stoop affects his posture when he's standing, but he looks like he could still do some damage.

his scars. It makes me feel strange. Sick sort of strange. If I met someone in the real world who'd taken a razor to their arms, I'd know they were mentally ill and it would be a thing. I'd probably do something, or say something, or make sure I didn't say something. But I don't know what it is here. I'm just sitting next to this guy as if we're all waiting for a bus that isn't coming. I guess I'm not yet into the whole guard thing enough to just dismiss it.

The detainee goes back inside. He gets out a little card, which I recognise as a phone card that gives you credit to call overseas, then he dials a number on a landline. Darren scribbles his signature at various points on the paperwork, while providing a running commentary. I'm not really paying attention; I'm more interested in the detainee who is talking on the phone in a language I don't understand. I can tell he's upset. His voice is rising.

Darren doesn't look up. He must have seen and heard everything in the centre by now, so it probably doesn't even register when the client starts crying. The man's speech gets faster and louder, and his crying quickly escalates into the territory of wailing.

It's not half an hour into my first shift. There is a Middle Eastern man with a shredded arm a few metres from me, bawling hysterically. What the hell am I meant to do? Darren still hasn't even acknowledged he's there. I'm worried other officers are going to come along and want to know what is going on, because the sound coming out of this guy is woeful. I guess I've only ever seen people cry while trying to hold it back, the British way, whereas this guy is fully into it, his grief like something out of a movie.

Eventually the phone call ends and the man's tears subside. He walks outside and sits on the step. The three of us are silent. Then the client lifts his head and says to Darren, "Can I have tea?"

I'm surprised by his good English. I guess after the phone

conversation, and considering no words had been exchanged up until that point, I'd assumed he couldn't speak our language. I say to Darren that I can make it, so he tells me to go to the lunch room, which is only a building over. I ask the man how he wants it, and he says black, three sugars. I go across, make the tea, then bring it back. It's a little too full, so rather than give it directly to him, I place it on the fold-up table.

"Thank you," he says, and smiles. A quick sensation of something flashes through me. I peg it as that feeling you get when you're recognised for doing something nice for somebody.

Then I think how stupid that is. Given his phone conversation, I wouldn't be surprised if this poor prick has family in Iraq or somewhere who've just been obliterated by a cluster bomb or IED. Compared to that, what is a cup of tea?

BARBARIANS

A few hours later I'm stationed in the canteen. It's a very low-key task where all that is required is my presence, but it does mark my first stint working as a guard for real.

Basically, I stand around while ensuring there is no trouble. The way the canteen works is that each week the detainees are given fifty credit points (roughly equivalent to fifty dollars), which they can redeem for various foods, hygiene products, smokes, drinks, phone cards and so on. Junk food seems to be the most prized luxury item.

Time and again a detainee walks away with a bag full of soft drinks or juice boxes, sees me and insists I take one. "Is hot, take, take." I must have refused offers from some twenty detainees for drinks and chips before one chap is so insistent he just leaves the drink on the rail and walks off.

After the canteen closes, I'm sent to the medical centre waiting room with about fifteen detainees. I don't really know what I'm meant to be doing. I suppose it's just another case of being a presence, a lot like the role of teachers in shitty schools, not really achieving anything, just hoping that enough crayons and bodies will stop the barbarians from burning down the buildings until they are sent home and become someone else's problem.

After a few minutes of waiting in the medical centre, it's a detainee's turn to see the nurse.

"MIL-98?"

I just about choke when I hear it. I see my colleague sitting at the desk with a folder and a list. It contains both the detainee's name and his alpha-numeric identifier. The name is tricky and the identifier convenient, but I just can't believe it's happening for real, even though we were told during training it's how things work. Honestly, anyone with half an education and the most basic knowledge of history should know better. Shit, anyone who reads novels or watches movies should know better.

The procession of refugees called by their boat identifier continues. I'm not comfortable with it, but what can I do? At least the refugees don't seem fazed. They just want to see the nurse or psychiatrist.

Hours tick by as I sit on my arse, getting paid, while the nameless barbarians are kind enough not to burn the building to the ground.

WAKE

I'm tired. There's not enough time. I didn't even drink last night. I realise now that my waking hours are going to be consumed by a twelve-hour shift, two hours of travel, half an hour getting showered and changed morning and night, then there's preparing dinner and eating it, which is at least half an hour unless you're a dickhead who eats two minute noodles, so, what, that leaves a bit over nine hours to fit in all leisure, all unwinding, all socialising, any chores, a quick wank, exercise and adequate sleep? Impossible.

Today I'm stationed in Red Compound. Bailey, a few years my junior, takes me under his wing. He's easy-going, and it only takes me about ten minutes to realise he's a pretty smart guy. I'm actually a bit surprised he works here. Sharp, young, personable—there's got to be better jobs he could be doing.

"How'd you end up here?" I ask.

"I'm from Fitzroy Crossing. Not that much full-time work there, so I found this job up here and they offered a better roster if you live in town. It's not too bad, but I dunno how much longer I'll stay."

"What else you planning on doing?"

"I'm thinking about going to uni, maybe doing a degree if I can get in."

"What area?"

"I'm not sure. My sister's a teacher, so maybe teaching. Or maybe something like film."

"Nice. What sort of films you like?"

"Everything. I just saw an old Australian film that's been rereleased. It's called *Wake in Fright*. It's bat-shit crazy, but probably the best Australian film ever made," says Bailey.

"Hell yeah, I saw it a while back, it was in some of the little cinemas." I'm quietly impressed. Your average bogan definitely would not know *Wake in Fright*.

"Hey, how young is Jack Thompson in it? He would have been a loose man back then," says Bailey.

"For sure. You look at that film, they must have all been pretty loose. They probably just found some shithole town and paid the locals to drink and fight for a week," I say.

"Yeah, no, I think they basically did, I read something about it, how it was shot on location. And you know that the roo-shooting scene was real? They went out with actual roo-shooters and shot the footage. I'll tell you something you won't see on the credits—that notice you normally get about no animals being harmed in the making of the film."

"Yeah, right, it looked pretty real," I say. "I thought they must have just gone out themselves: 'There you go, Thomo, go murder Skippy. And don't forget to smile!' "

Bailey laughs.

"You go shooting up here?" I ask.

"I used to, not much now though. I've got a mate on a farm out from Broome. He drove up a few months ago and brought his guns, so we went out with another mate. We just drove around in some empty paddocks shooting shit. Then there's these lights coming and we're like, 'Yep, not good.' This ute pulls up and an old cocky gets out with his gun. He wants to know what we're doing on his farm; he reckons he's going to call the cops. But my other mate sort of knew him because his son plays on the same footy team, so basically he just told us to piss off and never come back."

"Jesus. The old bastard could have shot the lot of you and buried you on his land."

"Yep."

This time I laugh. I suppose nothing we've said is exactly funny, but sometimes you laugh at things anyway.

The hours trickle by. Lunchtime, Bailey and I are stationed in the detainees' mess. Our job is to make sure nothing goes out apart from the detainee's cup, plate, bowl and a single piece of fruit. Two pieces of fruit could lead to an escape attempt, and three—almost certainly a riot. Which is to say, Bailey and I just stand around shooting the shit. We're talking about what the township of Derby is like.

"You know that Chris Rock joke?" asks Bailey. "The one about the difference between a black man and a nigger? 'Ain't nobody who hates the black man. But everybody hates a nigger.' Heard it?"

"Um, don't think so."

Bailey adopts a stance like he's addressing an audience. The clever bastard has memorised the entire monologue.

"See, there's black people, and then there's niggers. The niggers have got to go. You know the worst thing about niggers? A nigger will brag about some shit a normal man just does. A nigger will say some shit like, 'I take care of my kids.' You're supposed to, you dumb motherfucker!"

I laugh a true laugh because that's a clever little piece, and I can just imagine Chris Rock saying it in his deranged screech, but then I see an Afghani man glance our way and it occurs to me that here and now might not be the best time and place to be yakking it up over what might be considered—when told by a white man—a racist joke. I mean, of course you can laugh at race or racism and that is not itself racist. But a joke about scumbag African-Americans told by a white Australian who's shouting nigger this and nigger that? Honestly, I'm not sure.

Bailey's rendition of the Chris Rock monologue makes me think about a joke I haven't heard and haven't even thought about in a decade. When I was a kid it used to pass around every year as if it had just been conceived. I tried telling it myself, once, but my delivery has always been too flat, better suited to satire. It still got a laugh, but nothing like when my father told it. It went something like this:

> A truckie picks up a hitchhiker. The hitchhiker dozes off, when suddenly he's woken by a noise.
> CRASH! CRASH! BOONG!
> The hitchhiker sits up and says, "What's going on?"
> "Oh, we just hit an Abo," says the truck driver.
> "Oh, right," says the hitchhiker. "But what were the first two crashes?"
> "I had to go through two fences to get him!"

These days, your average urban Australian wouldn't think such a joke funny, but everyone thought it was hilarious when I was growing up, and I reckon it'd still get a decent reception if you whipped it out in the Manji pub or at a Harris family reunion.

Standing in the mess hall, looking about for displeased clients, I choke my mirth into a simpering grin, but I needn't bother. Nobody says anything. No one even looks irritated. Still, I wonder if I should say something to Bailey. Not bust his balls, just mention that maybe there's a time and place.

I decide to err on the side of caution and stay quiet, knowing that projections of rectitude rarely result in another man's mind being changed, and would definitely not endear me. I do, however, adopt a barren equanimity as Bailey delivers some advice.

"It's the same with the Indig' up here. I've lived in Derby three years now and some of them are ok. But you've gotta watch out for the coons. The other week I was on day shift, but the Indig' were having a party in the park, so I couldn't sleep. About 11 p.m. one of 'em started bashing his missus. Yeah, it was a pretty terrible sound, went on for a while. Then there was a bit of a commotion, and after that it was all over. Silence.

Yeah, mate, if you just keep to yourself and avoid the coons, you'll be right."

"Yeah, ok," I say.

I get Bailey's point—keep to yourself, don't get involved in shit you can't change anyway—yet I can't help but think, why didn't you do something? How could you stay in bed that whole time?

The hours tick by till, mercifully, it's home time. Jesus, these days feel long, long like the road back to Spinifex City, stretching out in a straight line till my vision fails ahead of the horizon.

SUGAR

I'm tired and bored and it's only lunch, only halfway through today's shift. I look around the mess hall, searching for stimulus. I see a couple of Sri Lankans get up and head my way. One of them walks ahead and extends his hand. We enjoy a manly handshake and I smile at the chap, thinking what a nice gesture it is for a detainee to welcome a guard.

The man asks my name and where I'm from. I begin to respond, but out of the corner of my eye I see his mate quickly walking past, sporting a bowl of desserts—also known as contraband. I realise that my welcome is no more than a diversionary tactic. I'm being played.

I peel off and stop the contraband runner. "Mate, you know you can't take that out."

"What, this, but I ..." he says, inching out the door.

"Oi, mate ..."

And he's off, single arm pumping, legs flailing, doing a runner. I watch him sprint away, a little shocked at the urgency of his exit, but mostly amused by the scene he's created. A dozen of his mates have now gathered—they all knew what he was doing. I shrug. What are we going to do: suit up the Emergency Response Team and bust down his door to retrieve a piece of chocolate cake? To be honest, I don't really get the whole contraband thing.

It's my job, though, and cracking down on the smuggling racquet is about as much excitement as I can expect. A little later I see an unusually light-skinned detainee with a handful of sugar sachets; he's not even trying to hide it.

"Mate, sorry, you're not meant to take them. You're meant to get the sugar from the office now."

He stands there, staring at me. "No?"

"Sorry, mate. No."

He nods toward Peter, who is in the middle of the hall.

"Yeah, go ask Peter."

The man walks over and speaks to Peter, who is the senior officer in the compound. Peter promptly waves to me to indicate it's fine. The man walks past, pocketing the sugar sachets. I shrug. He looks at me with what appears to be a mix of confusion and contempt.

Peter walks over. "Yeah, he's one of our special cases."

"Special cases?"

"His whole family died on that boat that sank off Indonesia a few days ago."

That boat — the one on the news. I'd seen the reports. A swag of asylum seekers were loaded onto some piece-of-shit fishing boat; it lost its engines, most of the people couldn't swim, so when it sank a few miles from the coast all but two people drowned. I thought it was unfortunate when I heard about it, but I guess unfortunate takes on a whole different meaning when it's someone's family.

I stand there, feeling stupid for enforcing such a petty rule. There's no one watching over me, no one forcing me to stop contraband from going out, so why did I automatically choose to follow the letter of the law and make life that little bit harder for the sorts of people who have parents being blown up in markets and siblings drowning at sea? Because I follow rules? Because I'm bored? Because I want to be good at my job? Not only are the rules utterly immaterial to my existence, they don't seem to have anything to do with safety.

If these are the stakes I'm dealing with — small graces to offset inestimable loss and pain — I don't believe I'll ever spot another detainee smuggling a goddamn thing. They could be walking out with the urn and I'm pretty sure I'd miss it. That's just how clever they're going to be, I guess.

MULTITUDES

I'm back at Spinifex City, cracking one of the last beers in the slab, when Roy wanders over, shirtless, sporting a handful of meat.

"Just put grease all over me doorknob, mate. Ah well, fuck it."

"Getting stuck in to some chook?"

"Yeah."

Roy rips into the chicken leg like a starving stray.

"You're a mad dog, Roy."

"Too right, mate."

I down my beer and Roy eats his chook, then I retire to check my internet connection and consult a site devoted to the appreciation of the womanly form.

Eight hours later I'm back at the centre, surrounded by dirt and tin. There's no sign of Roy. He's rostered on, but I didn't see him on the bus.

I'm standing at the door of the detainees' mess for the breakfast run. There are four other guards stationed in the hall. A detainee walks up to me.

"Officer, I am very sick, need Panadol," he says.

He's got a smile that reaches ear to ear. It doesn't look like the face of a sick man. I figure he must be taking the piss.

"Mate, you're taking the piss," I say.

"Need Panadol, officer."

"Well, mate, that woman up there, Grace, she'll be with you in five minutes."

"Five minutes?"

"Yep."

"Need it now."

"Yeah mate, in five minutes."

I guess it has begun—their testing me out to see how soft a target I am.

Roy finally arrives, two hours late. He's assigned to the same compound as me. I make him a cup of tea.

"Where've you been, mate?" I say.

"Had a shower, then laid back down on the bed. Just fuck'n nodded off, didn't I?"

He takes an interest in the cut-down knife I've been issued. It's a small blade shaped like a hook, the inner edge sharp, the outer edge and nub completely blunt. It is purpose-built for cutting nooses from necks. I show Roy the knob on the other end of the tool, used to break windows if ever trapped somewhere.

"What," says Roy, "use it for breakin' heads? Smack! Give 'em one in the back of the noggin. What's that? Bleedin' from the head? Where? Some bastard ..."

Ah, Roy, you hateful old prick. Yet I've seen him talking to the detainees and he's like a puppy around a new toy with them—I think he's excited just to have new people to talk to. Yesterday, I saw Roy playing table tennis with a group of Afghanis. He couldn't play for shit, but Roy still seemed to be having a great time, not a single broken head, severed limb or raped arsehole in sight. It's odd. I suspect Roy is a frustrated humourist, mostly frustrated from a lack of humour. His delivery is what gets me. Roy says everything with such gusto and conviction that you think surely he's a rapist with a sack of corpses in his backyard, yet the truth is, I don't think he means a single thing he says and I don't think he's any more set in his ways and opinions than a toddler.

Outside, we hear sounds of revelry. A group of detainees are celebrating something to do with the coming of Christmas. Roy asks Grace if he can go watch.

"Of course you can. But go with someone else."

That someone else is obviously going to be me, because I'm the only one who can tolerate Roy's verbiage. We follow the sound till we spot a group of about forty Sri Lankans gathered outside an activity room. They form a circle around a couple of men who are dancing vigorously. There is clapping and the beat of a drum. Soon as they see us, the Sri Lankans beckon us to enter the circle and show them our moves. We politely decline.

Grace wanders down from the officers' quarters. She watches for a while, then calls Roy over. There's a look on her face. She grabs Roy's hand and drags him into the circle. The Sri Lankans cheer "Dance! Dance!"

Roy is saying no, but his body and smile says yes. Then Grace abandons him, the sly bitch. Roy tries to retreat, but the circle closes and everyone is calling on him to dance. He pumps out a few hip thrusts, shuffles his feet and shakes his hands in the air.

I can't tell if it's how Roy dances, or how Roy thinks the Sri Lankans dance. I'm laughing and clapping from the back of the crowd. Roy then tries to flee the circle, but they won't let him. Roy clearly loves an audience, so he swings back into what might pass as a Bollywood shake of his head, throws up some half-arsed spirit fingers and finishes with a quick bow and wave. The crowd cheer him out.

Roy and I watch the festivities for a while. Roy is beaming. No doubt the highlight of his week. We walk back, Roy spilling words like a dog drinking water.

"You get to talking to 'em; good blokes, eh? Yeah I've enjoyed mixin' with 'em. Bloody good job, in't? You know, I can't blame 'em. If my family was bein' persecuted and raped and all that shit, I'd be on a boat, too. I see 'em and talk to 'em, especially the little Afghan ones. You're not meant to show sympathy are you, but you can feel it, can't ya?"

We get back to the officers' donga and make another cup of tea. I like tea but, really, it's just something to do. I ask Grace what the worst thing she's seen at the centre is. She tells me about the day sixteen Iranians protested over their lack of access to immigration officials. Opposite the administration compound, in the midday heat, they began cutting themselves with razors.

"That was probably the worst thing I've seen since being here. Blood everywhere. They were laid out on tarpaulins. I've had hangings and other things, but that was worse."

"I'd come in with a machete," says Roy. "*Schwt! Schwt!* You wanna slash-up? There ya go—get the machete into 'em, cut some limbs off. Just doin' what they wanted."

I stare, wide-eyed. What just happened to the man dancing with the detainees? What happened to the man who was sympathising with the detainees' plight? Roy is utterly schizophrenic.

A detainee from another compound has wandered over to the office where we're stationed. He knocks on the window. Grace slides it open.

"Yes?"

"Noodle?" he says.

Noodles are pretty much the only thing detainees can eat outside assigned meal times. Grace looks him up and down.

"You're not from Brown Compound, are you?" she asks, shaking her head. "Green? Red? Blue? What compound?"

"Green," the man says.

"You ask at own compound. Go away. Ask own compound."

Grace shuts the window. The man stands there a moment then turns and walks away.

Grace addresses me and Roy. "There's not enough noodles to be giving them out to clients from other compounds. They can fucking well get them where they're meant to."

"Up to me, I'd have 'em all locked down," says Roy. "I'd get the machete out. *Schwt! Schwt!* Back in there, you bastards."

Who is it that can tell me who I am? asked King Roy.

DEATHDAY

What is it about anniversaries? As if they are anything more than another shitty day. Yet some people can't help themselves. Some people even believe that the day is special and go to great lengths to make it so. I'm not one of them.

Besides, there sure as shit isn't anything special about being stuck inside a prison with this sorry lot. I've been sent to admin to file detainee request forms. It's a pathetic caper, their wants so small and insignificant when compared to their applications for a refugee visa. Yet little things have a way of taking on outsized meanings when that's all you've got.

I sort through requests for clothing, electronic goods, permission to conduct little events, all sorts of stuff far more pressing than reminiscing about Clem, who was dead yesterday and will be dead tomorrow. It's pretty strange to think it's been eleven years already, and I suppose the exact same thing will occur to me in another eleven years, and then another, until sooner or later there won't be anyone around to even know an anniversary has passed and it's just a day. Which—and anyone being honest with themselves has to admit this—is all it is now.

I nearly skipped right past it last year. Forgot the whole ridiculous caper till it was lunch. Some old bloke at the orchard I was working at had a pissy little transistor radio playing. A Slim Dusty song came on and that did it; straight away I thought of Clem. Then I realised it was December, but I wasn't sure of the exact date, so I asked the old feller. Almost got past one, but wasn't to be.

None of us could work out what it was Clem liked about those shitty country songs. They certainly didn't speak to Clem's life or worldview. Not enough scumbag and grifter and alcoholic. I always suspected he hated country music as much as Mum and Oli and I, but listened to it anyway just to piss us off, laughing all the way to the grave.

Mum said they played it at the funeral. "Looking Forward, Looking Back". Ironic for a man of Clem's ilk—for one who never did have much to look forward to, or look back on. I would have played "Lithium" by Nirvana. Or "Black Hole Sun" by Soundgarden.

The ghost of Chris Cornell screams his lament in my mind while I beaver away at my mundane task. He forgets the words to the song about the same time I come across an unusual request.

A group of twenty detainees are seeking assistance to find a clergyman to come to the centre and officiate a religious observance. A handwritten note says that the welfare officers tried to fulfil the request, but at this point they have been unable to find anyone with the means to reach our outpost. The request is denied, but the detainees may apply again in the new year.

It strikes me that there's not many places a clergyman wouldn't bend over backwards to visit if it meant tending a receptive flock, but it seems Curtin is one of them. You've got to hand it to the bureaucrats responsible for this place—they've certainly achieved what they set out to. When even an apostle says, nah, sorry mate, too bloody far, that's when you know you're isolated.

I feel some sympathy for the detainees because, in a way, I know how that feels—that sense of being cut off, waiting with ever diminishing hope for something that may never come. Knowing you are in it alone because, the truth is, you don't matter, not in this world.

It was my own fault. I'd made a half-arsed attempt on a comparatively modest Andean mountain, but I wasn't prepared for how much rock and ice climbing was involved. It looked so easy in the pictures. When I ran out of screws (probably a good thing considering I'm not a climber's arsehole and was in well over my head) I made my way down. With four days of waiting before my guide returned with his mule, and surrounded by endless mounds of grey, I soon grew restless and decided to find the route back to where we crossed a little river. I figured it would be a good spot to relax and kill time, maybe finish reading *The Brothers Karamazov*, which I'd lumped through four countries and was struggling to make a dent in.

Yet what had seemed so easy with my guide proved anything but, even with a compass and an old map. The only type of rivers I found were rivers of scree, the valleys and gullies filled with rock and rubble that looked the same in every fucking direction. There was surely a point where I could have back-tracked out of the mess I'd made, but when I finally admitted defeat—I later found out I had worked my way round to the other side of the mountain—that point was long past.

I recalled reading somewhere that as soon as you become lost the best thing to do is to stay put, or you risk making a bad situation worse. So after I'd already made the situation about as bad as I could, that's what I did. I waited.

Time moved very slow. You'd think that with no outside influences, no white noise, no interruptions, it would be an opportunity for expansive thinking about life, the universe, all sorts of wonderful shit. Wasn't like that. It was just the same handful of miserable thoughts on repeat. Thoughts about all the shit that was wrong with me, shit I'd messed up in life, the people I'd hurt, the opportunities I'd fucked up, the stupidity and ugliness of being me in that moment.

By the third day I felt a sense of aloneness that was utter

desolation. It was more than the fear of dying—it was the fear of dying without anyone to notice I was gone. And the thought that it was precisely what I had coming.

But I was just being melodramatic. On the fourth day the Bolivian bloke and his stroppy mule came looking for me. Turned out someone did notice, even if it was for no better reason than he was dead keen to get the other half of his guide fee. I was happy to give it to him.

I figure the poor mongrels in here must be feeling an acute sense of the same, surrounded by people yet utterly alone and completely cut off from every sphere of meaning in their life. When you're so isolated that even a clergyman can't be bothered, your prison is no longer built of ringlock and razor wire. It's become a prison of the mind.

So, yeah, they've definitely got it worse than me. All I have is a shitty father who isn't around anymore, who causes me a moment's grief once a year. These guys? Their whole lives are fucked.

DESIRE

When I finally get home at the conclusion of my first week's work, I don't bother with food, TV, reading, anything. I go straight to sleep. A long, deep, luxuriant sleep. The sleep of a man who's just been dumped somewhere he doesn't want to be and realises he's going to be stuck there a very, very long time.

When I wake up it's not with any sense of urgency and not to the synthetic chiming of an alarm. Today is my day off before switching to nights. We do six days on, twelve-hour shifts, then we get a single day to ourselves before swapping rosters. You keep ping-ponging back and forth the whole time, which means no one ever develops a proper routine, and there's never time for the circadian rhythm to fully adjust. I'm guessing that by next week it'll feel like I'm permanently jet-lagged.

I've showered and the kettle is boiling when there's a knock on my door. I open it.

"Hey," says Meg.

"Hi. This is a surprise. Is today your day off?"

"Mmhmm. Didn't you know?"

"No, I wasn't sure who'd be off."

I look Meg up and down. She's in little pyjama shorts and a matching tank top. The fabric is light and smooth, the garments hanging loose yet following the curves of her body. Meg's not wearing a bra, but her tits are still perky. I can see their outline. I can see her nipples. I don't think they're erect, but the top is so light they don't have to be.

Meg's not what most people would call hot, but she is definitely sexy. There's something about the way she carries herself, something about the softness of her body, her curves, the way she moves them. Something about the look she gives me out of the corner of her eye.

Meg knows I've looked her up and down. I'm not embarrassed. I smile at her and she smiles back. This is a much better morning than I had expected.

"So what's happening?" I ask.

"Nothing, just seeing if you were around."

"Cool. Hey, come in."

There's only one chair tucked under the little desk, so I shouldn't think anything of the fact that Meg skips straight inside and onto my bed, but it's hard not to. She pushes herself across until she's leaning against the wall, her legs outstretched, heels crossed. She looks nice. I can see the milky flesh of her thighs, whiter than the rest of her body.

"Want a tea or coffee?"

"Sure. I'll have a coffee. Thanks."

"How do you have it?"

"Black. Two sugars."

I make two cups of coffee then I sit down on the bed with my back to the wall, just like Meg.

"How was your first week?" I ask.

"It was really good. They've already had me up in the control room, so I'm learning how to do lots of stuff you normally don't get to do till you've been here for weeks. And I've made friends with some of the guys. Darren is really nice. Have you met him? He's one of the managers. He's going to let me work on the security screening on Monday."

"No shit. I've just been in the compounds."

"I've been in the compounds, too. I've been everywhere."

I twist my body around a little so I'm half facing Meg. It brings me closer to her. If she was to turn, our legs or hands might end up touching.

"What do you think of the detainees?" I say.

"Some of them are funny as hell. Especially the Iranian guys. But there's some weirdos, too. Some of the guys just stare at you. And some of them are way too touchy-feely, like wanting hugs and stuff, which is definitely not happening."

I wonder if it's a rebuke to me. To my own proximity to Meg and my covetous gaze and desire to touch her.

"Yeah. I'm a bit worried, myself. New meat and all. I've already had to rebuff the advances of a few fellers," I say.

"What! Who? When?"

I laugh. "My God, I'm joking."

Meg's wide-eyed stare thins into an affected wince as the penny drops. She slaps me across the chest with the back of her hand. The movement turns her a little so that her leg touches mine. Maybe she doesn't even notice, but I'm hyper-aware of that little spot where our bodies are sharing warmth.

"Errgh. I thought you were for real. There are gay guys in there," she says.

"Yeah. Scott is going on about it all the time."

"Oh my God, I really thought they'd been hitting on you."

"Well, it would only be natural."

"Oh, really? Do you normally have that effect on men?" she says.

"Ahh, no. On women. Haven't you seen the way they flock to me?"

"Mmhmm. Definitely. I thought I saw Grace checking you out."

"Eww. That's ... no."

"What about Karen? I think she might like you."

"Oh, come on!"

"And Leslie."

"No. No more."

Meg is just listing fat women. Not even fat—morbidly obese women.

"Ok, well you have to answer this," says Meg. "Would you

rather sleep with one gay Iranian guy, or be tied down and have Grace, Karen and Leslie tag team you?"

"Are you kidding? You're insane."

"Come on. You have to choose. What would it be?"

"That's not a fair hypothetical. I'd choose neither."

"No. You can't. If you choose neither then both the Iranian guy and the three women have their way with you."

"Jesus. So, basically I'm having consensual sex with an Iranian homo, or I'm getting raped by three trolls?"

"Mmhmm."

Meg leans over and touches my leg just above the knee. Her movement tilts her upper body and my eyes see down her top. It's like a flash of light in my brain as I glimpse those sensational breasts in the flesh. My mind is momentarily emptied. What is happening? What are we talking about?

"Come on," says Meg, "you have to choose. Grace is strapping on a massive dildo right as we speak."

"Whoa whoa whoa, hold on, if I choose the women are they wearing strap-ons?"

"No, but if you don't choose anyone then they will. Massive pink ones."

"This is ... Jesus. Well, obviously I choose the women."

"I knew it. I could tell you liked the bigger ladies."

"Well, I'll tell you right now, there'd be no sex. No chance in hell I'd be aroused."

"Viagra," says Meg, giggling.

"Oh, man. You are a terrible lady."

"Yep," she says, nodding. "Hey, what's the time?"

I check my watch. "Just after ten."

"I've gotta get ready. Gian is coming by in a bit and we're going swimming at the Derby pool. He's got a car. You wanna come?"

I don't even know who Gian is. First it was the Iranian homo and three trolls raping me, now some guy called Gian, the pronunciation a cross between a type of butter and the

Vietnamese-born comedian bloke who wrote *The Happiest Refugee*. Ghee-Anh. What sort of name is that?

"Um, you're going swimming?" I say.

"Yeah," says Meg.

Fucking Gian. Gian can fuck off.

"Ahh, nah, I don't think so. I need to do some stuff."

"Ok. Well maybe I'll see you later."

"Yeah. Sure."

Is Meg serious? Swimming with Gian? What was this then? What just happened? Were we just talking—is that all?

Of course that is all. Meg jumps off my bed and puts her cup on the desk.

"Ok, I'll catch you later," she says.

"Yep. Seeya."

Now I'm just pissed off. I close the door and proceed to have one of the angriest wanks I've had in a long time, as much in appreciation of Meg as in spite of Gian.

TOIL

It's about 11 when I finally head out of my room. I'm over my little tantrum. I was being churlish. Of course Meg would be making plans to do something other than sit in a tin hut.

I'm over tin huts, too, so I decide to walk to town. Spinifex City is on the outskirts of Derby and there's no bus at this time of day. I stroll off.

In forty-degree heat, absent a cooling breeze, I soon learn that one doesn't stroll. One toils. I toil toward town, taking in the scrappy landscape, contemplating the fact that the first Dutch and English explorers who visited the region deemed it wasn't even worth the cost of a flag. I don't doubt there really is beauty and value here to people born to the land, but to the rest of us it is no easy place to like, let alone love.

Rather than imagining beaches and camel rides, imagine a giant Brobdingnagian Joh Bjelke-Petersen dragging a hulking great chain across a beautiful land, grading earth and life to dust, then Joh taking a big maroon shit on that land and after about a million years it crumbling like dry dog turd and blowing far and wide. Then Aborigines find that land and some of the life has returned so they burn it and burn it and burn it some more. Then some white fellers come and drag another big chain across the land then burn it and clear it and burn it some more, then tenderise it with cloven hooves, get bored and let it be. That's Derby and surrounds.

After half an hour, I'm drenched in sweat. I reach the

main road heading into the centre of town. Now I have an important decision to make. Which supermarket?

It's not the decision itself that discombobulates me, more the fact this one-horse town has two supermarkets. There's no way they can both be profitable. What did Woolworths think, that the refugees would be making daytrips to Derby to do some shopping? So now the big green monster is siphoning off the wages of Derbards and sending the cash straight back to city shareholders, whereas the smaller shops recirculate some of that cash in town. I say screw the big green monster. I'll walk the extra half mile and go to the IGA.

As I toil onward I amuse myself by playing a game, trying to find the best demonym for the inhabitants of Derby. I start mentally listing candidates: *Derbite, Derban, Derbit, Derbian, Derbler, Derbole.*

So many possibilities, and now that I've started they come in a flood: *Derburger, Derbirker, Derblett, Derbois, Derber, Derbophile, Derbiot, Derblodyte, Derbucker, Derbidian, Derbiac, Derbman, Derbesian.* And *Derb.* I think I've finally exhausted Derby demonyms. They all seem plausible and sound good.

As I walk into the IGA supermarket, I notice that the indigenous population of Derbirkers are of a similar mind to myself, boycotting the corporate giant in favour of local entrepreneurialism. Good for them. I suppose that means that the white population shops at Woolies. But not me. I'm white and I'm at the IGA with six of my indigenous brothers and sisters. I am completely comfortable. We are all just shoppers, shopping.

I find meat. Big pieces of meat to cook—a pork roast, yes. And some mince, perfect. A few veges. Some tinned shit. Shit to boil. Gherkins. Peanuts. Sardines—love sardines. Bread. Cream. Couscous. Is that all? I should have written a list. I know there must be other things I'm meant to buy, but I can't think.

I buy my groceries, plus a postcard of King Sound that I see at the checkout, stuff it all into my backpack, then head next door and buy a bottle of whisky. My load is ridiculously heavy. I didn't really think this through. I trundle out of the bottle shop, head down.

I start walking on the sidewalk. Out of the corner of my eye I see two Aboriginal people sitting on the stoop of a shuttered shop. Probably gone out of business thanks to the green monster. But I'm not thinking of the green monster. I'm thinking about the black monsters I've been warned about—the ones who are high, unpredictable, violent. Best to just keep my head down, walk on.

But I can't. I'm constitutionally averse to ignorance. Despite the alarm bells ringing in my head, I lift my sweaty mug and look over at the man and woman sitting on the stoop.

"G'day guys," I say.

The man says something back to me. I don't know what he's saying.

"What's that?"

"Merry Christmas!"

Well, fuck me. That's about the last thing I was expecting, and not just because I'd forgotten it was that time of year.

"Yeah, Merry Christmas to you, too."

I feel good. It is a nice moment. It puts a little pep in my step for all of two minutes before I'm reduced to toiling under the midday sun as meat incubates in my backpack.

TOLERANCE

I get back to Spinifex City and put my pork roast on to cook at 250°C in the hope that my little salmonella farm can be converted into dinner. Then I wait around the common room during the afternoon, hoping to maybe bump into Meg.

Instead, I see Roy. I love Roy, but he is a lot of work. I was sort of hoping we would have different rosters, different days off, just so I would have a break—but no. He strolls in with a beer.

"Ayy, Nicko!"

"G'day mate. Where'd you get that from, you sneaky bastard?" I say, gesturing to his beer.

"That interpreter bloke gave me one. You want us to see if he's got any more?"

"Nah mate, it's right. How's things?"

"Lovin' it, mate. Makin' all sorts a little buddies. Some of the officers are dickheads, but. Left me fuck'n raincoat in the office, go back the next day, gone. Some prick's nicked it. Nah, it's bullshit. Reckon you can trust the refugees more."

"Well, it's a bit like anything. You get some good ones, get some bad ones."

"That's it, in't? I tell ya, talk to them fellers, what can you say? I heard that the DIAC department stands for Do I Actually Care. Eh? One of 'em is in there for two years, then he sees another bloke come and go with a visa in a month. It's bullshit, mate."

"If it was up to me, Roy, I'd make you a DIAC case manager."

"Yeah, no worries. Wouldn't be any negatives from me. Everyone would get a visa. Stupid in't? They say you gotta be wary of the bastards, not make any friends with 'em. But I reckon if I got into a scrap, some of them fellers would actually help me out."

Other colleagues come and go. I watch some TV, play some pool with Roy and eat some pork. Roy's interpreter mate runs out of beer, which means Roy runs out of beer, so I get my bottle of whisky and we have a few—but only a few, seeing as we've got to work tonight.

Mid-afternoon there's still no Meg, so I head back to my donga rather than just wait around like a pathetic lovesick teen. Not that I'm lovesick. A little lustful crush? Sure. I mean, so long as I'm in a shed in a desert it would be nice to have some female company. No doubt that's exactly what Gian is thinking while he plunges his dick into Meg.

I lie down on my bed. I have the aircon blasting; it's so chilly I need to put a blanket on. I'm normally a voracious reader, unless I'm bludgeoning myself with Dostoyevsky in the Andes, so I try reading a few pages of a novel I brought with me. It's Larry McMurtry; it deserves better than the scattered attention it's receiving. My mind keeps going back to my encounter with the indigenous population of Derby earlier in the day. It felt good at the time, but I'm perturbed by the unsubtle thoughts that were running through my head.

I didn't say or do anything wrong, but somewhere in my brain I was thinking it. Or maybe it wasn't me. Maybe I can offload responsibility to the little man pulling the strings behind my consciousness. But if that's also not me, who the fuck is he?

They're all me, which is why I'm uneasy. I used to be a merry little racist with the rest of the Harris clan. It's something a boy learns, much the same as anything. But eventually I came to see that none of it made sense, just hating people without any actual reason. By the time I got to uni I'd pretty much eliminated all the racial slurs from my vocabulary. I figured that qualified me as a decent human. I went one better by making a conscious effort to tolerate different races and cultures, being that at uni I was surrounded by all sorts of ethnicities, religions, skin colours and cultures.

But of late I've started to think that tolerance is just another symptom of the problem. If you're not inherently racist—if I didn't have that little fucker hiding somewhere in my amygdala telling me this black bastard is going to bash me, and that yellow bastard has sixteen billion brothers and sisters who all want to move into my backyard—what is there to tolerate?

The answers elude me, and it's easier to just stop thinking about it. It's probably a pointless intellectual hand job that means nothing to the world people actually live in. How about this: I resolve to try not to hate people unless they're cunts. Yeah, good policy, Nick.

I reach across and grab the aircon remote and punch up the temperature setting by two degrees. Wantonly wasting electricity is the high-water mark of stupidity. That's one of the few sensible things Clem used to say. I normally don't think of him much, but he's managed to find his way into my thoughts. They're rarely good thoughts, so I wish he wouldn't bother.

No doubt a virtuous son is expected to partake in a certain quotient of maudlin reminiscing and fairy-floss exhortations about familial love after his father's death. But whenever I think about Clem I tend to just remember what a bastard he was.

I've always wondered if he was bipolar, given he could go from happy to morose or friendly to enraged without provocation or justification, and did so on a daily, if not hourly, basis. That might have been ok if more had gone his way, but nothing did.

The truth is that he was an ill-tempered loser suffering

from delusions of grandeur, which is the very worst kind of loser, for there was forever something messing up his plans when all he wanted was to be the big man. But he didn't have the smarts, or the personality. My mother is the smart one, only Clem didn't know it and somehow she didn't either, and he probably went to the grave thinking he was smarter and better than all the people who thought he was a piece of shit.

Going to the grave makes it sound quaint, like he passed away after a long illness. Hardly. He killed himself. It was his own fault—the only time anything was, because it was the only time he wasn't around to argue the point afterward, to lay the blame on someone else. The daft prick was by himself, milling illegally cut timber on his portable sawmill after unseasonal summer rain. Mum found a half-drunk mug of homemade moonshine and brandless cola not far from his severed hand, which is probably why he bled out in the mud—alcohol being an anticoagulant and him being full to the hilt of anticoagulant pretty much always.

But, hey, he was still my father and one loves one's father despite everything... only I'm not sure that's true. Once, perhaps, when I was younger; but love is exhaustible. I know you're not meant to say that. There are entire websites devoted to platitudes about love being an inexhaustible spring that cures all ills. Well, sorry, it didn't cure shit in our family. Mum and Oli and I threw good love after bad, and it always ended up the same.

All I know for sure is that pretty much every person in Clem's sphere of shit was the worse for it. When he got himself killed it didn't suddenly make things great, but things did get easier. There was less money, but it somehow went further. You didn't get screamed at for no discernible reason. You weren't drawn into an endless array of plots, schemes and petty feuds with relatives and neighbours and strangers.

That's something else you're not meant to say. You're meant to profess how you'd give anything for just one more day with the dear departed. It's bullshit, the sort of romantic notion that sounds nice in a movie but pays no heed to the messy reality of shitty humans. One more day with Clem would be one day too many.

OLI

Thinking about my fucked-up family makes me think about Oli, one of the few with Harris blood in his veins who approaches something like normal. Our semi-regular conversations help me feel less like a bad brother, and bad son, and all-round bad human.

I take the Telstra SIM card out of my mobile phone and replace it with my old Virgin SIM card so I can find Oli's number and write it down. Then I have to put the Telstra SIM back in, because they're the only provider with reception up here. I make so few phone calls I shouldn't have bothered getting it — but it came in a package with my wireless dongle, and without wireless there'd be no internet, and without internet I'd be back to conjuring my own sexual fantasies, surely a violation of some human right that has always existed since it was discovered by a group of UN lawyers and pronounced immanent and immutable.

I head out to the only bit of lawn at Spinifex City. I dial Oli's number. It rings.

"Hello?"

"Oli, it's me. How you doing?"

"Nicko! Hey man. What's up?"

"Oh, just saying hi from prison."

"What? Shit, man, did you get in some sort of—"

"No, shithead, refugee prison. The detention centre."

"Oh, yeah, yeah, of course. Hey, listen, I'm driving so I'm gonna chuck you on speaker phone. Hold on."

A moment later I hear the fuzz of ambient noise.

"Nicko, you there?"

"Yep."

"Jen's in the car, too."

"Hi Nick," says a familiar voice.

Jen is Oli's fiancée, but I haven't been around to get to know her as well as I should. I think she has a perception of me as some fringe-dwelling crazy, but a friendly fringe-dwelling crazy. Anyway, I like her. She's good to Oli. And she's got a sense of humour.

"Hi Jen. How's things?"

"Good. We're on a date. So, what's it like persecuting refugees?"

"Pays well. Besides, they're not refugees. They're clients. I'm actually in the service industry."

"Is that so?" says Oli. "Hey, maybe after this you can start a bed and breakfast. What do you think, Jen, can you see Nick in his little white picket cottage putting mints on pillows?"

"I can see a customer asking for an extra pillow and I can see Nick telling his customer to go fuck themselves," says Jen.

I laugh. She's probably right.

"So what's it really like there? Is it as bad as the stuff we see on the news?" asks Oli.

"No, it's not really like that. It's weird. It's actually really low-key and cruisy most of the time, and the detainees seem to be pretty good value. I wouldn't say it's a nice place to be, though. I mean, it is what it is: a low-security prison in a desert. But I'm not risking my life or anything."

"You going to stick with it?" says Oli.

"You mean, am I going to quit like I always do?"

"No, I didn't—"

"Look. When I want a job, I get a job. When I don't want the job any more, I leave the job. That to me sounds like a rational model for living your life."

"If you have no possessions and no kids and no commitments," yells Jen, presumably because she thinks I can't hear her, but I can hear her fine.

"You know what? That's pretty much a perfect description of me. But anyway, I'm not quitting. The money's too good. I'm gonna be rich."

"Whoa, Nicko, rich? Have they been brainwashing you?" says Oli.

"No. But they have been paying me two grand-plus a week."

"Far out. That's more than I make."

"Yeah. I figure I stick it out for six months and I've got enough cash to pay off all my debts, and enough for a trip to Eurasia. I'm thinking Uzbekistan, Tajikistan, Kyrgyzstan."

"Basically all the Stans, hey?" says Oli.

"Maybe even Iran."

"Yeah? Westerners are allowed in?"

"Apparently."

"You'll have to grow a beard. Oh, that's right ..."

"Yeah, fuck you. Anyway, you should come. You too, Jen," I call out.

"Gee, thanks, Nick. Invite me to a place where I'm considered property and have to cover my face in a veil."

We chat and banter for a while, talking about my job, my trip to South America, about Oli and Jen's plans for an extension to their little cottage in Melbourne. Then there's a brief silence and I hear what sounds like Jen whispering something to Oli. Then I'm pretty sure she hits him.

"Hey, so, Nick," says Oli, "you should call Mum."

"Umm, yeah. I will."

"No, really, you should call her."

"Ok."

"Promise me you're going to call her."

"I'm going to call her," I say.

"When?"

"Fuck, dude, when I feel like it."

"How about soon as you get off the phone with me?"

"Why are you on my arse?"

"Well, when's the last time you spoke to Mum?" Oli asks.

"I dunno. Not that long ago."

"Nicko, it was January. Almost a year ago."

"Was it? I've been sending postcards."

"Just call her. She wants you to call her."

"Did she say that to you?"

"Not in so many words. But she wants you to call her," says Oli.

"All right. Jesus. I'll call her."

"Good. Good. Hey, we're pulling into a carpark, so I better get off the phone. I love you, man." Oli is a lot more sentimental than me.

"All right. I'll talk to you. Seeya guys."

I hang up, and almost immediately remember I was going to say Merry Christmas or Happy New Year or some shit, but forgot. It doesn't matter. They're bullshit days anyway. It's probably a good thing that at Curtin the management is—calendrically-speaking—completely unprejudiced. Every day is the same up here, and that's fine by me.

I pace the lawn, juggling the mobile phone in my hand as I contemplate what to do next. Calling one's mother should not be this hard. I tell myself that it's all in my mind. Mum wants me to call. If Oli says so, it's true.

But I've conjured all these recriminations. Barbs that no person will ever stick me with. They don't need to. I'm a practised self-flagellator. Ultimately, it always seems easier in the moment to push it away, yet the more I do the worse it gets.

It's been five years in the making. At first I kept in touch with phone calls every few weeks, then every few months. I started sending postcards instead. That way I never had to hear about the others. I never had to hear about how some Harris was destroying their own life and managing to drag everyone around them into their misery, and I didn't have to think about my place in it all. I just don't want to deal with it, any of it.

Regular contact gradually frittered down to what it is now.

Once or twice yearly. Yet when I do call, she never judges me, never asks me to come home, never mentions how much my absence hurts her, and somehow all of that makes me feel so much worse till now ... going back seems impossible. Even calling seems impossible.

But at least I send postcards.

I tell myself I'll call Mum tomorrow, or maybe on my next day off. I head back into my tin shed, lie down, switch my lamp off and close my eyes. I can still get maybe an hour's sleep before having to get ready for night shift. It's going to suck.

RIOT

I wander over to the bus stop just before 5 p.m. About a dozen others are already gathered. I don't know most of them. I'll be on my feet most of the night, so I crouch down and sit on the concrete kerb. I notice a small, middle-aged woman with a quick smile standing in the shade away from the rest of the group.

It's daytime and everybody is wide awake, so there's a lot of chatting and joking. Conversation turns to events of the night before. Seems there was some sort of incident. Apparently an Iranian man felt that an Afghani man had pushed ahead of him in the queue to use a phone, so he hit him on the head with a stick. Sounds reasonable enough to me.

Then a little later in the Red Compound mess hall, a group of Afghanis were intent on having words with the Iranian who'd earlier wielded the stick. A scuffle ensued and was eventually split up. Later, there was a showdown. A group of Iranians approached from one direction and a group of Afghanis from the other. Just how many may be the subject of exaggeration, but the number of one hundred and fifty is bandied around. It sounds high. Anyway, a fight erupted between the groups. A couple of men were injured: a broken nose, busted lips, bruised and bloodied faces. No officers were hurt.

At the bus stop, the fact of the fight, or riot in some accountings, is invoked as ready evidence of the barbarity of the detainees, which is stupid because there are Australian riots just as there are English riots just as there are French riots just as there are Curtin riots. I contemplate pointing out how stupid what they're saying is—how a little scuffle doesn't prove shit about anyone or anything—but figure there's no point.

Talk turns to gossip, a favourite subject up here.

"How about Janet, eh? She's got no problems with the Iranians. She really likes 'em," says a fat, balding man wearing glasses and a smirk.

"Likes 'em ...?" asks a Kiwi woman.

"*Likes 'em,*" the man repeats, in case his meaning isn't obvious. Apparently it isn't, so he makes himself sledgehammer clear: "Spends hours with 'em at a time, hours, just disappears into their rooms."

"Eww, that's disgusting."

"Yeah she loves her Arab boys all right. She took a holiday in Jordan. She's obsessed with 'em."

"That's fucked-up, man."

"I can't understand how anyone would go near 'em."

The middle-aged woman who is standing apart from the group finally speaks up. "They're not all bad. A lot of them are good people."

"Mary," says the balding man with the overweening grin, "they are not your friends. Remember that. They are not your friends."

It is one of the ingrained principles of being a detention worker: empathy not sympathy, friendly not friends, et cetera.

"Yeah, I know that, but—"

"Mary." Somehow he has found a yet-higher tone of condescension. "They. Are. Not. Your. Friends."

"I know ..." Mary begins, before trailing off.

Other voices join in.

"They all play up. All of them, given the chance."

"I heard that they want to introduce Sharia Law here."

"Already have in England."

"There you go," says another.

"The other week I saw that they were asking for it here in Australia," says the Kiwi.

"They come here and try to take over."

"Yep, that's how it happens—get citizenship, get elected to parliament, then they bring in Sharia Law and take over."

My colleagues don't know what they are talking about. I suppose I could say something, correct their mistakes, massage some of their misgivings, but there's no point. I'd just be pissing in the wind.

Instead, I focus on the long shadows draping away from scraggly trees and the rich quality of the light in this world of reds and silvers. It's still hot, humid and dusty, but there's something pleasing about this time of day. Of course, it won't last. It'll just be hot, humid, dusty and dark soon, but I should shut up and try to enjoy something while I can.

MOB

Meg runs out just as the bus is pulling up. I'm already seated toward the back when she gets on. She seeks me out and sits next to me. I ask her how her swim was. She tells me, then she tells me about Gian, Gian's car, Gian's room in an actual house, Gian's housemates, Gian's DVD collection and various other Gian-centric trivialities, such that by the time we get to the centre I feel like I really know Gian. Meg has even promised to introduce us, which sounds just great.

I get my allocation, then listen for Meg's. Once again, I'm in the compounds. Once again, Meg is not. She's working in the office with Darren, which suggests to me that Darren is trying to fuck Meg, just as Gian is trying to fuck Meg, just as I am trying to fuck Meg.

Is everybody trying to fuck Meg?

Frankly, yes, I think every man in Derby is trying to fuck Meg.

It's the male population, our inherent vice — all of us trying to fuck everything all the time. It was all right when it was just me, but now I feel like I've been dragged into some seedy confederacy.

I'm resolved. I am not going to try to fuck Meg.

That said ... I'm not going to try to not fuck Meg.

I mean, if she wants me to fuck her, then I should fuck her. If she asks me, I'll definitely fuck her. But I'll stop *trying* to fuck her. Big difference. I'll just be cooling my heels, acting like a normal human around her.

See, I'm better than these brute machines unable to rise above their pursuit of carnal gratification. I can just be friends with a sexy girl. The sort of friends who don't have subtext and subterfuge. And if that means forgoing the pleasures of a woman's touch so long as I am up here, no problem.

I feel better having made the decision. I bid Meg "*Bonne soirée*," to which she says, "Whaaat?" to which I say, "Have a good night," to which she says, "See you later," and then I head straight to the mess hall in Blue Compound where my first nightshift begins.

Tonight, I'm delegated the important mission of standing next to the cordial machine. I mentally inventory the fact there is green cordial and red cordial and also plain cold water. I'm onto this caper. I'm going to monitor the bejesus out of these enormous cordial machines. Which is my job, right? The only other possibility is that I'm lending my presence to the good work of discouraging barbarians from burning down the village. There was a scuffle-cum-riot-cum-putsch last night, after all.

Ninety minutes is a long time to stand next to a cordial machine. After about half an hour I grab a chair and sit down. I'm now sitting next to the cordial machine. That lasts for about five minutes till Benedict, the swingiest of swinging-dicks, walks into the hall. He's roaming the compounds, checking up on things, putting the little details in order. And he's straight on to this little article of disorder. He walks across, taking big strides. He stops and points his clipboard at me.

"You can't be sitting down. See the other officers?"

I look around the hall at the other four officers. Only three of them are standing; a fourth is seated behind a desk, marking off names as detainees enter the hall. But I'm pretty sure I get Benedict's point.

"Ahh, yeah," I say, standing up.

"What are they doing?"

"Standing."

"And why do you stand?"

Oh good, the Socratic method. My favourite form of condescension.

"So you can see?"

"So that you are prepared. If I attack you and you're sitting in that chair, how are you going to move out the way or defend yourself?"

"I don't know." I also don't know if it's a common thing for officers to be attacked while defending a cordial machine.

Benedict grabs the chair I've been sitting on and puts it back under a table. "If you can't handle standing for ninety minutes, then you can't handle this job."

He strides away to have a word with the other officers while I guard the cordial machine in a suitable state of upright readiness. I don't know why, but standing while bored is infinitely worse than sitting while bored.

After dinner, I'm in the officers' donga. A detainee knocks on the window and asks Leslie to unlock some activity rooms. Leslie gives me her keys, which I put on my lanyard. She sends me off as if it's no big deal. But it sort of is a big deal. It's the first time I've done something completely on my own, no other officers in sight. It also happens to be night. A dark night, at that. And it's only twenty-four hours after the incident.

I weave through the unlit alleyways formed by the rows of dongas, not entirely sure where the activity rooms are. The further I get from the imagined safety of the officers' donga, the less comfortable I feel.

I remember what Warren said in training. At night you should always travel in pairs. Yet here I am, sort of lost, on my own, sporting a set of compound keys. I might think standing next to a cordial machine as if detainees are about to riot at the sight of red and green is pretty much ridiculous, but the truth is I still don't really know anything about the detainees; I don't personally know what they're capable of, whereas I have been told at least a dozen stories by experienced officers about detainees attacking officers, attacking each other and their penchant for setting fire to shit. Misgivings start to manifest as a genuine fear. It is a goddamn prison.

Up ahead I see a group of detainees, thirty or more. I grab the radio from my belt so that it's close to hand if I need to call for assistance. I'm not at all sure about this. My gut says turn around and go get an officer buddy, but my pride says toughen up and open that door, you pussy. As I step into their midst I'm not quite panicking, just experiencing a rectum-tightening anxiety.

"Hi."

That's what I say to project my authority and confidence. Just a general, "Hi," to a group of strangers. I look at the faces to see if there's any malice, without knowing what that malice would look like. Insincere smiles? Scowls? I've no idea. The detainees just look like people.

"Is this the door?" I ask.

A number of voices say yes. Then it occurs to me that they could be lying. I don't know which one is truly the activity room. Maybe I'm about to open somewhere completely off-limits to the detainees. I don't want to look stupid, though. I'd rather risk letting them into somewhere they're not meant to be than seem like a new chum who doesn't know what he's doing. So I start trying keys in the door. My back is to the mob. That's also something you're not meant to do. This whole situation is fucked.

I finally find the right key and the knob turns. I pull the door open and stand aside. The refugees start streaming inside. As they pass, each and every person says thank you, some with an unexpected enthusiasm that suggests they are genuinely grateful. In fact, they seem to think I've done them a favour.

My panic subsides and I feel like a good bloke for having

done a nice thing for these chaps in spite of my misgivings. I ask one of the men who has a notepad in his hand what they are doing.

"English class," he says.

Oh. My dangerous mob is a mob of aspiring anglophones. Their teacher with the key is late. I see.

I slip back through the anonymous alleyways between tin sheds, telling myself this is the last time I will be some pathetic little scared white man standing in fear of an imagined horde.

WASTE

The next night, I'm in Green Compound. It's the biggest but quietest compound, mostly populated by Afghanis, who have thus far left an impression on me as a polite, gentle, humble people. Many of them don't speak any English—apart from maybe "Hello, Maggi, thank you"—so interactions between officers and detainees are a little more limited than in the other areas where there are more Iranians and Sri Lankans with better language skills.

The night starts off in the usual way, standing around the mess hall guarding cordial machines and trays of desserts. Not all detainees show for dinner, so after the mess shuts it's our job to go check that anyone who didn't show is still alive. I'm given a name and room number and sent off—again, on my own. I guess that's how it's going to be, which I'm sure is fine. Like I said before, I'm not going to imagine bogeymen where none exist. Simple fact is, detainees prefer to hurt themselves than officers.

I eventually come to the correct row of dongas. They've got a nice series of gardens in front of them, roped off with twine. The light is good here from all the spotlights around the compound, and I see various flowers, different ferns, creepers, other plants I can't name and a few chilli bushes sporting dozens of plump little red firecrackers. The most appealing part of the garden, though, is the plot of sunflowers. It's one of dozens of such plots I've seen around the centre. They seem to all be coming to bloom around the same time, and they do about as much as anything to brighten up this shanty town. Mind, they're not a patch on the sunflowers down home.

Back in Manji, an old Italian bloke named Vic was a minor local celebrity for his sunflowers—twenty-foot monsters like something out of *The Day of the Triffids*. I remember when the people from *Guinness* came and measured them. It was a big deal for a little town, and seemed like the pinnacle of human achievement to a boy of seven or eight. For about five years he officially had the record for the world's tallest sunflower.

I suppose a sunflower doesn't need to be twenty feet tall to do its job, and the comparatively stunted varieties around the camp are certainly doing theirs. Actually, I'm quite impressed that the detainees manage to grow so many different plants in this friable desert dust. The miracle of water, I guess.

I notice a hose spilling its guts in the garden, its rate of flow completely unchecked; it must have been on a long time, as the ground is soaked and the water has begun to create a shallow lake in the yard formed between four rows of dongas. I follow the hose to its tap and turn it off. I get the impression both detainees and officers think water is an inexhaustible resource at Curtin just because it's coming from an underground aquifer. Every day and every night there are hoses left running. Fire hoses, too. Some detainees figure it's easier and quicker just to give a blast of a geyser and flood the entire area rather than carefully water individual plants.

It bothers me. Even vast aquifers eventually deplete. In a country like Australia, every drop should be considered precious. It sure as shit was precious when I was growing up. If you wasted so much as a glass of water in sight of Mum she'd be interrogating you, asking you what you thought you were doing, why you didn't put it on a plant that was crying out for a drink. I was the sort of kid who tended to take on the worries of my parents—worries about money, family hatreds, battles with the council or absurd shit like who could claim rightful ownership over grandad's old McCulloch chainsaw. Anyway, after enough crises, I became a little water Nazi, too.

I remember in year nine at Manji high school our dickwit gardener, a little redheaded bloke with a big beard and stocky limbs, used to put the sprinklers on and leave them running for hours during the middle of the day, and I'm talking the height of summer, easily forty degrees. Wasting all that water to evaporation was pointless and stupid, but what really pissed me off was the fact I knew where the water came from, and it wasn't some inexhaustible aquifer. It came from the same stream that ran through the back of our fifteen acres: Karlup Creek.

Over the past few years it had started drying up into a series of pools during late summer. We didn't (and Mum still doesn't) have a connection to the town water supply; we depended on rainwater and, if that ran out, we depended on the creek. Every time I saw that sprinkler spilling our water on the school oval I would sneak over and turn it off.

One day a group of us were kicking the footy on the oval and the leprechaun gardener happened along. He saw his sprinkler was off—again—and he also saw us, so he stormed over and demanded to know who did it. It should be said, every one of us hated that little leprechaun. He was humourless and angry and weird, and because he was a gardener, not a teacher, we didn't even pretend to be respectful. Now, if he'd cornered just one or two of us, things might have gone different, but you don't try to exert authority in front of a group of adolescent boys, especially the lippy ones who live to peacock for their mates and believe they become invincible in a mob. Of course we started taunting him. We told him he was a leprechaun. We asked him where his pot of gold was. We ended up telling him to piss off. He said he was going to the deputy principal, which is possibly the lamest thing he could have said.

He was walking away when a tallish kid named Wayne ran up behind the leprechaun and stole his hat. Wayne didn't run away, didn't throw the hat to another one of us, he just stood there holding the hat high in the air while the leprechaun feebly reached for it. To a mob of year nine boys, it was a stunning turn of events. We were cheering Wayne on like we had fifty on Makybe Diva to win and she was rounding the last bend.

Then it went to shit. The leprechaun grabbed Wayne and put him in a headlock and dropped him to the ground. Even back then you couldn't do that to a student, which is precisely why Wayne had the balls to steal the hat in the first place. But the leprechaun did it and Wayne started screaming, "Let me fucking go!" And the rest of us started screaming, "Let him go!" and Wayne dropped the hat and the leprechaun got off him, picked up his hat, walked over to the sprinkler, turned it back on and left. Never said a word to the deputy, and nor did we, though from that point on it was outright hostility every time we saw him. Anyway, right before we all moved off to the safety of the basketball courts, I slinked back over and turned that fucking sprinkler off. It makes me smile just thinking about it.

So I wouldn't quite say I'm pissed off at seeing the hose running into the detainee's garden, but it does exasperate me. Once I turn off the tap, I roll up the hose so that it's not draped across the pavement, waiting to trip some poor bastard. I walk over to the room housing the detainee who was missing from dinner and knock gently. The knob turns and the door pushes ajar. I draw it open enough to poke my head inside. A thickset Afghani man is sitting at a desk. He doesn't say anything, but he is looking at me.

"Hi. Are you Wasef?"

"Yes."

"You weren't at dinner. I was just checking to see if everything's ok."

"Ok?"

"Yes, is everything ok? Is there anything I can help you with?"

He stares at me. He doesn't smile. "You cannot help me with anything."

"Right."

I wonder if there's something more I should say. If there is, I don't know what.

"Ok, well, that's all. Good night," I say, and close the door.

Because there's so much self-harming and so many attempted suicides, we are expected to be constantly monitoring the mental states of detainees. If we see anything that suggests a man might be contemplating self-harm, we are meant to report it. That's why talking to detainees is encouraged. That's why Roy can't be faulted for heading off to play table tennis with a group of Afghanis. All part of the job. Wasef is clearly not a happy man, but he hasn't said anything to trigger the need to write him up.

I head back to the officers' donga, report that my man is present and alive, then head back out to get some air, to try to enjoy a bit of quiet in the night. We're meant to be constantly conducting random patrols anyway, so I am in fact doing my job by aimlessly wandering the grounds. I suppose it should be with a buddy officer, but I'm not about to ask someone to hold my hand to go for a stroll.

Half an hour later I'm leaning against a pole, trying to figure out where I've been, where I am and where I shall go. A detainee approaches. I don't recognise him.

"Before. You ask if you can help," he says.

"Hmm, what?"

"You come into my room, ask if you can help. Are you my personal officer?"

"No, I'm not your personal officer," I say.

"Why you ask if you can help?"

I finally realise who he is—the guy missing from dinner who I checked up on. He's still not smiling. In fact, he looks even more pissed off than he did before.

"What if you were put in cage, like animal? And the person

who put you in cage come and he say, 'You have enough water, you have enough food?' You are still in cage, you are still treated like animal."

"I understand. I'm sorry ..."

"What do I say to my son in Afghanistan? Three year old. He ask me when I come home, when I come home. What do I tell him? I am here twenty month—twenty month—and I see some come, get visa after two month. Where is justice? What can I tell my son?"

"I don't know."

"You help me ..." says the man, as he walks off shaking his head, dismissing the notion in disgust.

I feel a bit shit. I thought I was being nice by trading niceties, when it only served to remind the man how little control he has over his fate. His agency extends to whether he has dinner or not. My agency in his life extends to whether I give him noodles or not. None of these things mean anything when all you want is to tell your family you've found a way to make their lives better.

I walk across the courtyard between four rows of dongas. The red dirt is muddy underfoot from yet another hose left on. I find the tap and turn it off. I think it might be the same hose as before. I'm not sure.

I keep walking.

SMILE

Tonight I've been allocated to Brown Compound, along with Meg, Scott, Gabriel, Grace and a new kid called Jayden. This is the first time I've worked in the same compound as Meg. I don't think I like it. She's cool when it's just the two of us, but she can be a bit bullish and outspoken when in a group. Sort of like she's showing off.

I'm not sure what I think of Gabriel, too. He's one of those thirty-odd-year-old men who's suddenly realised he and his kind rule the world. The big man, the important man, the man who should be listened to and followed, except he's not even in charge tonight. I can see that riles him, as he's hovering around the paperwork.

Grace is in charge. She portrays an air of insouciance that comes from having worked in various detention centres for years. She is old, fat, flippant and foul-mouthed. There is a distinct bitterness to her. When she says such and such is a dumbfuck, it's not in the nice way that you sometimes call someone a dumbfuck. She means you are worthless and dumb and should go die. But, you know what? I like being around bitter old fat bitches. They tend to have earned their nastiness through varied and shithouse lives, and they own their mean streak rather than playing to someone else's idea of how a woman should be. Certainly they're more interesting than the vast majority of people who present a vacuous niceness that veils deep seams of petty spite and cruelty.

It's after the dinner run. While Scott is outside having a smoke, and Jayden has nipped off to the dunny, the other four of us are in the officers' donga enjoying the cool of the air conditioning. A detainee knocks on the sliding window. Grace tells me to open it, so I do. I think the man is Afghani. They're pretty easy to tell because they've got very full, rosy cheeks, and their eyes are a little narrower than a lot of Middle Eastern people.

"Hi. What would you like?" I say.

The chap says something to me, but it's a garbled mouthful of pidgin that I can't understand.

"Sorry, say that again?"

It's no better second time round. I feel a bit silly. We look at each other with plaintive expressions. I'm already out of ideas.

"Umm, Grace, do you know what he wants?"

"Jesus, clients are fucked," she says. "Absolutely useless."

The detainee is just standing there, dumb smile on his face, the same smile I wear whenever I'm in a foreign country mangling a language as I try to ask for something. Grace yells past me, "What do you want?"

The detainee says something. I don't know whether Grace understands it any better than I do.

"Go away. Go away! Fuck off," she says.

The detainee seems to get the gist. He nods meekly and walks away.

APPLES

Grace sends me, Scott and Meg to complete a task. She's given us a list of rooms in which we are to conduct unannounced searches. It's real guard work—a good old-fashioned prison throw-down to check for contraband. I'm surprised Gabriel isn't also assigned because, truth be told, we don't know what we're doing. Well, at least I don't, and if I don't I can guarantee Scott doesn't. Meg? She takes charge from the get-go.

Scott has the clipboard with the list of rooms and the paperwork that needs to be filled in as we go. Meg and I are doing the actual searching. Meg knocks at the first room. The detainee opens the door and Meg explains that we are going to conduct a search. He seems completely indifferent. In fact, he just sits on his bed until we ask him to stand outside. His room is immaculately kept, so the search should be easy.

Meg and I start on opposite sides of the room. I look under piles of clothes, in his bedsit drawers, under his bed, under his mattress. The man has no contraband, and I can see that Meg hasn't found anything on her side. I say to the man, "Thank you. All good," and walk out.

But Meg is still in the donga, now searching my side of the room. I don't know why. Maybe that was in the training—that you're meant to have two people go over the same area. Anyhow, lo and behold, she finds something.

"Contraband," she calls.

"What?" says Scott.

"Fruit."

The Afghani man pokes his head inside, as curious as me to know what's going on. Meg picks up three apples from a pile of four apples next to his bed. She faces the man.

"You can't have these," she says in that loud, distinct way of Westerners speaking to foreigners. "One apple only."

"No apple?"

"No. One apple only."

Is that a rule? I know the detainees are meant to only take one piece of fruit from the mess hall each meal, but if they put it aside to eat another time, then across the course of just over a day they amass four pieces of fruit—surely there can't be a rule against that. And if it really is a rule, is Meg seriously enforcing it?

"Ok, ok," says the man.

Meg puts the three apples in a big blue bag we've brought along for contraband. Scott makes the requisite notes on the paperwork. We go through the rest of the searches. In one room we find a razor hidden in the bathroom. I've no argument about the razor being confiscated. In one room we find too many chairs, so they're confiscated. And one room has additional sheets—good for tearing into strips for hanging. They're confiscated.

Once we're finished and walking back to the officers' donga, I say to Meg, "Hey, why did you confiscate those apples from that guy?"

"Because he's not meant to have them."

"Yeah, but they're apples."

"Well he might have been hoarding it to make alcohol. Did you know that they do that?"

"Like, hooch?" I say.

"Yeah."

"Ok. But it was three apples. Who gives a shit?"

"It's against the rules."

Of course, no rule is meaningful unless enforced, and

enforcement is always a matter of discretion. I'm surprised that Meg's discretion tends toward complete, unquestioning conformism. It seems totally at odds with her personable, happy-go-lucky outlook.

Me? Ever since the incident with the sugar sachets and the man whose entire family drowned, my discretion tends toward carte blanche: take what you like, do what you want, so long as it poses no danger to self or others. I don't think I would have cared if the guy had a distillery set up in there. I'd say Scott is the same. But Meg exercised her discretion and took his apples.

COFFEE

I don't get up till 4.30 in the afternoon.

With only about twenty minutes before the bus arrives, I need to get my shit together. I need to wake up. I boil the kettle while I shower.

I'm not joking when I say the first coffee of the morning — or, in this case, the afternoon — is something I think about every night before going to sleep, and it's the first thing to come into my head when I wake.

It's my one unshakable bourgeois habit, ever since a young doctor in training named Mason Lonnergan introduced me to the French press. Before then I'd never had a coffee where there was undissolved gunk leftover after making the drink; I'd certainly never had a coffee bought from a shop. Yet I still thought I was a cut above, given at home we drank Nescafé when a lot of other people were drinking International Roast and Maxwell House. During senior high school I moved on to Moccona instant. I believed I had reached the pinnacle of the coffee experience. I looked down at the commoners and their inferior blends.

Then I got to the big smoke and found a whole other world of coffee appreciation. I dived more readily into learning about coffee than I did learning about medicine.

These days, I like my beans freshly ground just before brewing on either an aeropress or French press. The beans should be a light–medium roast so that you're not burning away the oils and leaving an ashtray flavour more suited to stouts (for which ashtray is de rigueur). My preference is single-origin Central American or northern South American Arabica beans grown above twelve hundred metres. They should be roasted as close to consumption as possible. And, yes, I'm aware I sound like a wanker, but I don't care.

I love coffee, I live for coffee, yet I'm back to drinking Moccona instant. The only saving grace is cream, which can mellow and improve the shittiest flavours. I've always had cream in my coffee. One of our neighbours was an old Slav named Merv Sulich. He'd retired from farming but still ran a couple of dairy cows and kept bees; it earned him a few bucks and kept his mind and body active. In fact, last I heard, Merv is still alive and still keeping bees and he's somewhere in his eighties, so I'd say he's got the right idea. Anyway, once a week we'd go over and get a bucket of fresh cow's milk from Merv, then we'd boil it up on the stove and a nice layer of yellow cream would congeal on top. That cream is so different in taste, consistency and colour to what normally passes as cream that it doesn't deserve to share the name. It's magnificent stuff. Sometimes when we hadn't decanted the milk into a jug and I was pouring it straight into my tea from the pot, a little bit of cream would slop in. It tasted good, and soon enough I was scooping cream into my tea; then, when I started drinking coffee, I put it in my coffee. The beauty of cream is that it is low in lactose and doesn't overwhelm the palette with sweetness, while at the same time the lipids elevate all flavours, much like salt in food, as well as adding a mouthfeel equivalent to a rich espresso. Unbeatable.

I scoop a spoonful of coffee granules into a cup and add near-boiling water. I open the bar fridge and grab out the carton of cream. You've got to be kidding—I can tell just by the weight that it's empty, the last little dribble of liquid having set solid.

Fuck! Why didn't I buy more cream?

I feel a surge of anger, and I know I shouldn't, I know it's just a stupid drink, but it really pisses me off. Am I meant to go to work without having had coffee?

I pick up my cup of black coffee and look at it like I'm staring at dog turd. I feel actual hatred for that cup of coffee. I part my snarl and blow then take a ginger sip. Yep, tastes like dog turd. I put the cup down next to my nearly empty bottle of whisky. I look at the two. I've never had a black Irish coffee. It could work. The sour burn of alcohol might just fool my brain into thinking it's detecting the odd citric tang of an Indonesia-grown Robusta bean. That, or at least I'll be tasting dog turd *and* whisky. I open the bottle and pour a dash into my coffee. I take a sip. Yep, tastes like whisky in instant coffee. The two flavours really don't merge at all. I drink it anyway.

The funny thing about booze is that even when it tastes like shit, it triggers something in the head that convinces you it's a good idea to have more. I'm very nearly on autopilot as I make another coffee and put it in my travel cup and add a splash of whisky. I put the bottle down and screw the lid back on, but there's so little left it seems pathetic leaving it. I drizzle the last of it into my cup. I'm still angry at the coffee. I feel like this is my way of saying, "Fuck you, coffee." I also know that that makes no sense. I don't care. It makes me feel better.

CONVERSATION

About 3 a.m., you can expect to be either semi-conscious or delirious from sleep deprivation. I'd say we are the latter, as a few officers and I discuss the new recruit, Jayden, already designated the officer-most-likely-to-be-raped. He's a very pretty boy, a boy to whom some of the detainees have taken a particular shine. He's also expressed an interest in joining the centre's Emergency Response Team.

"That guy doesn't need shields and batons and all that shit, he needs a Kevlar chastity belt," says Gabriel.

"If you were out there and it turned to shit, I reckon the best thing to do would be just throw Jayden to 'em and run. They'll be too busy raping to come after you," says Bailey.

"Nah man, what you do is when you're all lined up with your shields and marching forward, you put Jayden out the front, pants down, arse facing the rioters. They'll be queuing up for that shit. They'll be taking tickets. 'Oh, me next, me next,' " says Scott.

Then, without care for any sort of segue, Rash says, "Do you know what the scientifically proven best way of taking a shit is?"

"Huh?"

"I will tell you. The best way for the body to take a shit is if you are standing on your head."

"That's scientifically proven? Dude, come on," I say.

"No, it is. I read it."

"How do you take a shit standing on your head? You'd have

to practise, like, projectile shitting, or it'd run down your back."

"What do you shit into? Where do you aim?" says Scott.

"I don't know, but it's the best for you."

"So you're going to take all your shits standing on your head?" I say.

"Maybe. Gabriel, can I have your keys?"

"What for?"

"I need to go take a shit."

"Ah-huh. But what do we always tell the clients?" says Gabriel.

"What?"

"What — do — we — tell — the — clients?"

"Umm ..."

"Please."

"Please ...?"

"Why can't you say please?"

"I just want your keys."

"And I'll give you my keys when you learn to say please."

"Why don't you just give me the keys?"

"What is your problem? It's polite. It's simply being polite."

"And I politely asked for your keys."

"Well I'm not giving them to you, then. Not if you can't say please."

"All right, can I *please* have your keys?"

Gabriel unclips the keys from his lanyard and hands them to Rash. Rash leaves the donga.

"What a cocksucker," says Gabriel.

PIECES

Bus. Shed. Sleep. Another day passes unseen.

I wake up that afternoon, having forgotten that I'm out of cream. I spoon some coffee granules into a mug then pour hot water. I open the bar fridge, and that's when I realise.

I'm furious. I tip the black coffee out in my bathroom sink and stand there, fuming, an idiot looking at his idiot cup. The anger is irrational and pointless but so very real. All I can think to do is break that miserable cup and it'll be done. I look for somewhere I can throw it and really there's nowhere that won't cause more problems and that just makes me angrier so I think fuck it and turn and throw the cup at the wall as hard as I can. It shatters into pieces that rain down on my bed.

I feel no better. Just angry. I'm standing there, looking at the shards of porcelain and the dent in my wall, when an unbidden memory of an axe and broken glass flashes into my mind.

Jesus, why am I thinking about that? I squint like there's light in my eyes but the image only comes on stronger.

I must have been eleven, or thereabouts. I got up that morning and the first thing Clem said to me was, "The wood box is empty," like it was on his mind. Like he'd been brooding on it. I said, "Yeah, I know, I'll get it in a bit, Dad." He didn't say anything. He went out the back.

I knew it was my responsibility to keep the box full, but the fire wasn't even going, and it was almost nine. *Pinky and the Brain* was about to come on. It's not like I was one of those kids who sits inside all day. I'd watch one cartoon then I'd get the wood and I'd be outside until evening.

Clem came in about halfway through the episode. Brain had devised yet another ingenious plan to take over the world. Oli was in his pyjamas, sitting beside me on the couch.

Clem looked at me and looked at the TV and said, "Got that wood yet?"

I said, "No, I'll get it after this. It's almost over now."

It wasn't five minutes later when the back door flung open and this time Clem had the axe in his hand.

"Got that wood yet?" he yelled.

I just looked at him. I didn't understand.

"Got that wood yet?" he repeated in the exact same voice, like he hadn't said it the first time.

I said, "No," in a little voice that makes me angry when I think back to it.

Clem walked across to the TV and swung the axe. The screen exploded. He turned and stared at me and didn't blink.

"Got that wood yet?"

Oli burst into tears. Mum came in and saw what Clem had done. She screamed at him. He screamed back, and then Mum was in tears, too. I took Oli to his room and told him he could listen to the Walkman I got for my birthday, then went and got the axe. I went to the wood heap and cut the wood and filled the box.

There was a replacement TV by the next day. Not new, but not much different to the old one. Clem never said anything. It was like it never happened. Like a lot of things never happened.

That was fourteen years ago. Standing here, looking at the broken pieces of that memory, all I want is to be able to go back to that time as the man I am now. Then I'd have a place for all the anger I can summon. Instead, I walk across to my bed and start cleaning up my mess.

PITA

By the time I get to the centre, I'm calm and level and back to human. I know I'm not like that—like him. It's being in this dust-filled shithole and this climate and doing this job with its long days and longer nights. It'll do your head in if you let it. I think I just need more sleep. That, or a decent coffee.

I get my allocation. I'm shitkicker number five in Brown Compound. I'm in the mess hall for dinner, standing sentry on the exit. The detainees seem in good cheer tonight. I'm pretty sure it's because there is pita bread out instead of the usual shitty loaves. I struggle to understand why the caterers normally serve white bread when you've got Sri Lankans, Afghanis, Iranians, Iraqis and Palestinians making up most of the population in here, and all of them prefer pita to those godawful loaves of foamy horse semen. It's a little thing, but I know it matters to the detainees.

I figure there will be some smuggling tonight. Though I have vowed not to stop any detainee taking whatever food they like from the mess hall, I like to know what's going on, so I watch closely. These guys don't know I'm going to let them get by, so hopefully they will be at their sneakiest, which means I need to be extra watchful to catch them. It's a game—a way to pass the time.

The first to make the dash is an old Afghani man. The pita bread is tucked beneath his shirt and pants; he holds his plate and bowl against his stomach to stop the pita falling out. Head down, he makes for the door at a furious shuffle, crinkling the entire way because the pita bread packet is made of cellophane. He wears the most conspicuous look of guilt I've ever seen. An unsubtle mob are keenly watching to see how the old-timer fares; they burst into laughter as he crinkles past.

Spurred on, the Sri Lankans are next. Just a few metres from where I'm standing, a portly man is stuffing a pita packet into his pants. I quickly look away, but the Sri Lankans know I know, and I know they know I know. The portly Sri Lankan proceeds to take the packet of pita out of his pants, remove the plastic, wrap the pita bread in paper towels and stuff it back in his pants. Very subtle. He waits till I'm talking to someone at the door, then shuffles out, exchanging conspiratorial glances with me, though I am studiously absorbed in conversation.

As for the man with whom I'm conversing, that's Tarik, an Iranian chap. Scars everywhere—face, arms, body, I presume from cutting himself. Yet he seems a fairly chipper sort. Tarik especially likes talking about women.

"You have girlfriend?" he asks.

"No. I don't."

"In Iran I have twenty girlfriend."

"Twenty?"

"Twenty. One not enough. Two not enough. Twenty—one after other, jiggy jiggy. She come in, jiggy jiggy, out she go, next come in, jiggy jiggy ..."

I shake my head.

"You, no? Have problem with ..." says Tarik. The gesture of a fisted-arm raising like a drawbridge adequately conveys his meaning.

"No problem. My problem is no woman."

"No have girl?"

"None. Zero."

"Oh, what about officer girl? Officer Karen."

Tarik glances at the officer seated at a desk on the other side of the room. Karen, like many of our peers, is obese.

"You and officer Karen, jiggy jiggy?"

I laugh. "No. Karen eat me."

"Oh, you don't like big woman."

"You like big woman?" I reply.

"I like woman," says Tarik, sharing a knowing nod. He grasps me by the upper arm in affection and leaves, a packet of pita dangling from his hand.

INTERVIEW

After dinner, I'm sitting on the bench in front of the officers' donga drinking a very average cup of tea. I'm shooting the shit with a fellow guard who has the salt and pepper hair of Ray Martin and the face of some bloke whose name you can't remember, except I do remember his name and I don't expect I'll forget it anytime soon because that name is Quincy.

I mean, what were his parents thinking? Did they hate the boy? It sounds more like a fruit you make jam with. Actually, now that I think about it, that's what his face looks like, too—a fruit fit for jam.

I hear Benedict stomping our way before I see him. His walk makes me think of the SS. Each leg bends high like a crankshaft then pounds stiff into the ground with the force of a pile hammer. I reckon you could put him in a field with a stump-jump plough strapped to his back and you'd have a pumpkin patch in about twenty minutes.

All Benedict says when he sees us is, "Gabriel inside?"

"Yep," I answer.

He's in and out in under a minute. Then Gabriel comes out and tells me I've been allocated two interviews. I have not been looking forward to this.

Basically, there's this bureaucratic shit sandwich called the personal officer scheme. Every day and night a certain number of detainees have to be interviewed so that a form can be filled out providing a rough and ready assessment of the detainee's mental health. It's meant to be that an individual officer is permanently assigned to a specific group of detainees so that a rapport builds and knowledge grows over time. But the staff turnover up here is monumental. In which case, the interviews are randomly dished out to whichever officers happen to be in the compound on the day.

I've been with other officers while they've conducted interviews, but these will be the first of my own. You're required to ask a bunch of questions about how the detainee feels and what their problems are. Without fail, the detainees who report that they are miserable, depressed or upset cite the length and indeterminate nature of their detention as the problem.

No shit! They're not meant to like it, or what would be the point of locking them up in the first place—in which case, why are we asking? The whole thing's just awkward and stupid.

I knock on my first door, wait a second for the entreaty, then let myself in. Farhad is in his room with three friends. They're sitting in a circle, talking. I explain that I'm here to do Farhad's personal officer scheme interview. Though he's been in detention for eighteen months, Farhad's English is still sketchy, so his friend translates. I ask Farhad if everything is ok.

Farhad speaks at considerable length in his native Pashto. I gather from the tenor of his voice that everything is not exactly ok. Farhad finishes, and his friend translates for me.

Farhad is worried about his family. They fled from Afghanistan to Pakistan, where they now live in a small village with intermittent electricity. He has trouble contacting them, and he is concerned about his sister, who is suffering from some sort of illness. They cannot afford medicine for her. The whole family was relying on Farhad to send money, but he was denied a visa and has now been at Curtin for over a year waiting on the outcome of his appeal, so he is unable to help.

It gets worse. His family don't understand why he fails to send money home now that he is in Australia—as a good son and brother should—because Farhad has not told them he is in detention. Too ashamed.

Yes, Farhad is suitably miserable. I jot down bits and pieces, though I know it serves no purpose. The last thing I ask is, "Any other problems or issues?" As if what he's said isn't enough.

Farhad answers. His friend listens, then looks at me and smiles. "He says, 'I pray that no longer we have to live in this cage.'"

I don't put that on the form. I finish with Farhad and then complete my other interview, head back to the office, make a cup of tea, laugh and joke with the other officers and try not to think about shit over which I have absolutely no control.

MATTHEW

Another night, but things are looking up. When I get my allocation I'm surprised to hear that I've been designated rover, meaning I'll be roaming the compounds, general dogsbody. Moments later that idea is deflated as I'm told that I won't actually be roving. They need me to spend the night with a detainee named Matthew. He's just been placed on constant watch, which means he's considered at imminent risk of either self-harming, harming others or causing a disturbance. He must be within arm's-length (which is bullshit) and line of sight at all times. It's something different, at least.

I find Matthew in the Green Compound mess hall. To begin with, I just stand awkwardly close to Matthew while he eats his dinner. He talks to his friends, I talk to my colleagues. Being watched makes all detainees uneasy, so after a few minutes Matthew departs. At that stage I properly introduce myself and accompany Matthew back to his room.

Rather than have me stand at the door watching him as he goes about his evening, Matthew invites me in. His English is surprisingly good—exceptional, in fact—and Matthew proves friendly, courteous and very open. Once I realise he is not your run-of-the-mill detainee, I ask him questions about how he came to be where he is today. He tells me everything.

In 2001, Matthew was sixteen, and he went by his birth name of Majeed. He was one of tens of thousands of Afghanis fleeing across the borders after the American invasion and the civil war that followed.

There were established corridors through which the refugees moved, but it was still a dangerous journey. The first border was with Iran, an old enemy, where the police shoot to kill. Matthew tells me it was fine, no one shot at him. He travelled overland to the Turkish border, where it was mountainous, rocky and very cold. They travelled at night and slept in caves, making their way by foot. Other smugglers helped them through to the Mediterranean coast. Before that Matthew had never seen the ocean. Without any trace of shame, Matthew tells me that when he looked out upon the Aegean Sea, dark blue without an end, he was scared. So much water, and such a little boat.

The boat that the Turkish people smugglers put Matthew and over a hundred others onto had no working engine. In the dark of night they set out, towed in the wake of a tug, past the Greek islands, bound for Italy. By the time they reached deep water it was apparent that their motor-less vessel was leaking at a rapid rate. Two diesel generators were set up to pump water. They ploughed on. Hours later, the first generator died. Not long after, the second generator died. The boat was sitting lower and lower in the sea, while more and more water appeared in the hull.

It was daylight when the tug dropped the towline and they realised they had been abandoned in a sinking ship without enough lifejackets to go around. Matthew describes mass panic and despair. Most people on board could not swim. He could not swim.

Before the boat sank, another arrived, sent by the people smugglers. The refugees were loaded on board, then safely ferried to the Italian mainland. I don't mention to Matthew how lucky he was. How many stories I have read in the news of people smugglers cutting their losses and abandoning sinking vessels, only for the human detritus to wash up on a Turkish beach or Greek island a day or a week later, like so much more flotsam.

From Italy, Matthew travelled by train to France, and from France to England. When he arrived he had no visa, so could not avail himself of any of the rights of citizenry or residency, but he had the help of Afghani friends and a community of expats who'd made the trip before him. He found an off-the-books job. Because he was young, he rapidly acquired the language. He started dating an English-speaking girl. And then an Afghani friend who had converted to Christianity showed Matthew some verses from that strange book the English called the Bible.

"When I looked at the Koran, I saw just another piece of cardboard," he tells me. "But when I read the Bible, it was straight away, I knew."

I guess that's what is meant by revelation. Matthew felt he belonged with the Christian God, simple as that. So he read the Bible and was eventually baptised a Christian. To make the break final and complete, he forsook the name of Majeed and became Matthew. "Like the apostle," he tells me.

Matthew lived in England for years. Eventually, he applied for a refugee visa in the hope of formalising his residency. He was surprised when his application was rejected. The English had sent troops to fight in Afghanistan; they knew it was a country at war with the world, and at war with itself. He applied a second time, was rejected a second time. After that, there was nothing more to be done. Matthew was deported to Afghanistan after spending six years on English soil.

He returned an apostate. When I mention I'm an atheist, Matthew tells me that an Afghani man would be killed for such a thing—as would a Muslim who had abandoned his faith. Matthew had no option but to keep his conversion a closely guarded secret while he set about constructing a new life.

Things happened quickly. He became a husband and, soon after, a father. That's what convinced Matthew to try again. His son inherited his Hazara ethnicity. Even if the war ended, the tribal conflicts would never disappear. The boy could expect a difficult life, or perhaps no life at all.

Once he had enough money to pay his way, Matthew crossed to Pakistan, then flew to Indonesia. After a wait of months in a concrete shoebox, constantly fearing that the Indonesian police were coming to extort his remaining money or simply arrest him, Matthew was taken to an old, decrepit boat.

Déjà vu—except this boat had an engine. A single outboard. It didn't have enough drinking water, and the captain didn't have navigational equipment beyond a compass. It was grossly overcrowded, with barely room to sit, let alone stretch out.

After two days chugging south, the engine quit. The boat drifted. Days passed. The asylum seekers were distraught. They knew others had perished this way. Matthew didn't know which was worse—to die of thirst, or to drown. "Perhaps to drown while thirsty," I say, and Matthew laughs.

On the sixth day of drifting in the sea, the men and women spotted a plane, then it disappeared from view. Four hours later, an Australian naval vessel sailed over the horizon. They were saved.

When he was finally deposited on Australian soil, Matthew understood that he would first be sent to a camp. But he did not understand when the Australian Government rejected his claim for refugee status. He is a Hazara man. An apostate. A man with a wife and son from a land that has gone crazy killing itself. If not all that, how much danger would be enough? Nor did he understand why Australia chose to lock him in a prison, when he'd been in the same situation in England, living free.

Isolated from his family, unable to support his two-year-old boy, not knowing if any of them have a future, Matthew told an officer conducting a personal officer scheme interview that he was depressed. He told the officer that he had thought about self-harming.

Almost immediately, he regretted saying it. He took it back

as silly talk that didn't mean anything. A joke, a sick joke. It didn't matter; the bureaucracy was already in motion. The officer was obliged to report his comments up the line, automatically triggering a constant watch, and that's how I got here.

Matthew tells me all of this, then quite unexpectedly says, "I am going to sleep now." He immediately lies down and closes his eyes and becomes very still.

ROOM

Last night was good. I think I made a friend. My first refugee friend.

Tonight, in furtherance of my career as a humanitarian, I've been asked to help a new arrival, a young Iranian man named Samir, find a different room. The room he was moved into in Green Compound has no flush on the toilet, which he only found out after depositing a generous refugee turd.

The problem is, there are no other vacant rooms in green, only rooms with another occupant. Nearly all of those occupants are from Afghanistan. That doesn't faze Samir; he's willing to cohabit with any religion or ethnicity. He's easy-going.

The Afghanis see it a different way. I talk at length with one Afghani man who arrived at Christmas Island on the same boat as Samir—which sort of makes him a friend. But there is no way in hell the Afghani will let Samir stay with him. Rooming with an Iranian is unthinkable; his countrymen would ridicule him.

And so it goes with another seven or eight others: for religious and cultural reasons they are accepting only of fellow countrymen. I hadn't anticipated that there could be so much prejudice between these people, not here, on Australian soil, where they have no tribal lands or traditional communities, where they are seeking the same thing and enduring the same hardships. If white people were expressing those sentiments toward Samir, we wouldn't hesitate to call it what it is: racism. Genuine, pointless racism.

Of course, we could just tell these guys it's too bad, that we'll do as we choose, that they have no say in the matter and if they want to be part of this country they need to leave their bullshit prejudices at home, but, so long as there are still spare beds, a harmonious resolution probably makes better sense.

I take Samir across to Red Compound where there are more Iranians. The officer in charge suggests I ask a detainee named Ali in room thirty-four. Samir and I go to the room. I knock on the door and a tall man with a thick moustache answers. I explain the situation. He says, "Yes, of course, this is fine, this is good," and with that Samir has found a bed, and hopefully a friend.

I spend a few minutes with Ali and Samir sharing small talk. Ali's English is excellent, whereas Samir's is not. But he's very eager to learn.

"How much English I speak?" Samir asks me, each word an effort.

"Well, I'd say about twenty percent."

"Twenty?"

"Yeah, about that."

"Twenty good?"

"Twenty is very good."

"Ok, good. You talk me, I am better. Yes?"

"Absolutely. Anytime. You'll need to pull your finger out if you want to catch up to Ali, though."

Samir looks at me, then looks at Ali. Ali speaks quickly in a language I don't understand, then Samir nods and turns back to me.

"Yes. I learn. How you say?"

"Learn?"

"No. What you say."

"Pull your finger out?"

"Yes, yes. Write, I learn, please."

Samir finds a pen and piece of paper and I write down the phrase: "You need to pull your finger out." I explain that it means a person needs to hurry up or work harder. Samir likes it.

"Thank you, officer. I learn. Officer, what your name?"

"Nick."

"Officer Nick. Thank you, Officer Nick. You are perfect man," says Samir.

"I think you mean, 'you're a good bloke'. Not 'perfect man'," I say.

"Yes?"

"Yeah. A good bloke."

"Good bl ... blo."

"Bloke."

"Good bloke," says Samir.

I shake hands with the two men and leave.

A little later in the evening, on my way to admin, I see Ali, or perhaps it is he who sees me. Ali asks for a light. These guys are always looking for a light because they smoke like it's the 1960s, yet are banned from having lighters. I carry one around, even though I hate cigarettes. Lighting a detainee's fag is a nice little thing you can do, and that simple exchange often leads to a conversation.

"Thanks for taking Samir into your room, Ali, that was good of you."

"No, it is good. I am used to many people. I have a big family and we never have a room to one person. Never."

"How many brothers and sisters?"

"Four sisters. Two brothers. But now, one brother. He will come after me. Then my mother, I want to give her a house."

"Oh, boy, ok. Well you're gonna need a good job."

"Yesss, a good job. I will work."

"What about your father?"

"No. He is with my other brother. In heaven. Though if they hear me say that, they are very mad."

"You're a Christian?"

"Yes, for three years."

"But your family's not Christian?"

"No. I am the only one."

"And what do they think about that?"

"They worry very much. I am here, yes?"

"So, what happened to your dad and brother, if you don't mind me asking?"

"The Basij," says Ali, the word very nearly hissed. "Like police, but worse. They take them to prison and they do not return. They tell us they do not have them, but they do not return. This is common. The Basij are very bad men."

"Wow. Jesus. That's ... fucked."

"Yes, thank you, Nick. 'Fucked.' I say this too."

Ali draws on his cigarette. "You have family, Nick?"

"Yeah, I've got a brother and my mum. No dad, like you."

"Ahh, also the Basij take him?"

I laugh. "Yes. The bastards. Anyhow, mate, I should get going. Take care, all right?"

"Yes, of course, Nick. Maybe I see you tomorrow."

"Day off tomorrow."

"Ahh. Yes. Me too, I think I take a day off. Go to Derby. Go to the shop and buy a new shirt."

"Really?" I say.

Ali laughs. I look at him, then the realisation of what he's saying dawns on me and I laugh, too. Ali isn't going anywhere.

GLOW

When I wake up to my day off I'd like to say it is with a sense of refreshment, vitality and joy, but I open my eyes to a glowing tin shed and think:

Fuck you, tin shed.

Fuck you, Derby.

Fuck you, climate striving to kill me, us, all life.

I hop into the shower. The water is good and straight away I feel better. I need to keep this shit in perspective. This place may be a shithole, and the job may be boring and sometimes bothersome, but I'm raking in almost two and a half grand a week. That's ... well, that's still less than what I'd be earning if I was a half-decent doctor, but, hey, it's the most money I've ever seen, and probably more than I ever will again.

I dress and grab my phone and wander outside. A wave of heat crashes on my face and after a moment of blinking and a handful of shallow breaths I realise there's no coming up for fresh air, it's this fetid greenhouse concoction or nothing. I'm instantly returned to my "mood". That's what Mum used to say: "Found a mood? Good or bad?" I don't remember being particularly difficult, not unusually sullen or temperamental, but I must have had my moments, like any kid.

I do remember one time, locking myself in my bedroom. That was about the most rebellious I ever got. I don't remember exactly what it was for, but Clem had given me a good dose the previous night, probably because I'd forgotten something or fucked up something, and I must have disagreed and pushed back a little. It ended with him telling me to get to my room and to stay there, and that I couldn't go fishing with him and Oli in the morning if I was going to be such a cunt. He certainly had a way with words.

I went to my room and, with considerable trouble, barricaded the door with a clothes drawer. Then when it came morning I don't know if Clem had forgotten or Mum had talked some sense into him or what, but he called through the door to ask if I was ready, like there'd never been any doubt I was going.

Normally I would have just pretended it hadn't happened, that whatever was said the night before didn't matter, the way we always did. But for some reason I wasn't letting this one go. I was becoming me, I suppose. And so I called out, "No!"

He tried to open the door and couldn't. He yelled, "What the fuck's going on?"

I was emboldened by the fact he couldn't get in, though of course he could if he really wanted, he was a strong man and an even stronger one when he was riled, but I was thinking like a boy for whom moving that big set of jarrah drawers had been bloody near impossible.

So I said, "I'm not coming! You said so."

There was silence for a moment. Clem must have been standing there, thinking. He could have said any number of things to placate me, or he could have gone ballistic, but he went right down the middle of those two options. "I don't care," he said, not to me, just in the hallway, to himself, and walked away.

I heard him getting ready outside and then talking to Oli and then Oli ran inside and up to my door and banged on it and screamed as if we were separated by six brick walls. "Nick! We're going! Come on!"

He waited and I said nothing, so he said, "We're going to Windy Harbour! Nick!" Then he ran down the hallway and called, "Mum! Nick's not coming."

I heard Clem come in and he said something to Mum. If he hadn't been angry before, he was now. He was always angry if given the chance to brood and figure out a way in which anything and everything was a personal insult, how it was the shitty world lashing out at poor old Clem yet again.

Mum asked him to be calm. She suggested he try telling me, in a nice way—not in an angry way—that he wanted me to come. Instead, he had a go at Mum, about how she was turning his boys into spoilt sissies, as if my not forgiving him immediately was utterly inexplicable and weak and irrational. She said fine. Just leave him at home. Take Oli and go fishing, because you've worked yourself into a foul mood and you'll take it out on Nick if he goes with you.

He slammed the front door and I heard the car engine gunning and then gravel flying. Mum knew to give me a bit of time to calm down. It was probably half an hour later, once the boredom of being inside had started to set in, when she knocked on the door.

"Sweetie?"

"What?" I said, even though I wasn't really angry anymore, just sad and sore that I'd been left behind with no attempt to convince me to go.

"Seeing as it's just us, I thought I'd make some little custard tarts. The ones you like. But if I do, we have to eat them all before your father and brother come home, or they'd get too jealous. Do you think you can eat three custard tarts in a day? If not, we'll just have to wait for tomorrow, when they get back," said Mum.

"Yes!" I called through the wall. "I can eat three. I can eat more than three!"

"What's that, honey? I can't hear you. I guess I'll just wait till tomorrow," she said, and I heard her footsteps going, then I was huffing and heaving to move those drawers, and I finally got them across just enough to squeeze through a sliver of the open door. Mum was standing at the end of the corridor.

"I can eat three, Mum!" I yelled, but I was yelling out of excitement, not anger or sadness.

Mum smiled and I realised that she had just done that for me — her little performance. I understood that she was getting me to do what she wanted, but also what was best for me, the same way she would get the roos and goats and chooks to do what she wanted. Yet it didn't feel like manipulation, which was a word I hadn't learned yet. It just felt like she cared enough.

Mum made a batch of custard tarts with my help. I ate my three and one of hers, and we didn't tell Oli and Clem when they came back the following morning. And then the best thing was that she made another entire batch that day as if she had just thought of the idea, and I ate six custard tarts in two days! It was so indulgent and meaningful, and yet it was such a harmless and silly little secret.

I look at the phone in my lap. It's not like that anymore. A batch of custard tarts can't make anything better. Does she even make them anymore? I feel like I should know the answer to that question.

I slide the phone into my pocket.

TIDES

In the afternoon, I hike into town to get some supplies. I head
to Woolworths. I feel a bit guilty about it, but Woolies isn't as
far to walk. I just cannot be arsed going the extra yards to the
IGA.

I strike it lucky when I spot a fellow Spinifex City resident
who happens to be a car owner. I ask if he's heading back, and
if he might give me a lift. Yes and yes. I quickly stock up. Three
cartons of cream, two bottles of whisky, a block of beer, some
food. Set.

Back at Spinifex City, I'm chucking my food into one of the
communal fridges when Roy wanders in.

"Comin' to the pub, mate? Heard a few others say they're
headin' down."

"Yeah, for sure. Which one? The Tide's Inn? I think that's
where the other guys go."

"Fuck'n oath, sounds good, Nicko."

Roy and I are lucky. Our day off falls on the weekend, so
there might actually be some life in town. I've certainly been
looking forward to a few restoratives.

"Get a good sleep, mate? Tires yer out, dunnit? If I could, I'd
sleep in till nine or ten every day. Then I'd get up, have some
breakfast, 'n watch one of them shows where they sell stuff,"
says Roy.

"Advertorials?"

"They're the ones, but I only watch 'cause I fancy the blonde sheila selling the stuff. I mean, they're trying to sell you a ladder. Who wants to buy a fuck'n ladder at that time of day?"

Roy and I have a few beers then swing a lift into town. The Tide's Inn is easy to identify thanks to the massive boab tree growing out front. Its trunk is short and as wide as a car; its limbs are gnarled and spastic. I can't tell if its dead or if that's just how a healthy boab looks. It's this climate—it turns everything ugly and angry. Soil turned dust and rivers churned brown and beaches turned mud and crabs that can and will rip your dick off.

I know that I should be more reverent. That old ugly boab could be over one thousand years old. There's one down the road that's meant to be fifteen hundred years old. The inside is hollow and apparently they used to lock Aborigines in there. Not sure when. Given the sentiments I've heard around Derby, I'm guessing they only stopped sometime in the 1990s.

Roy and I head inside and grab a seat at the bar, order a jug and get to drinking. There's a good few people, probably twenty of whom are from Curtin. I see Bailey come in. I wave him over.

"Where've you been, mate? Haven't seen you in the centre for a few days," I say.

"Yeah, I've been doing the ERT training. I'm back tomorrow," he tells me.

"You mean training to be in the riot squad?"

"Yep, full kit, batons, shields, helmets. And we've been learning all the formations and combat skills."

"Nice."

"What's that, headache? Knee some cunt in the head," says Roy, acting out the motion with his usual vigour. "Oh, sorry, you slip? *Crack!* One in the back of the skull. Be a bit of all right, wouldn't it—get time off to learn that sorta shit?"

"Yeah, it's been good. Late starts in the morning, early finishes in the afternoon. It's been interesting. Learned some nifty holds and grappling, that sort of stuff."

"So, are you in the squad now? Like, if there's a riot or whatever, do you get called in?" I ask.

"Yep. And I get extra pay for it. And if there's a riot or big disturbance at another centre, then I can get sent there, too."

"That'd have to be good money, wouldn't it?"

"Oh yeah. Big money."

Roy drains his glass.

"Jug?" he says.

"Yeah," I say.

I see Karen across the room and nod a greeting. When the person she's talking to starts talking to someone else, Karen excuses herself and comes over. Karen and I have nothing in common, but I like her. She's a sweet, gentle lady, who also happens to be extremely uncomfortable in her own skin. The thing about Karen is she's fat—as in, morbidly, perhaps super-morbidly, obese—and it is something that clearly occupies her thoughts and concerns every waking moment of her life.

You see it in her personality, but also in little movements: a frequent slight tugging at the corner of her shirt or the occasional two-fingered pluck where it sticks to her belly, almost paranoid hoisting of the back of her pants, frequent checks of her upper lip for sweat, an over-cautiousness when passing people lest she brush them with her gut or hips or rump.

I feel very sorry for her, but that itself is unfair. People shouldn't be pitied. Whatever their problems, all anyone wants is to be treated like other normal people—with basic courtesy and engagement. Frankly, I'm surprised to see Karen in the pub. Good on her.

"Hey Karen," I say. "How's it going?"

"Hi Nick. Hi Bailey. It's quite busy in here, isn't it?"

"Gets busier," says Bailey. "And messier. About eleven you can just about guarantee a fight."

"Oh. I don't think I'll be here that late," says Karen.

Roy turns around, armed with a jug of Emu Export. "Oh shit,

look out, trouble here. You been training for the riot squad, too?"

"Sorry?" says Karen.

"Want a glass, love?" replies Roy.

"Um, well if that's ok, I'll have a glass, thank you. Just one."

Roy reaches over the bar, pilfers a glass and pours the beers.

Karen asks Bailey something about this riot squad business, and Roy mutters something to me about bashing someone or something, and I glance around the room to see who's in the pub. I spot Chantal sitting at a table in the back. I haven't bumped into her since the first day we got here. She's billeted in a different camp, and she's on the opposite shift rotation to me. I haven't seen Danny, either, and I won't.

He was fired a couple of days ago for posting something on his Facebook page about Muslims swamping Australia and how they should return whence they came. Yeah, he's a smart bloke and has a good sense of humour, but he's prejudiced through-and-through—but so are the people he's prejudiced against. Those nice Afghani fellers who smile and say thank you—in the right circumstances I reckon they're capable of a pretty decent pogrom or two. Anyway, the whole brouhaha was on ABC news, as if a Facebook post that pretty much reflects government policy is of any material importance.

I feel sorry for Danny. He's got a wife and newborn to provide for at home. Still, he should have known better. You don't write racist shit on Facebook—you say it in person inside the detention centre.

I leave Roy, Karen and Bailey talking among themselves. I make a beeline for Chantal. She's sitting with Jayden, the new recruit I met a few days ago.

"Hey, Chantal."

"Nick!"

She jumps up and gives me a hug. It's nice, not to mention completely unexpected. I honestly didn't think we were that well acquainted. As I look her over I'm reminded that she was the most attractive girl at the Northam racecourse, and she's the most attractive girl both in this saloon and at our prison. The same would probably be true if she did a tour through every small Australian town north of the 30th parallel. I think. Certainly that's my honest opinion at this moment in time.

Chantal sits back down. I glance across the table.

"Hi," I say.

"Hi," says Jayden.

I sit and we chat about the job and Derby and some of the odd people we work with, and I tease Chantal a little about how scared she was of being raped — and that sounds fucked-up, but it's fine, it's funny, Chantal laughs and agrees that there really is very little to be worried about.

I'm actually getting the vibe that Chantal might be interested. She's laughing at the things I say. Smiling at me. Her body is twisted around in her chair so she's facing me, which means she's not facing Jayden. He doesn't seem to have much to say, anyway, and I don't try terribly hard to bring him into the conversation. Sorry, Jayden.

Then Roy staggers over. Roy has another full jug (which raises the question, what happened to the rest of the last one because I certainly didn't see more than a middy). Like myself, Roy takes a seat at the table without invitation.

"Hello, what we got here; young Chantal, is it? You old enough to be in here? Where's your chaperone?" says Roy, clearly joking.

"Yes," says Chantal. "I'm eighteen."

"I think it was my buy, mate," I say.

"You get the next 'n." Roy tops up my glass. "Anyone else?" he asks, holding the jug up.

"No thanks," says Jayden.

"I'm drinking vodka and lemonade," says Chantal.

"Want us to get you one, love?" asks Roy.

"It's ok, I'll get her one," Jayden says. "I'm getting one for myself, anyway."

"Thanks," she says.

There's a pause in the conversation. Roy scans the room. He hones in on something, his whole body stiffening and leaning forward like a pointer dog. He throws an elbow into my ribs. "Oi, there you go."

I look at what he's looking at. It's an Aboriginal woman.

"A bit of the old black velvet. Eh?"

"Not sure people say that anymore, Roy."

"What's black velvet?" asks Chantal, looking around.

"Yer dunno black velvet? It's what the darkies feel like. You know, on the old..." Roy makes a whistling sound and arches his eyebrows to finish his sentence.

I don't outwardly react, but inside I cringe. Why, Roy? Why say that to Chantal? Why say that to anyone, ever?

Chantal sits there in silence, clearly thinking, trying to work out what Roy means. Finally she says, "I've gotta go to the bathroom," and she gets up.

Fucking Roy. Chantal may herself be racist, but when you combine racist and lecherous it tends to scare away pretty eighteen-year-old girls. She probably thinks Roy is a rapist. Being that I'm his mate, that would make me friend-of-rapist, so I guess I'm shit out of luck.

The only thing to do is catch Roy up in the drinking. I down a glass, pour another, top up Roy's, then head to the bar for a new jug.

VIBE

GUYRA PUBLIC LIBRARY

I tally six jugs between us. Could be seven. It's about 9.30 when Meg comes in. She's accompanied by the much-talked-about Gian, which is fine, because I'm not trying to fuck Meg.

I wonder if I should go in for the hug, all spontaneous and friendly like Chantal, but it's potentially awkward with Gian there, especially if Gian has just finished excavating his cock from Meg.

"Hey," I say, trying to sound as sober as I can and not too eager. "I was wondering if you were coming tonight."

"Totally. We were having some drinks at Gian's."

"Hi. Nick," I say, extending a hand.

"Yeah man. Gian."

"Quite the grip you've got," I say.

"Gamer's grip," says Gian, chuckling. "I've got the thumb of a Jedi master."

"Yeah, I can think of another reason," says Meg, smirking.

"Wanna do some shots?" asks Gian.

It's resolved to do shots. While Gian orders drinks, I chat with Meg. She tells me about her afternoon; about Gian driving her out to Lennard River where they went swimming in a natural rock pool.

"What about crocs?"

"It's in, like, this rock gorge, and it's got these falls above it and below it, so apparently the crocs can't get there."

"Ok ... but you walked there, right?"

"Yeah, obviously."

"So crocs have four legs, they can walk. I mean, think about it—they stalk cattle and run them down up here. So why couldn't a croc just walk around the falls? If I was a croc, I'd just walk to the pool, then I'd eat your tasty arse."

"You'd eat my tasty arse?"

"No, I mean, I'd eat you."

"So you want to eat me?" says Meg, cocking her head, pursing her lips.

"If I was a croc."

"Which bit?"

"Huh?"

"Which bit of me would you eat first?"

"Umm ..."

There is momentarily nothing in my brain apart from that which I cannot say: tits and arse, tits and arse, tits and arse ...

"Yo, shots!" calls Gian.

He means that in the plural. I don't even ask what they are, I just slam them down.

The night rolls on, there's lots of Curtin officers at the pub, lots of locals. I spread myself around like the affable drunk I am, though for a large chunk of time I'm with Meg. I'm starting to get the impression that Gian and Meg might indeed be friends and nothing more. She's a lot more touchy-feely with me than him, and I think maybe, just maybe, Gian is gay. I'm not entirely sure why I think that—it's just a vibe, I guess. But he does have splotches of tousled hair, dyed blond. And he wears a necklace. And he moves his upper body less rigidly than some guys; he sort of sways and swoons. I dunno—he might just be a cool dude, or a dude trying to be cool, or he might indeed be gay. I've never been good at picking a person's sexuality.

Meg, though, is definitely straight. She stumbles a bit and I grab her. She steadies herself by holding my arm and leaning on my shoulder. I think she's acting drunker than she really is. I smell her hair, perfumed like vanilla and coconut. I let simple gravity drape my arm around her back, then rest my hand on her hip. It's natural and easy. Meg's fingers find mine. She bends her head back a little, and looks up at me with big brown eyes.

I see her lips, shiny and perfectly curved like two segments of blood orange, and I badly want to kiss her. I think she wants that, too. I hesitate, anxious I don't misjudge the moment.

That's when I hear a voice holler above the din. It sounds like Roy.

ENTERTAINMENT

Last I knew, Roy was playing pool with his interpreter pal. Now he has his arm around the neck of some bearded Derbard, trying to choke him, while the Derbard kneels on the interpreter, hand grabbing at his face. A large crowd has formed a loose circle around the fracas, the faces of the spectators filled with the sort of wild glee you'd expect to see in the Colosseum. I guess this is about as close to entertainment as you get in Derby.

Roy seems to have things under control, but then I see a Derblodyte push through the crowd—and it's not to get a better vantage for viewing. I slam my glass onto the bar and skip through the throng, shouldering bodies. By the time I breach the human cordon, Derblodyte man has gone from trying to rip Roy off the Derbard, to landing two punches in the back of Roy's head. Roy seems unfazed; he's still got hold of the bearded fiend who's now sporting a touch of periwinkle around his lips.

"Oi, fucktard!" I yell.

The Derblodyte looks up to see my fist heading for his face. He reels back and I clip him across the brow. He staggers and I keep going, using my momentum to shirtfront him into the pool table. Then some other Derbirker punches me in the back of the head, and I just don't know why Derbiots persist with back-of-head punching because I guarantee the dark side of a man's skull is harder than any fist. I reel around and throw myself at the little prick and we tumble to the ground. We spill onto Roy who's still clutching the bearded Derbard-turned-blue; they sprawl on the floor, which makes a grand total of half a dozen drunk men thrashing about like goldfish on carpet.

Before I can get to my feet, three big bouncers arrive. They drag me from the floor, my arm twisted around my back; they prise open Roy's chokehold and do the same with him. We're rushed through the crowd, out the back door, and deposited in the car park. They tell us to bugger off and never come back. Then they stand at the exit, glaring at us.

"You all right, mate?" I ask Roy.

"Yeah, think he broke a chair over me or summin'; fuck'n shoulda killed that bloke."

"Well, you nearly did, mate."

"Appreciate yer jumpin' in Nicko, yer a fuck'n good bloke. Not like them other sheilas."

"And you're fuck'n mad, Roy. I'm gonna call you Mad Dog. Mad Dog Roy. Once he latches on, won't let go."

"Too right. You know how to handle yourself, eh? Bit o' the fight in ya?"

"Bit."

A facility with fists is about all that's left of the Harris legacy, and I claim my share.

Out of the blue, Roy reels around and calls out: "Cocksuckers!"

"That's the way. You tell 'em, mate."

SALTY

Roy and I limp around to the front of The Tide's Inn. We see one of the three bouncers standing guard at the entrance. No point trying to sneak past—never works.

Roy and I could just call it quits and walk home, but we've both got a belly full of grog and veins tingling with adrenaline. We don't feel like quitting. There's a drive-through bottle shop attached to the pub, so we pop in. While Roy pretends to be a car, I buy a bottle of whisky, and they let me. God bless those Derbuckers.

Now, I'll say this about myself: I am a very malleable drunk. If I'm with women, I'm a drunken womaniser, warm and charming. If I'm with bogans, I'm a voluble dero. If I'm with the educated middle classes, I'm obnoxiously erudite. If I'm by myself, I'm an absurdist philosophiser. My drunkenness adapts to its surrounds. With Roy, I'm feeling loose. I feel like we need to do something stupid. Even more stupid than getting in a bar fight.

Without ever actually agreeing on a plan of action, we stomp through town, headed for the pier. We reach the road that is the single accessible trail across the mangroves and tidal mud flats. It's raised up by dint of God knows how many truckloads of rubble.

"Don't you fall in, Roy," I call, as the old bastard stumbles off the road and sinks a boot in the mud, "I'm not haulin' your heavy arse out!"

"Quicksand, mate! Shit, she's got me, the bitch's got me," says Roy, play-acting being caught by waving his hands in the air, his face a perfect repose of stupidity-crossed innocence.

We traipse on and eventually come to the pier. It juts a few hundred feet into the churning shit-stained tidal waters of King Sound. It used to be a port, I think. Maybe it still is. Right now it's deserted, though it is lit end to end by the fluorescent glow of street lights.

We pass two signs. One is a drawing of a person swimming inside a big red circle and cross. The other is a picture of a crocodile swimming. It looks happy.

Roy and I make our way to the edge of the pier. I lean over the railing, looking at the water. It's choppy and brown. We share the bottle, taking swigs of cheap whisky, the sort with the smell of metho and burn of turps.

"Carn!" says Roy, slurring badly.

"What?"

" 'Av a swim, mate! Take a fuck'n dip! Cool down!"

"Go on, then."

"Nah, both us."

Roy makes as if he's going to climb onto the railing. "Carn!" he yells.

"What, I'm getting roped in?"

Roy slumps onto the railing. I take a swig of the whisky. We share an animated silence, then Roy says, "Let's chuck a few bombies, Nicko!"

Again, Roy motions to climb up, but doesn't. He's got clown face and googly eyes that look in two directions at once. And he's not merely slurring; his native cockney accent is coming back. He's barely intelligible. He's barely intelligible at the best of times, but now he's barely intelligible in an English way. He's probably so pissed he wouldn't know which way was up. I climb the rail, sit on the top rung and swing my legs over.

"What you reckon, mate, double pike?" I say.

The sense of danger I feel while sitting there is good, though

I have no intention of actually jumping off.

"I reckon 's fuck'n salty, yer daft prick!" says Roy.

"Eh?"

Roy reaches across and takes the bottle from my hand. Then he points a wavering finger at something bobbing in the water about twenty yards out, just beyond the light cast by the lamps.

"Bullshit. It's driftwood or something," I say.

"Sure?"

"No, I'm not fucking sure."

"Yeah, 'n go on."

"Well not if there's a salty there!"

Not anytime. The water looks like it might swallow a man and never spit him out.

" 'Ere."

Roy reaches out with a steadying hand. I begin to swing my legs back over. I'm right in the precarious position of having both legs in the air, no footing, when Roy gives me a mighty shove.

At first I'm unsure what's happening. I don't seem to be sitting on the railing anymore, nor standing on the pier. My ears fill with the riotous laugh of a maniacal clown. I can see the stars. I suppose I must be falling and it reminds me of a song—*Catch a falling star and put it in your pocket, never let it faaade away. Catch a falling star and put it in your pocket, save it for a rainnny day*—then there is darkness and it is wet. My eyes are open but I see nothing. My chest fills with an acid burn as I realise this is not water, this is King Sound, a soup of brown watery shit and fuck!

Oh fuck!

I need air.

I thrash arms and legs and imagine my head pointing to the surface but I don't know which way it lies, only there's a rule, a trick, something you do, something Mum told me, something to save for a rainy day. For Christ's sake, Mum, what is it, just tell me! I still the paroxysm of aimless thrashing which is as sure to attract salties as push me from the light and I wait for the answer while I remain suspended in a consuming darkness. But that is it, and the irony is exquisite for I remember the trick, to still oneself and slowly, very slowly, you rise and then you see the light, and I do and I swim and I imagine myself breaching the surf as a humpback flinging its full body from sea but I don't, I limp into air and breathe and it's ok, it's all ok.

Only Roy is screaming.

"Salty! Salty! Fuck'n salty! Git out! Git out!"

I look up at the pier and I see Roy pause to guzzle the last whisky from the bottle and then he cocks his arm and I see splintered light refracted through a glass prism and then I hear *plop*, perhaps the bottle, perhaps something bigger.

"Take at, y' bas'd!"

I look left and right to the pylons, big concrete monoliths marked brown, red, green and yellow in merging striations, only I don't see a ladder, why is there no ladder?

I swim furiously for shore. I can't see the salty but somehow I can feel it, feel it as a weight in my legs, like I'm trailing a buoy, dragging the beast with me. I'm ten yards from the bank when my cupped hand scrapes mud and I try to stand but it really is like quicksand, Roy was right, and I sink to my knees and then I have to thrash and flail and swim my body out, continuing to the shore with breaststroke till I beach. I scramble the way I've seen sea lions on documentaries scramble across the volcanic mud of barren islands, pounding my flippers into the sludge and pulsating my body and pushing from my feet, making miserable progress up the bank and not once stopping to look behind, not till I'm over the embankment and onto the mud flat-proper and still I beat my way forward knowing now I'm just common Brahmin to be stalked and run down and savoured as tartare. Eventually I scramble to my feet and only then do I look behind. I see nothing.

I wade and stomp my way back round to the road and drop my body on dry ground. I see Roy strolling my way.

"Where'd it go?" I yell.

Roy responds with the dance of a drunken sailor. When he reaches me he says, "Sorr' mate, finish'd it. Was jus' a drizzle lef'."

"Where's the salty?"

"Eh? Wo' salty?"

"The fucking salty!"

"Eh?"

And with my arsehole reamed wide as a church door by the jest of an irreverent simpleton drunk off my own drink, we begin the long trek home.

DOZING

Yesterday, the day after the night before, may qualify as one of the worst hangovers of my life. Quite a few people at work remarked upon my poorliness. They were kind enough to expect little of me. I was still made to stand guard over the cordial machine, but I did it sitting down and no swinging-dick came by to tell me otherwise. Three times during the day I went around to the back corner of an unused building in a little no-man's-land section of the centre between Brown Compound and Green Compound to doze in a chair. I must have spent almost five hours like that. That's how critical my role is to the functioning of the centre: I do nothing or disappear and everything ticks on as per usual, while I rack up a bit over four hundred dollars for my day's contribution.

That contribution, which amounts to simply lending my presence, is still a damn sight better than Roy's. He didn't make it to work. I was in dire straits, but I still dragged myself out of bed at the usual 4.30 a.m.; I even banged on Roy's door to try and rouse him because I knew he would sleep through his alarm. He didn't or wouldn't answer. So I went back to my room and took stock of the devastation. A pile of mud containing my clothes sat in the middle of the floor. There was mud on my white sheets, on my towel, on the walls, it was everywhere. My shoes—my only pair of shoes—were of course soaked in mud, so I had to wash them in the shower then wear wet, stinking shoes all day.

But today I'm ok. Not great, still fatigued and listless, but ok. Roy is ok, too, but he did get in a lot of shit for skipping work and not calling in. He received a formal warning. It's actually his second. He received one last week for failing to respond when hailed over the radio, thus triggering a Code Black where all officers in the detention centre frantically began the search for one Mad Dog in case he'd been clobbered by a client. Two warnings in just over two weeks — Mad Dog is on borrowed time. Poor daft bastard.

I see Mad Dog at lunch and he's doing fine. He's brushed off the formal warning, which he considers an inexplicable persecution not of an entirely different kind to that experienced by a refugee. We recount the fight in the pub, a fight I consider to be of the best kind for it was mostly drama and scuffling without anyone getting properly hurt. Mad Dog explains how it began, telling me: "The bloke had it coming." I press him on the matter and he tells me that one of the Derbards he and the interpreter were playing pool against made an unsportsmanlike, possibly racist, comment toward the Iranian interpreter. The interpreter may have said something like, "Fuck off," which was enough to get the Derbard going, and that set Mad Dog off, which set the other Derblodyte off, which finally set me off. I ask Mad Dog if there really was a croc when I took my dip off the pier. He says, "Yer went swimming, did ya?"

As for me and Meg, she's acting like nothing happened between us, which is true. Nothing did happen. Something almost happened. But nothing did. Somehow that is a worse state of affairs than if nothing was going to happen in the first place. Once you get to the jumping off point and for whatever reason you don't jump, it's damn near impossible to get back up there. Relations never go back to that place of innocence from where they began; there's suddenly a self-consciousness and awkwardness that seeps into every action and interaction. Though you think it'd be sort of cute or sweet or somehow tantalising to share knowledge with someone of your wanting them and their wanting you, once that knowledge becomes explicit it's just weird.

I also have a tender swelling the size of a fist on the back of my head.

BUM

I've been in a few scraps over the years, but I actually abhor violence — or, at least, the kind perpetrated for the sheer sake of it. Fighting for fighting's sake is either the mark of stupidity or the product of the worst disillusionment, and too often it ends in harm, not hurt. The only defensible violence is defensive violence. When I fight it's because the fighting has already begun and I'm either defending myself or my mates or someone who cannot defend themselves. All of which makes me a kind of saint, really, like Joan of Arc.

That said, depending on how one looks at it, an outsider might judge me partly responsible for some of the fights I've gotten into. My tendency to speak my mind and not suffer fools lightly, especially but not exclusively when drunk, does seem to rile a certain type of person. A few terse or brusque comments have preceded a number of the scraps in which I've been involved, but that is purely an observation of chronology, of correlation and not causation. I contend that a fight does not and cannot begin with words. A fight begins with the first punch thrown. Frankly, the sort of moron who cannot defend against words with his own words is the sort of moron who deserves a good thrashing.

So it is somewhat unexpected, and entirely peculiar, to find that not only has the story of my little scuffle turned into the legend of an epic pub brawl, but those exploits have attracted not a word of disapprobation and more than a few of admiration, and not just from manly men who think fighting is a fine thing.

Yesterday Karen told me she thought it was very good of me to defend Roy. This morning on the way into the centre one of the female managers who I've barely spoken to smiled at me and said, "Hey there, Plugger. We're going to have to get you into the ERT."

And right now I'm talking to Allison who till now has always looked straight through me. Allison is a bit younger than me, I'm guessing about twenty-three, and quite cute. Because she's had a lot of experience she is designated a rover, though today I notice she's spent a fair bit of time in Blue Compound, where I'm stationed. Currently, it's just the two of us in the office. Allison tells me bits and pieces about the eighteen months she spent working at the Christmas Island centre.

"It was ok before it got really overcrowded," she says, "but then clients started sewing their lips together and there were fights and protests and the whole place just became fucked. It totally screws people up."

"The clients or the staff?"

"The staff I mean. That's why I asked for a transfer, even though the money's better over there. Some of the guys are just constantly like ..." Allison balls both fists together as her face adopts the far-off look of insensible rage. "If you start off a bit of a cunt, then odds are you'll be a major one by the time you leave."

"You seem pretty sane to me. Potty-mouthed, but sane."

Allison laughs. "Yeah, that's something else. I never used to say the 'c' word. Now I can't stop. I accidentally said it on the phone to Mum the other day and she lost it."

"What a cunt," I say.

There's silence. Then Allison bursts out laughing. Close one.

Another officer comes into the office and Allison goes back

to filling in some pointless form. When the officer leaves, Allison turns around, catching me looking at her arse.

"So where are you from?" Allison asks.

"Do you know Manjimup? It's in the south-west."

"Oh yeah, it's near Pemberton. I've driven through there. Like, with the karri trees."

"Yeah."

"It's nice. I'm originally from Kalgoorlie. We don't have trees."

"Oh shit, Kal ... so you'd be right at home here."

"Exactly. Except it's never really humid in Kal. But, yeah, I'm pretty used to being surrounded by red dirt and coons," says Allison, chuckling a little as if she's made a joke.

"Hmm," I murmur. It's the best I can muster given I want to convey some sort of censure, but she did just give me a pass, not to mention I want to keep flirting with her. Why do all the pretty girls have to be so racist?

"So do you still live there?" says Allison.

"Where?"

"Manjimup."

"Oh, no. I don't really live anywhere."

"Like ... what do you mean?"

"Well, before this I was travelling in Central America and before that I was travelling up the coast of New South Wales and Queensland, just working when I had to, picking fruit and that sort of thing, so I haven't had a fixed address for a while."

"So are you, like, a bum?"

"You mean a bohemian."

"Like a Jamaican or something? No, a bum."

"I'm not a bum. Are you a bum?"

"What? No."

"Well, exactly."

"Ok ..."

"Do you know where the term comes from?" I ask, my tone a little harsher than I intend it to be.

Allison gazes at me. She has the look—a look I recognise

from experience — of a person on the verge of transitioning from perplexity to antipathy. I don't care. I hate that word, and intend to plough on regardless. I've been called a bum too many times by too many dumb people who think honour (as if honour matters) only lies in the stolid pursuit of misery through unending employ in meaningless labour. Fuck them.

"'Bum' is an American term for a homeless person who doesn't have the resolve or moral fibre to do an honest day's work and drag their arse out of the gutters, which is obviously not me because I'm in this shithole right now. So, no, I'm not a bum."

"Awesome. Congratulations."

"Do you know what bohemian means?"

"Apparently not. But it sounds like you're dying to tell me."

"A bohemian is someone who pays no heed to rote rules or the expectations of society and finds their own individual way in life instead."

"Great. Can't wait to use that in a sentence," she says.

"Sorry, I just mean, I'm not a bum. I'm sick of fuckheads calling me that."

Allison snorts and her eyes glare.

"Not that you're a fuckhead," I backtrack, trying to find a light-hearted tone. "That's not what I mean. I mean some people who are fuckheads have said that to me."

"So I'm not a fuckhead and you're not a bum."

"Yeah," I chuckle pathetically, as if the levity hadn't already dissolved.

Allison doesn't say anything else. She just walks out of the donga. I sit there, brooding. We were having a nice conversation. We were flirting. Why did she, out of the blue, have to accuse me of being some piece-of-shit bum?

Oh — and have to be a racist?

Fuck her.

NOODLE

A few minutes later a detainee knocks on the window. I slide it open.

"Maggi," the Afghani man says.

First time I heard this, I hadn't the faintest idea what the detainees were on about, till someone explained they wanted noodles, even though the Maggi noodles were replaced with some cheaper brand years ago.

"You mean noodles," I say.

"Noodle?" the Afghani man says.

"Noodles," I respond.

"Noodle," he says.

"It's noodles. Nood-lll-sss. Noodles."

"Noodle-ss?"

"Yes, noodles. How many do you want?"

"Two."

"Two packets of noodle-sss. 'Two packets of noodles, please.'" The man nods.

I grab two packets of noodles from a box and hold them up.

"I want two packets of noodles," I say, intending for the man to repeat the phrase. He doesn't. "One packet of noodles," I say, holding up a single packet, "two packets of noodles," I say, holding up both packets. "Noodles. Sss. Noodles."

"Yes. Noodle-ss."

I pass the noodles to the man, but I don't let go, suspecting that he knows "please" and not "thank you". He tugs on the noodles but I hold tight.

· "'Thank you.' You say 'thank you' when someone gives you something."

"Thank you," he says, looking at me with the same look Allison gave me. I let go of the noodles before yet another bout of perplexity mutates into something unintended. The man walks off. I go back to sitting and brooding and that is how my day is spent.

RATTLED

There's no rhyme nor reason to the mood in which a man wakes. Sometimes the sun is shining, and sometimes the fucking sun is shining.

By the time I get to work, just before 6 a.m., rays of hellfire are already tearing into the landscape. Sweet Mother Nature is wielding her cat o' nine tails, the tassels lush, golden and coruscating as they strike man and mongrel alike, no doubt a gift in another's eyes, but a wickedness in mine. Such flagellation by abundance must be lovely in Broome as one strolls a lovely long beach of squeaky white sand. But I'm not in Broome, our glamorous neighbour. I'm in a prison at a place called Curtin, surrounded by scrub and fences and tin and dust where such sunshiny splendour is merely cruel and miserable, a burden to be endured. All I can think about is respite from the heat and glare, and that lies solely inside the four walls of a tin shed, hardly respite at all.

I've never hated the sun, it makes no sense to hate the sun, but right now I do. I hate the sun. I hate it as I hate the oily sheen on my forehead and the damp where my belt pushes pant against waist, as I hate the beads of sweat that simultaneously course the furrows of my chest and back. The sun is an enormity upon this land.

If it would just rain. We've been bringing our rain jackets every day and every night since we arrived, told to expect spectacular storms, storms that sweep away the humidity and heat. From time to time we've seen thick banks of cloud in the distance, but as yet there's been not a drop of water, except for the shallow ponds formed by dickhead detainees who themselves come from lands where water is precious yet leave our hoses running just the same. I turn a hose off—has it been running all night, for fuck's sake?—and begin my headcount, the first of three welfare checks we'll be conducting over the next twelve hours.

It's the same every morning. Each officer in a compound gets a list of detainees and their locations, then we go room by room, cracking the door open, checking if they are inside. Normally we find them asleep. We mark their name off a list, thus certifying them present and alive. And they always are—alive. Detainees seem to need time to work up to self-harming or suicide, so mornings are relatively low-key.

At first, it bothered me going into detainees' rooms unannounced. Their personal spaces are never private and that must have some sort of psychological effect. But I suppose there is no alternative. Besides, if you knock at 6 a.m. it would just wake a man who only benefits the fewer waking hours he spends.

I go about my checks, not bothering to make certain the detainee is breathing, unless they are one of the nutjobs. It's a safe-ish assumption that most of them are fine, and to be absolutely certain would mean creeping into their room, crouching next to the man and listening very carefully for his breath. That's weird and I'm not doing it. It's also pointlessly time-consuming and no one wants to be last to complete their welfare check. Why any of us should care who finishes first and who finishes last, I don't know. Perhaps it's a misplaced sense of pride in work. Perhaps it's just a way to find interest where there isn't any.

I notice this morning that many of the doors are locked. In one section, four doors in a row are locked. The detainees are breaking the rules. It's also inconvenient. I have to get my keys out and find the right one amóng a bunch of ten or so, then carefully unlock the door without waking the detainee. It slows me down. In a very short space of time I find my frustration building. The detainees know how this works—why are they making my job harder?

I come across another locked door and it's just ridiculous by this stage so I get out my keys and jangle them like crazy. It's 6.15 a.m. The man groggily opens the door before I get the key in the lock. I nod at him and frown. Sorry pal, but you make me go to all that effort of using keys to open your bedroom door, then you get woken up. Simple.

I'm almost through my list of rooms when two other officers find me. Gabriel, who is running the compound today, sent them out to help me. Everyone else is finished. It pisses me off.

SOLITUDE

It's mid-morning and I've calmed down. There's one more personal officer scheme interview to be done. The name and number seem familiar. I check the client photos. It's a man named Soheil. Every time I see him in the mess hall, Soheil shakes my hand and asks me how I am. We don't really talk beyond a few pleasantries, but there's an intelligence in his eyes and something in his calm demeanour that intrigues me. Talking to him will be good.

I knock on Soheil's door. Soheil greets me warmly, invites me in and offers me a drink. I notice how meticulously his room is kept. Not an article out of place. And clean. I take a glass of water from Soheil; I put my clipboard on the floor. I want to speak to him as two humans, not as an officer following a script.

I ask how long he's been at the centre. Seven months, he tells me. His application for a refugee visa was rejected at the first interview; Soheil cannot articulate the reason for this, if there is one. Like many of the men in here he is now waiting on his review—and he has hope, because the review stage frequently results in applicants being awarded a visa.

I ask Soheil if he knows how long he will have to wait for the decision. He thinks it will be six more months, but isn't sure. To me, it is an unimaginably long time when all you're doing is waiting.

"I'm sorry," I say.

"It is no problem. I wait," says Soheil.

There is a quietude about Soheil. He moves gently, he speaks gently; his eyes have both warmth and reservation. I ask Soheil why he chose to come to Australia. Without giving me specific details, he tells me that it was very difficult in Iran. I ask about family and friends. He tells me he has a brother in Europe, but that much of his family died in Iran. He doesn't say who, or how.

I ask if there is anything I can do for him. Then I remember how well it went down last time I asked a man that, so I qualify my question with another question.

"Maybe there is something from town you need?"

"Thank you. No. Nothing. Thank you."

I get up to leave.

"Ahh, sorry, there is something, please," says Soheil. "I live in room on my own. Just me. Soheil," he says, tapping his chest. "This is good for me. Best for me. I am alone, it is ... this is best. To think. And sleep is very hard. I sleep two, three hours every night. No more. I have nightmares. I go, I see mental health every week, they give me pills. I want to stay in room on my own. Can you make request for this?"

I tell him I will do what I can. Soheil is grateful. He tells me that I should come and join him and others playing table tennis sometime. I tell him I'd like that.

NO

That afternoon I remember what Soheil asked about his room. No doubt he's worried because quite a few detainees from Christmas Island have been transferred over the last few days, with more to come, and they all need beds. So I tell Gabriel that Soheil has asked for an exemption from having a second person move into his room.

"He's trying it on," says Gabriel, as he continues filling out paperwork at the big desk in our little office.

"What do you mean?"

Gabriel rolls clockwise in his office chair. He rests his feet on the desk.

"There are two key phrases in this place that tell you they're trying it on, and one of them is, 'I need my own room.' Soon as you hear that, you know they're trying to get one over you. It's bullshit. The answer is, 'No, fuck off.' "

"And the other?"

"The other one is, 'I need to move rooms.' They don't need to do fuck-all."

"Well, Soheil said he's been seeing mental health, and has been taking sleeping pills, and still only gets a few hours of sleep each night, so ..."

"Mate, you'll learn, these guys see a new bloke, they try it on. Just look out for those two phrases, 'I need my own room' and 'I need to move rooms'."

Gabriel drags his feet from the table and swings back around to his paperwork. It's pretty much the same advice all the managers in the centre have given me. Every request is an attempt to get something out of the new guys who don't know any better. Our job is to go through the motions where necessary so as not to get in strife from the higher-ups, while otherwise politely telling clients to go fuck themselves.

As far as it goes, there's probably some truth to the advice—why wouldn't (and why shouldn't) a man in prison take every shitty little advantage he can seize? It doesn't bother me if that's what's happening. But I don't think that is what's happening. Soheil is a modest guy, and when he tells me he has anxiety and sleep problems, I believe him. It doesn't matter, though; there's nothing more I can do. Gabriel isn't just some shitkicker like me sounding off. A few days ago he was promoted to client service manager. What he says carries weight.

ACACIA

Later that afternoon, Gabriel brings up the fight Mad Dog and I got into. He's heard that I was up against four or five locals. I laugh when he says that, because I love a story that grows in the telling, especially one that flatters me.

"Yeah, give or take a few," I say.

"Better watch your back, mate. Them Derby locals keep a grudge."

"It wasn't even me, mate. It's Roy who started it. I was just helping out."

"Oh, that retarded faggot. What is wrong with him? He was in my compound the other day. He's walking around opening doors on cupboards muttering shit to himself, talking about tasering people, then disappears for an hour. He's not the full quid. Ended up I wanted to fuck'n kill him."

"Yeah, he's an interesting one. He's all right. Probably just dropped on his head a few times when a baby."

There's no one else in the office so I tell Gabriel—in confidence—how Roy pushed me off the pier the other night. We have a good laugh about it, especially the part where I swam for my life, chased by an imaginary crocodile.

"Nah, there probably was."

"You reckon?"

"Yeah, there's a fairly big croc that sorta lives down there. Most the times I've been there I've seen him or some other croc around the pier. You wouldn't see 'em in the dark, but he was probably there."

Huh ... well, still funny.

It's about an hour before knock-off when an old Afghani man knocks on the window of the donga. I open it and the man peers in, seeing who is inside.

"I speak with," says the man, pointing.

"Gabriel?" I say.

When he sees who it is, Gabriel gets out of his seat and rather than just going to the window he opens the door and walks outside. The two men sit on a bench and talk. After a few minutes, Gabriel comes back into the donga and says, "I want you to come with me. Got a little job we need to do."

"Sure."

We move at a brisk clip and as we do, a whole-of-body transformation comes over Gabriel. His chest puffs up and his chin juts forward and his impish smile becomes something stern and resolute. Gabriel's not a very tall or broad-shouldered man, but there's muscle on his frame, enough that most would think twice before diving into a blue with him. I know he used to be a real prison guard, so I can only assume that that's the persona he's now inhabiting.

"So, what are we doing?"

"That old feller, he's all right. He got shoved in with this Iranian faggot who wants his room back to himself. So he's been harassing him, telling him he's gonna bash him, that all his Iranian mates are gonna bash him, and so the old man keeps pleading for me to get him another room. I told the Iranian to knock it off the other day, but he's still at it, so I'm gonna sort him out. The way we took care of it in Acacia."

I don't know what that means, but I'm about to find out. We get to a room and Gabriel tries the door. It's locked. He uses his keys to open the door and walks in. He switches the light on. The detainee is lying on his bed. He sits up.

"Come in, shut the door," Gabriel says to me.

He walks over to the detainee. "Stand up."

The detainee looks at Gabriel.

"Stand up," he repeats, in a voice that sounds like authority.

The detainee slowly gets to his feet. He's got the look of a teenager who knows he is about to be chastised, and yet couldn't give a shit.

"What'd I say to you the other day? Hmm? I fuck'n told you to leave the old man alone. Didn't I? Didn't I?" says Gabriel, now jabbing a finger hard into the detainee's chest.

The detainee looks at where Gabriel is poking him and his face changes. I think he realises this is not the same lecture he received a few days ago. This is something altogether different. Gabriel takes a step closer. The two men are only inches apart, face to face.

"If you say one more thing to him, a single fuck'n word, I'm gonna make your life hell. You see this?" snarls Gabriel, pulling the badge pinned to his shirt toward the detainee. "I'm a manager. Man-ag-er. I can put anyone I want in this room. Any more trouble and I'm gonna move the old man out just like you want and I'm gonna put a big Iraqi faggot in here. Yeah, you know what that is? A poofter. A homo-sexual. A big Iraqi homosexual with a big cock and he's gonna rape you every single night. You understand me? Hmm? Do you understand me, fucker?" says Gabriel, as he stabs the man in the chest with his finger, again and again.

The man steps back but there's nowhere to go, only the corner of the room.

"If I ever have to talk to you again you're gonna get that new roommate, and I'm gonna make sure you don't get a visa. Yeah, no visa. Understand? Go on, tell me you understand."

The man nods. Gabriel stands there a moment, glowering, then turns and walks away.

"Let's go," he says to me.

The moment we're outside, Gabriel turns to me and smiles. The prison guard persona has vanished, the transformation some sort of magic trick.

"What do you reckon?"

"Umm, I think, I dunno, yeah ..." I say in an unsteady tone, unsure of my own reaction to Gabriel's performance.

"Yeah, you can't baby 'em. Just gotta lay it out sometimes."

Gabriel takes a deep breath. He's relaxed, but his chest is still puffed out. He's proud of what he's done.

"You thinking of playing footy for Derby?" he says. "Preseason starts soon."

"Oh, I dunno. I'd only be able to train with them every second week, I guess."

"Yeah, well they always need the numbers so you'd get a game. I played last season."

"Ok ..."

"Actually, I just bought a new Sherrin in Broome a few weeks back. It's beautiful, mate. We should have a kick sometime."

"Yeah, ok. Do you think ..." I start, but stop.

"What?" Gabriel looks at me. He sees the unease.

"Nothing."

We make our way back to the donga. Just another day at the office.

OBSERVED

His name is Amir Hosein—the man threatened with a big Iraqi cock up his arse. I know this because it's a day later and I'm conducting the second of six scheduled checks on Amir. He's been placed on the psychological support program, meaning he's been assessed as being of moderate risk to self-harm. It was triggered last night. I don't know exactly what he said, whether it was a threat to cut himself if he didn't get this or that or whether he just indicated that he was thinking of hurting himself. At any rate, he got what he wanted. This morning the old Afghani man was moved into another room. Amir is on his own.

I conduct the fourth check of the day and find Amir lying in the dark. This is what I've got on the form:

6.21: client observed in bed in room sleeping.
10.09: client observed lying in bed in room.
11.45: client in bed in room.
2.37: client observed lying in bed in room.

In a detention centre, lying in bed is pretty much the universal signifier of protest, depression, sickness, anger, boredom—you name it. So that's what gets written down on just about every welfare report ever written. It's a meaningless and thoroughly unedifying paper trail.

What makes it worse is that I'm fairly sure no one even reads this shit. It's arse-covering bureaucracy. So when it comes time for my next check I figure on adding a little colour to the bald fact that Amir is — no surprises here — lying in bed in a dark room. I use a piece of scrap paper to sketch out my "observation" before it's ready for the form:

4.00: The client lies in a dim-lit room
No light no sun, only the Curtin gloom.
Though he says nothing and nothing is said
He touches a hand to his shaved head.
Hand! Head!
Then hits the newsstand: CURTIN CLIENT NOT DEAD!
I write it down that this man does live
Not much but enough and enough I give
(To this report, this avoidance of tort
Due diligence discharged in short).
Of more there is nil
Nothing else to spill —
On vigour or desire
Or thoughts gone haywire.
The client lives and lives as he lies
In the room of a prison made of endless Curtin skies.

The better part of an hour is taken up writing the shitty poem that would have made Mrs Kennedy from year eight English very proud. Before I transfer it to the form, I give it a final read, and that is when it occurs to me: I have lost my fucking mind.

If someone above the level of shitkicker were to actually read this, I would surely be reprimanded and maybe even shit-canned, so I screw up the paper and bin it, then retrospectively fill in my four o'clock entry and — fudging the time only by a handful of minutes — add my final entry after poking my head into Amir's room for the sixth time this shift:

4:00: client in bed.
5:25: client in room in bed, audible breathing, appears to be asleep.

COLOURS

It's my third straight day in Red Compound. Amir is still being monitored. Gabriel gives his file to me.

Over the course of two days, Gabriel has gone from barely knowing I exist, to acting like he wants to be my mate, to treating me like a dumb underling. I think it's because I didn't react how he wanted the other day. I didn't say anything out of sorts, but I wasn't slapping him on the back, and I've found it hard being around him since. He's obviously noticed.

It's mid-morning. Amir didn't show at breakfast, which makes four meals in a row that he's missed. That means we're now obliged, according to some arbitrary bureaucratic rule, to formally inquire of Amir if he is on a hunger strike. Off I go.

I gently knock on the door (in case he's sleeping). As usual, there is no answer. As usual, the door is locked. I open it up with my keys and go in. Though the lights are off, I can see that Amir has finally dragged himself away from his bed, which is where he's been, seemingly without moving, for the last two days. He's now sitting cross-legged in the middle of the floor. There's something not right about the scene, but I'm not sure what it is.

"Amir? How we doing?"

He says nothing.

His face doesn't look right, but I can't really see because not much light comes in from the corridor. I switch on the light. I turn back around and I see blood pouring from a gash on

Amir's shaved head. Two thick streams diverge around his ear then rejoin to form a single stream at his neck. I see that there is blood on his hand. There's what looks like a razor still in his grasp.

I take a step back. At training we learned that if he's got a razor he must be treated as dangerous. He could use it to attack. Keep your distance, call for back-up. I pull the radio from my belt and hold down the transmit button.

"Code umm ..."

I can't remember the right order for the transmission, and I don't know if it's a Code Blue medical emergency or a Code Black officer needs assistance situation.

I need to stay calm, keep my nerve. Everyone in the centre hears these transmissions and of course you're being judged on how you handle it. I start again.

"Control, this is Red Six, Code ..." I want to say Black, I want other officers to come, but it's fine, he's just cut, other officers will come anyway, so don't sound like a scared baby, "... Blue, medical assistance required, room sixty-eight, Red Compound."

This sets off a brief flurry of radio communications as various staff are summoned to the location. I stand in the doorway of Amir's room, watching him bleed. I know it's probably not as bad as it looks. The detainees cut their heads because the scalp bleeds profusely, the same way and for much the same reason as professional wrestlers do; a harmless little nick can look like an ear has been lopped. But the fact there is a lot of blood isn't even what's off-putting. It's that a human did this to their own body.

Amir, for the first time since I met him in the company of Gabriel, looks at me. He looks at me and smiles. Not a happy smile or a greeting smile; a grim smile. What does it mean, I wonder.

Fuck you?

See what you've done?

Happy now?

I don't know.

Bailey is the first on the scene. "Right, step back," he says to me.

I move out into the corridor while Bailey pulls on latex gloves. "Amir? What's going on in there?" he says.

Another officer arrives. It's swinging-dick Benedict himself, then another officer arrives and another. I slink away to watch from a distance, knowing I'm neither needed nor wanted.

It only takes them a few moments to control the situation. Benedict and Bailey walk Amir out of his room, a big hunk of gauze pressed onto his bleeding scalp. They're taking him straight to the medical centre.

One of the officers left on the scene is a manager named Paul. He's also a union rep, so I know he's on the side of the worker. He asks me if I'm ok and I tell him I'm fine, but I guess he can see something in my eyes or some look on my face that he's seen countless times before. I wonder if he can tell how hard my chest is thumping, or if he notices that my hands are jittery. I don't want him to think I'm weak. I'm not queasy and I'm not shy and I'm not the sort to get scared of something. I honestly don't know why my body is so jittery, because this is all no big deal. I mean, come on, I saw human cadavers dissected back when I was studying medicine. This is nothing—literally nothing. No real danger. No serious risk of death. No confrontation.

"Is that the first Code Blue you've called in?"

"Yeah."

"Well, if you want to take some time, you can. If you want to take an hour just to get a cold drink and sit somewhere and let your nerves settle, that's fine. There's no shame in that. And if you want to talk to someone, we can arrange that, too. There's no shame in it at all."

"No, I'm fine. I'll ... I might get a Coke or something, take five. I'm good."

I get a cold can of drink and sit alone under a tree for a while, until my hands stop shaking and my chest feels normal. I think about Amir cutting himself and I realise, based on the amount of blood I saw and the freshness of the flow, Amir must have been waiting for me. He was sitting in darkness in his room, a razor in his hand, waiting to hear the jangle of my keys as I unlocked his door. Only then did he take that razor, press it into the flesh of his head and cut down, wearing that grim smile while he mutilated his own body. It's an unsettling thought knowing it was for me — that he waited to hurt himself as some sort of performance for me. I don't know if it was because of what Gabriel and I did, or because he was angry that I kept disturbing him with the welfare checks, or if I'm just an officer, any officer, nameless and faceless, a representation of something much greater, much more malevolent, than any single one of us.

By the time I go back to the office, my jitters are gone. I feel a bit funny, as is always the case after adrenaline has been in the blood, but I'm steady. I act out the sort of nonchalance I've observed in the more experienced officers and go about completing an incident report. I describe in simple terms exactly what I saw upon entering the room, followed by my reaction, then what I observed once other staff arrived on the scene. I don't mention anything about the conversation between Gabriel and Amir.

Later, I ask Gabriel if he knows why Amir cut himself.

"Because he's a fuckwit. He knows that if he slashes up then he gets put on the at-risk list, so he gets exempt from having a roommate. He's playing the system," Gabriel says.

OVERDUE

It's my "day off". I finished work last night at 6 p.m. and will be starting work tonight at 6 p.m. That's not a day off. That's a sleep-in.

I make a cup of coffee, pick up my book and walk outside. The glare of the sun hurts. I sit in a plastic chair and open to a dog-eared page. I read a few chapters. The story is engaging and the writing is quintessential McMurtry—a good thing—but every now and again I have to reread a paragraph after catching my mind wandering, eyes and internal reader on autopilot as some other part of my brain thinks about the long-overdue call I promised Oli I'd make.

I wonder what Harris bullshit there is to catch up on. Oli knows not to keep me apprised, that I've moved on and don't want to be dragged back into those interlocking spheres of shit. The less I know, the better. But even after everything, I don't think Mum really understands how I feel. The rare times when I call she still manages to surprise me with some new nugget of Harris lunacy.

Last time we spoke it was Esther, Clem's dear sister and my aunt, though we've never called her that. Mum told me Esther had been in a fist-fight with her best friend, Didee. Esther wouldn't say how it started, but the going theory in town was that it concerned a tin of missing drugs. Probably pot, but with Esther you never know.

Didee's a big woman, has the build of a bloke, and she put

Esther in hospital. Mum took in Esther's shithead kids for a week while their mother's face mended. Lo and behold, some antique watches handed down from Grandad went missing. Mum figured they could have been misplaced by accident (like the missing tin of drugs ...). Or then there's my theory—that some little Harris reprobate stole them. Anyway, Esther's oldest son, Ricky, could have taken the younger ones in and saved all the hassle, but Mum wouldn't have a bar of that. It's no mystery why.

Some people think it's a funny story, but I'd say it's more bothersome than funny. Esther's son, Ricky, fucked Belle. She's his cousin, the daughter of Filthy (that's what everyone calls Phil, Esther and Clem's brother). Belle got pregnant because they didn't use a condom, and then she went and got an abortion in Perth with Ricky's help. Word ended up getting out, because there's no such thing as a secret in a small town, and then it was a huge deal because not only had two cousins fucked each other, but the whole age thing was dicey.

Ricky was twenty. Based on how far along the pregnancy was, they worked out that Belle was right on the cusp of her birthday when it happened. Nobody knew whether she was fifteen or sixteen, and neither Belle nor Ricky would admit to anything. The difference of a few days was the difference between a child molester and just a sleazy loser who manipulated a stupid girl who happened to be his cousin into having unprotected sex.

I was twelve or thirteen when all that was going down. It was pretty much the end of Esther and Filthy because Filthy took his daughter's side and Esther took her son's side, which still boggles my mind, as if there was any way to defend Ricky. Mum, of course, took no sides, because she's always been diplomatic and knows that taking sides doesn't change a thing.

Not Clem. He took his sister's side, even though they were in the middle of their own falling out. Said that kids just do that sort of shit, even though Ricky wasn't a kid—Belle was the kid. I think he wanted to spite his brother, who he hated even more than Esther, because they'd always had a difficult relationship. Filthy thought Clem was a liar and scammer, and Clem thought Filthy was a cruel, unreasonable bastard. Both were right.

I wonder who's fucked who this time? Or maybe it'll just be who's fucked up their life, more than it was before.

If I think about it too much I'll convince myself not to call, so I walk back to my room and grab my phone. If Oli said so, then she wants to hear from me.

I dial the number that I know off by heart. The phone rings a long time. I wait. Mum is normally outside working in the garden; sometimes she doesn't bother to answer the phone at all.

Finally, someone picks up.

"Hello."

"Mum?"

Maybe it's a bad line. Maybe I've forgotten what my own mother sounds like.

"No, this is Kylie. Is that Oliver?"

Jesus. I certainly didn't think I'd be speaking to Kylie Harris, wife of Filthy and mother of cousins Belle and Beau.

"Um, hi. No, it's Nick. Is Mum there?"

"Nick. Oh, goodness, yes. Oh, I can't believe it, we were just speaking about you. That can't be a coincidence."

Well, obviously it can. And why was Mum speaking about me with Kylie Harris? Actually, I don't even want to know. I shouldn't have called. This is the reason why—because there is always something with the Harrises, always some unpleasantness, some dispute, some hateful gossip being spread, and now Filthy's wife is with Mum and she's already confirmed they are talking about me, about the incident that is still a raw wound after five years. I don't want it in my life. If I just pretend hard enough, it's like it isn't.

"Is Mum there?"

"Yes, yes. It's good that you called, Nick. Just hold on a

moment. I'm going to get the other cordless phone and give that one to her, and then I'll hang up this one."

"Righto," I say.

I guess Mum has a cordless phone now. That's about the extent of the family news I can handle. I hear another handset click onto the line.

"Hello?" says Kylie.

"Yeah."

"Ok, I'm going to hang up the other one now."

After a moment I hear a phone clumsily pressed back onto its receiver, then I hear the sounds of Kylie walking through the house, clearly taking a circuitous route, for it seems to take forever. Just give Mum the phone, I think. Finally I hear muffled voices, then:

"Hello, baby boy."

And it breaks my goddamn heart every time.

MUM

It takes a few minutes to wear away the distance, then it's like it always is. A son talking to his mother. She wants to know about me. About my travels. About old friendships and new romances. Somehow she always sees the good in everything I do. My current job is fantastic. A once-in-a-lifetime experience.

Fact is, I could probably tell her I just harpooned the last blue whale and she'd find the upside—a unique experience, a historic moment. I've missed this, that feeling of being loved unconditionally.

And despite not wanting to be brought back into the never-ending Harris intrigue, I do miss the stories that remind me of the country life I grew up with. Mum tells me about Merv's bees deciding to relocate from his hive to our shed. Our ancient dog, Dingo, found the beginnings of the new hive when sniffing out a skink. She got bit about thirty times, but she recovered fine and it seemed to get rid of her fleas and scabs. Mum thinks bee stings might have some sort of untapped healing power, which is no doubt an idea her hippie friends flamed, so she tried them herself on some persistent itch or rash or some such. I ask how she caught the bees. With great difficulty, apparently. Then I ask what the rash was. I remind her that I am practically a doctor. Probably just an irritation, Mum says.

She tells me about wild pigs that had been rooting in the mud on the banks of our creek down back. Jakey Orrington, just a little kid from down the way last time I saw him, managed to shoot one after about a week of stalking. He didn't know anything about dressing pigs, so he tried to skin it and, well, that was a disaster, so Dingo now has about a year's supply of wild pig in the freezer. Best-fed dog in Manji.

"Hey, so what's Kylie doing there, Mum?"

It's out of my mouth before I can think what it is I'm asking. Instantly, I know it's a mistake. Why bring it up when no good can come of it?

"Just helping out. She's been really good to me, Nick. When Phil had the accident last year we spent a lot of time together and we really mended some fences ..."

"Wait wait wait, *what* accident?"

"Oh, I thought you knew."

"No. Nobody said anything to me."

Why didn't Oli tell me?

"It's fine now, Nick. He's recovered, mostly. He lost the vision in one eye. The scars are still quite bad. He has to have more surgery, they think. Another skin graft. They took the skin from his hip and put it on his face. They're probably going to have to do it again, at least one more lot."

"Yeah, but what happened, Mum? Jesus," I say, then regret it immediately. "Sorry. Sorry. Just, what was it?"

"The chainsaw hit him in the face. He was cutting firewood and they think it must have hit a knot and kicked back. You know what he's like. Wouldn't think of wearing any protection, so it got him right up the side of his face. Took the flesh and some bone."

"Shit ..."

"He was on his own, too. It's lucky he survived. It's that Harris will. Strong men, the Harrises. Tough as nails. He had to drive back into town with bits of his head falling off. He was in a bad way. Kylie was a mess."

"You're not joking or something?"

A sick, fucked-up Harris joke.

"Ask your brother. It was even on GWN news."

"When did it happen?"

"Well ... I think it was the weekend after the Australia Day thingy they have in town. Your cousin Leroy won an award, so I went along. End of January, I think. Or maybe early Feb."

"A year ago?"

"Yes, something like that."

I didn't think my family could truly surprise me anymore. I thought I'd seen and heard everything. But Filthy almost killing himself in a similar way to his brother Clem? I'm floored.

Then a thought strikes, and it is dark. "The chainsaw. What chainsaw was he using?"

"I don't know. A decent one to do that."

"Would Kylie know?"

"I don't know, Nick. Why do you—" Mum says, then stops. She knows what's in my head. "Nick, oh Nick, it doesn't matter anymore. Too much time has passed. Let sleeping dogs lie."

My pulse is racing and I feel that taste of saliva in my mouth, the taste of fight.

"Nick? Nick?"

No. I'm not doing it. I left that behind. I'm not that man. Mum's right. It doesn't matter. It's not what is important.

"Yeah. No, you're right. Sorry. But so ... what do you mean Kylie is helping you out now? With what?"

There's silence on the other end.

"Mum?"

"I'm fine, but I haven't been that well lately."

"What is it?"

"It's not important. It's nothing serious. I don't want you to worry."

"Well, I'll worry less if you tell me what it is. Practically a doctor, remember Mum."

"I don't know, Nick. And I'm fine. There's nothing for you to worry about."

"What are the symptoms?"

"Honey, I'm not going to talk about this with you, all right?

I'm fine. And everything at home is fine. Better than fine. It's good. The only thing missing is you."

Mum never says anything like that to me. I don't know what to say, so I say nothing.

"Nick, I know you've got to live your life, and I'm very proud of you, the way you've found your own way in the world. But when you're ready, come home. It's been long enough. And not for me. I don't want you to worry about me. For you. Come home for you."

There's something in her voice. If I was a different person, a better person, I'd ask what. I don't.

"Ok, Mum. I'm coming home. Soon as I get out of this place."

McCULLOCH

After I finish talking to Mum, I can't get Filthy and the accident out of my head. I can't get the chainsaw that did that to him out of my head. All the trouble and bullshit—it all started with that fucking chainsaw, Grandad's McCulloch, which is still wreaking havoc on the Harrises.

It was exquisite. A yellow monster made of steel. Not a hint of plastic, heavy as hell. Sounded like a Harley Davidson and had so much power she near tore out of your hands when you throttled up. You could just sit her on a thick jarrah trunk and pull the trigger; she'd melt through with nothing more than her own weight. Brilliant chainsaw; sort of chainsaw men go to sleep thinking about, dream about through the night and when they wake there's a sticky damp patch in their jocks.

There came a point when Grandad had to stop using it. It was too heavy and his arthritis wouldn't stand the vibrations. This is before he'd even decided to sell the farm—or before his kids decided for him. He started using one of those plastic chainsaws he'd always hated. But he kept the McCulloch and wouldn't pass it on to either Clem or Filthy. He wouldn't say who was going to get it when he died. Maybe he hadn't decided, though the thought has crossed my mind that he would have been in his rights to forego both those bastards.

Maybe it was meant to be me. He used to let me hold the trigger, throttle it up while it was sitting in the vice. I loved it, the noise, the sense of power, how it could do so much violence but didn't—because you were controlling it. I remember telling him he should name it, but he said no, that's ridiculous, it's just the McCulloch.

Yet it wasn't just the McCulloch, just a farmer's tool with a specific purpose. I think it came to be a symbol for the things in his life that had mattered—and still did. A sort of totem, though he would never have put it in those words.

And then it just up and went missing from his shed. It seemed obvious that either Clem or Filthy had taken it. Clem always maintained that the chainsaw should be his because he was the only brother who made a living from timber. That's ironic because Clem made fuck-all of a living from selling timber, and died trying. Clem was what he was, and everyone knew it: a grafter, delusional, prone to wild swings of mood and rash actions. From the outside looking in, I can understand why others must have thought he'd taken the chainsaw. But I know my father. If he had it, he would have boasted about having it when he was pissed, and he never did. The opposite. He'd drink and get angry as hell, or sometimes just wake up sober and angry, ranting about that chainsaw. He was certain Filthy had it and that it wasn't just lost or stolen or that Grandad had given it away or sold it and forgotten in his mounting senility. Clem reckoned that Filthy had always wanted it as bad as he did, but that Filthy is the sort of piece of shit to take something that isn't his and then convince himself he's done what is right.

There were months of toing and froing, accusations, threats, the usual bullshit. But apart from Clem's ranting and evermore elaborate conspiracy theories, it was old news. Whoever got the chainsaw was going to keep the chainsaw.

Only, Clem wasn't a man to let a good grievance go. I remember the precise day it came to a head. We were watching the AFL grand final. It was Essendon versus Melbourne, and the entire town was glued to their TVs, because Manji is through-and-through a footy town. It was half-time, Essendon was up by about forty points, and it was a great day because I loved footy and even though I barracked for the Eagles I had a soft spot for Essendon. I didn't even care that Clem had a few of his dero mates over. They were amiable enough. Everyone was happy. Even Clem was happy.

Then Presto, a pot-smoking loser who used to make jokes that even a kid knew weren't funny, told Clem he'd heard a rumour about Filthy having the old man's chainsaw. Now, my bet is that Presto heard that rumour from Clem, but had forgotten that, and was reciting it as if he'd found a fresh source of intrigue.

Being that Clem was drunk, and a shitty drunk, it was all the ammunition he needed. He didn't say anything. Just got up, grabbed the keys and walked out the front door. I knew straight away what was happening. If Mum had been there she would have tried to take the keys off him, but she had no interest in being around Clem's mates, so she'd gone to a friend's to watch the grand final. It was just me and Oli, and Oli didn't know what was going on. I ran after Clem. He heard me coming. He swung around and said, "Don't you fucking say a word, boy."

"Can I come?" I said.

It was all I could think to say. Clem stood there a moment, the idea finding its way to favour. Clem was gonna show his boy what he was made of. He was gonna have an audience for his mightiest victory.

"Oli! Oli!" Clem yelled.

Oli is only two years younger than me, but he was as innocent a child as ever lived. He ran out of the house grinning, probably thinking we wanted to play a game of backyard something-or-other.

"Get in the car," said Clem.

Oli and I got in and Clem drove off, tearing ruts in our gravel driveway. Oli asked what we were doing, so Clem spent the next twenty minutes recounting all the ways in which Filthy had wronged him. The way Filthy used to pick on him when he was a kid, punching him in the kidneys and ribs and spine and whenever he complained to Grandad he was told to defend himself and not be a sissy; the way Filthy broke his kite on purpose the day after he got it for Christmas; the way they had a running race when Clem was fifteen and Filthy was seventeen and Clem won but Filthy lied about it and then refused to have a rematch for the next twenty years; the way Clem was much better looking and much better with the girls and when he was sixteen he rooted Kylie Norris at a party, then later that night, with a gash dripping Clem juice (they are Clem's precise words to his sons aged eleven and thirteen), Kylie made out with Filthy, who then became her boyfriend, who then married her, and yet Kylie and Filthy pretended like Clem had never fucked Kylie. I don't even know how that last one figures as a grievance, but in Clem's mind he was wronged. Clem then explained to us that Filthy only went on and married Kylie, tainted and all, because he was such an ugly man that he had to take the first woman dumb enough to say yes. But that's unfair on Kylie, because she's actually a half-decent person, certainly better than your average Harris.

So, we got to Filthy's block on the outskirts of town. Clem parked out the front in a blaze of dust and stones. He slammed the car door shut and stomped over to Filthy's shed, threw the door open and started rifling through Filthy's shit, looking for Grandad's chainsaw. Kylie came out the house and saw us boys sitting in the car. I could see the confusion on her face. Then she heard Clem in the shed and I think she worked out pretty fast what was happening. She called out to her husband. A moment later, Filthy walked out wearing socks and rugger shorts and no shirt, holding a can of Emu Bitter. He had a small potbelly gut, but you could still see the stringiness of his body, the look of sinew, sort of how wild stock reared in the bush look.

Filthy didn't even go over to the shed. He stood on the verandah and called out. "Oi, Clem. Clem!"

I heard the metallic clatter cease. Clem rushed out.

"Where is it?" he yelled, moving toward Philip. "You're lying. I know you got it."

"I haven't got nothin'. Now fuck off. Get off my lawn."

Clem squared up about ten metres from the verandah. He looked at Kylie.

"Kylie, you should go inside. You don't wanna see this. I'm gonna beat the shit out of your husband if he doesn't give me that chainsaw."

That's what did it. Filthy's face got even redder than it normally was and he threw his can of beer at Clem.

"Come on, cunt! Come on," yelled Filthy, jumping down the steps of the verandah and striding toward Clem. "I'll make you piss like I used to."

From the car I watched the two men close in till they were so close there was nothing left but to fight or retreat with tail between legs, humiliated. I knew Clem wouldn't back down, not with that much drink and anger in him, and I knew Filthy wouldn't back down, because he was proud and mean and he meant to teach my father a lesson just like he used to before Clem got too old to bully and then fucked his wife-to-be.

Filthy knew what he was doing. He goaded Clem into throwing the first punch, a slow, looping right hook that Filthy leaned away from with far too much ease. He leaned back in and swung his own right fist. It connected with Clem's face just above the eye; I saw it and I heard it, the sound like a block of sheoak thumped with a mallet. Clem dropped to the ground as if someone had flicked his off switch. He was just a crumpled pile of human, prostrate on Philip's mowed lawn and we were two boys watching their father get beaten. Oli sat with his mouth agape, scared and staring and still, but I opened the door and ran. I knew my dad ruined everything and I was old enough to understand that he was nothing like the man I'd imagined or even the man he'd imagined, yet I was still young enough to believe in family and to love my father in a blind, childlike way, so as to want to protect him and fix him and make everything all right.

Filthy stood over my father, leering, his fist cocked in case Clem got up, but Clem didn't get up. He didn't move.

"I warned you, boy. I fuck'n warned you," Filthy said.

Then he turned and walked back into his house and I thought it was over. Clem finally started to move a little, so I spoke to him in a soft voice, "Dad, Dad, are you all right? Dad, Dad," but he didn't say anything, he just wriggled like he didn't know what he was doing and groaned, and I kept asking, "Dad, are you all right?"

I looked back to the car and saw the look of horror on Oli's face, a look that burns my chest when I think back to it because Oli was such a beautiful boy, sweeter and nicer and purer than any of us, and he'd just seen the worst thing in the entire world and it crushed him. But it wasn't the worst, not yet, that was still coming. Filthy tore the flyscreen door clean off its hinges in his fury to get back out, a long brown leather belt dangling in his hand. Kylie was grabbing at his arm, trying to stop him, trying to hold him back, saying words that were just sounds to me. He didn't stop and then he said something to Kylie but I don't know what, only that it was angry, then he said something to me as I hovered over Dad's body, and I don't remember what, just the sound, the snarl. I remember seeing past Filthy into his house and finding two faces looking out, Beau and Belle, as surprised and confused as me. Then their father started and the faces disappeared. He used the buckle end of the belt, hitting Dad as hard as he could. I tried to get in the way and I did, for a moment, till Filthy grabbed my arm and threw me across the lawn then went back to strapping Dad's arms and shoulders and back. Dad didn't try to get away.

Kylie was screaming then she was holding on to the belt, holding on like a drowning woman holds on to a life vest, and Filthy stopped. He looked at his wife and I thought he was going to hit her, but he didn't. He let go and walked inside. I heard Kylie crying, then I heard Oli whimpering, the tearless sob so high-pitched it was almost a whistle. I thought I could hear crying inside, too, but then it was drowned out by the TV. Filthy must have turned it up so he didn't have to hear all the carry-on and I still remember the sound of the crowd roaring as the Essendon Bombers kicked another goal.

After a while Dad got to his knees and I helped him reach the car. Kylie told us to wait, said she was calling Mum, but I said Mum's not home and she asked where she was. I told her, but I didn't know the phone number. Kylie said she'd look it up, she'd find it, to just wait, but Dad had enough consciousness back and wouldn't wait. He got in the driver's seat and tried to turn the car keys, but fumbled them. I said, "I'll drive. Dad, I'll drive," because I could, he'd taught me. And he didn't argue, he didn't say anything. He just crawled over to the passenger seat and I got in and drove home, telling myself as I went that one day it'd even out, that one day there'd be a punishment, Filthy would know what it was like to be beaten and humiliated.

When Mum got home and saw the welts and swelling on Dad and saw the marks on me, she wanted to call the cops. Filthy Philip Harris had beaten the shit out of her husband and flogged her boy. But Dad said no. He said his brother would get what was coming, sooner or later. Mum looked at me, sitting next to Dad as he drank a mug of homebrewed liquor and no-brand cola, and years later she told me how sad it had made her seeing my stern little face, my eyes the puffy red eyes of a boy who wouldn't let himself cry, and she knew, and I knew.

When Dad died, killed by his own severed hand, I readily accepted the one thing he bequeathed me. I became the holder of the grudge. The boy and then the man obsessed with a chainsaw that wasn't just a chainsaw.

It's been missing for a dozen years, and yet still it follows me around.

CONTROL

It's a few hours later. I'm at work and the briefing is wrapping up. I listen, wait for my name, then come the words "Brown Five". I'm relieved. I'm in a different compound to Amir.

The evening begins in the usual way: the guarding of the dinner cordial, rounding up of stragglers, talking shit with fellow officers. Quincy says he's going to conduct a patrol, so I head out with him.

The humidity is bad tonight. Quincy and I are sweating. The fact it's getting worse must mean the overdue rains are coming. I sure as shit hope so. It seems like the wet has been coming ever since I got here. At this rate, I'll be gone before it ever does. Mine is a three-month contract. Of course, short stints have a habit of stretching out to years when the money is this good. There's plenty of work if we want it. But stay at this place too long and I reckon anyone would eventually lose their sanity.

Quincy and I follow the line of the fence separating Brown Compound from the perimeter. Every layer of steel mesh is topped with razor wire. Each razor is comprised of two small triangles of steel joined together at their narrowest points, the long sharp blades facing outward. The shape makes me think of Luke Skywalker's X-wing starfighter. It's an incongruous image, far too glamorous and noble for the ugly little blades. They make my skin crawl.

I talk to Quincy about the centre. He's a man with sense and perspective. He gets it.

"It's been heaps different to what I thought it would be like," I say. "Sorta worse and better. I tell you what, though, I've heard some fucked-up stories about things that have gone down that I never heard on the news."

"Exactly. The thing is, up here everything is hush-hush, Nick. The media only gets fed what the company wants to feed them. They're clueless, they subsist on dribs and drabs. It's like a manager said to me when I first got here. 'Curtin is like Fight Club. The first rule of Curtin is you don't talk about Curtin. The second rule of Curtin is you don't talk about Curtin.' And it's true. It's a closed book."

"Did someone deadset say that to you?"

"Absolutely. It's how it works. What about that new guy the other week, fired for posting something on his Facebook page."

"Yeah, Danny, we did the training together."

"Right. Us guys lose our job if we say anything public, so people outside don't really know what happens in here. They just make up their own idea of detention. So, you know, the pro-refugee lot make it sound like a Nazi concentration camp, and then the other side makes it sound like an all-expenses-paid vacation."

We walk past one of the open-air porticos. I see Soheil and three others playing a game of table tennis. We take a seat on a bench and watch. They're good. Soheil is the best, playing with short, sharp strokes. He returns a serve with a smash, winning the point. We applaud. Soheil turns around and sees us.

"Nick! Come, play. Here, yes, come."

"Oh, no, you guys are playing."

"Please, come. Here, I show you."

Quincy stays seated while I jog over. Soheil hands me his bat and a detainee loops a ball over the net. We tap it back and forth until I hit it too hard and it sails a metre clear of the table.

"Here, like this," says Soheil, and he shows me the arc my bat should be travelling, nothing at all like my wrist-heavy swing.

We keep playing till I hear my radio crackle to life. I hand the bat to Soheil and excuse myself. I listen.

"Control, this is Red Two; Code Blue, Code Blue, room sixty-eight Red Compound, sixty-eight Red Compound. Client is complaining of back and stomach pain."

I recognise the room number, but it's not my compound tonight, so not my worry. Soheil hands me the bat. I play for a while, getting better as I go. I've got the hand-eye coordination, now I've just got to control my swing so I can get the ball on the table.

"Come back tomorrow night," says Soheil.

"Thanks. I'll try."

Quincy and I head back to the officers' donga and put the kettle on in anticipation of another long, pointless night.

THIRST

During briefing we get a rundown of all the detainees who are on some form of welfare watch or who've showed signs they might be unstable. There's always a few, sometimes as many as a dozen, and generally a new one every day or second day. Tonight, one of the clients Benedict tells us about is Amir.

It turns out Amir not only cut his head with a razor; he is on a declared hunger strike. According to the nurses, Amir has not eaten for four days. That means he hasn't eaten since Gabriel and I saw him. That really isn't a big deal. On average, a person can go two months before organ failure and death. Boredom sets in well before that, and almost no one lasts the distance. So Amir hasn't eaten for four days? Big deal.

But it's also believed that Amir is refusing fluids. That's a much more serious proposition. Depending on the climate, activity level and individual physiology, a person refusing fluids has as much as a week until they are either critically ill or plain dead. The physiological process starts with the blood plasma reducing and toxins concentrating; the heart has to pump faster and harder to push that toxic soup around the body, brain function decreases, body temperature can't regulate, the kidneys fail, the heart goes into cardiac arrest and they are gone. Dead as a headless cat.

It means that Amir's "hunger strike" is the real deal. Short and brutal. While I hope he doesn't die, my main hope is that he's someone else's problem tonight. I just don't want to have to deal with him. The whole situation is ... unpleasant.

I wait for my name and there are the words: "Red Four". To make it even worse, my number one is Gabriel. Once I get to the compound office and drop my bag off, it takes Gabriel all of about twenty seconds to hand me Amir's file.

Amir is not at dinner. Why would he be? He's on a hunger strike. As soon as the mess hall closes, I head to his room to conduct the first welfare check. When I get there a nurse is speaking with him, so I figure that rather than go in I can just ask the nurse if he's still alive (presumed to be the case on the basis of her conversation with him) and why he's not eating. She comes out.

"Hey," I say. "I've gotta do the PSP on Amir. Do you know what's going on? Why he's not eating?"

"Oh, that's confidential. No, I can't talk about a patient."

"Yeah, sure, no worries. I just don't want to have to go in and disturb him and ask him the same stuff you were talking to him about."

"It's confidential."

"All right ... but he is still alive though?" I joke. There's even a smile on my face.

"No, it's confidential."

"That he's alive?" There's no smile on my face. "You can't confirm that he's alive?"

"Oh, no, yes, obviously he's alive, I mean ..."

"Yeah, thanks. Don't worry about it."

I knock on the door. There's no answer.

I try the doorknob. It's locked.

As I jangle my keys out of my pocket, I hear, "Fuck off!" then stuff starts slamming into the door. Amir must be throwing every object to hand. I don't enter.

I head back to the office and tell Gabriel. He says that we've confirmed he's alive, so to hell with him. He can throw a tantrum if he wants. Not our problem.

A little later I see Soheil. I ask him if it is ok if I come and play some more table tennis with him tonight. He tells me to head over to the portico in Brown Compound at about 10 p.m., and I tell him I'll definitely do that, unless something comes up.

It's just after ten and I'm walking over with Scott, who is also keen to have a game. I'm yards from the portico—I can see Soheil and the others slapping balls—when a Code Blue reaches out and plucks me away. It's in room 68, Red Compound.

By the time I get there, Amir is already being stretchered out. Gabriel called it in—he went to check on him, given my last failed attempt. Like last night, Amir says he has terrible back and stomach pain, unbearable now. I watch him as he is carried off. I know what back and stomach pain means. He's not taking water.

There's something deeply unlikable about Amir. Something in his face and his posture. Something in how he moves and speaks on the few occasions he does either. But mostly something in the calculation of his actions. No, I don't like the prick, not at all, but that's a damn sight different to wishing him ill or actually causing him harm. This whole drawn-out mess is starting to get to me. I can't shake the thought that all this started with that little conversation.

He must have believed Gabriel. That stuff about the big Iraqi poofter. I mean, Amir comes from a country where homosexuals are jailed and whipped. Sodomy is punishable by hanging. Who knows, maybe it's Amir's biggest hang-up? Given the Iranians and Iraqis hate each other, a dirty great Iraqi cock aimed at an Iranian arsehole would have to be terrifying. Hell, it terrifies me.

And that's bad enough, but it's probably not even what set him off. If he believed Gabriel really could and really would stop him getting a visa—and why wouldn't he? Amir doesn't know how this system works, no one does—then it's tantamount to our taking away his sole fragment of hope.

Amir may be a bully and a coward. He certainly scared and humiliated the old Afghani man. It may even be that he was a piece of shit in Iran and is destined to be a piece of shit throughout any sort of life he makes in Australia. But I still don't think it justifies what we did. It was cruel. It wasn't without purpose, but it was cruel.

I don't bother with table tennis. Not in the mood anymore. I hang around the office, doing nothing of use, drinking cups of shitty coffee followed by cups of shitty tea. About midnight, a call comes through. It's Benedict. Turns out the nurses found something in Amir's pocket: a bed sheet, torn up and tied into a noose.

PINK

Red Compound. Again.

I think the managers must be allocating certain officers to certain compounds so they become familiar with a particular set of detainees. My lot has been lumped with the detainees of Red Compound and Brown Compound. I guess it's all right. It's where most of the Iranian guys are. Most of them are talkative and like to joke around. But they are also the most volatile, like Amir.

Thanks to Gabriel, I'm assigned to hold Amir's hand. He's been escalated to a constant watch, considered a "high imminent" threat of suicide or self-harm. I sit outside his door, watching, occasionally tugging at my shirt and wiping the back of my hand across my face. This miasma. This dirty Curtin miasma. Just rain, you motherfucker.

For hours Amir barely moves. He's still not eating. I suspect he's secretly taking some fluids, or maybe the nurses had him on a drip, because, well, he's not dead. He doesn't look good, though.

Midnight comes and goes. It's man versus tedium. Sure, it sounds like a cushy job, just sitting around doing nothing, but you can't get up to take a stroll or make a cup of tea. You're stuck, watching. Counting time. And when you're aware of time, it's like a quantum trick: it slows down. The sort of slow where you watch the second hand on your watch and it takes two seconds before it jerks from twenty-two to twenty-three.

I know it's impossible, but that's the mind.

A turtle rushes into a police station. "Come quick! Three snails just attacked me!" he shouts. "Calm down and tell me what happened," says the constable. The turtle shakes his head. "I don't know, it all happened so fast."

Little details become events. When a pathetic breeze wicks some of the moisture from my upper lip I figure I've just enjoyed the highlight of my evening. But, no, there is better. There's a group of Iranian men sitting on a bench under the stars, just out of sight. One of them is inspired with what appears to be a spontaneous, original ditty. The song drifts on the breeze.

Everybody, I want a pink whore,
I want a pink whore.
Everybody, I want a red whore,
coming to my room for fuck,
ooh, ooh.

He sings it thrice, and only on the third time am I sure it's a pink whore and not a pink unicorn. From where I'm sitting, I think a pink whore sounds lovely. I would be most pleased to see a pink whore right at this moment. Any shade of whore. In fact, any human who might stop and talk. Something—other than staring into a dark room at a man who in all likelihood hates me and who really wants to die and knows that I know those two facts are related, or who is so disturbed that he's decided the best thing he can do for himself is to pretend he wants to die, which is a drastic course of action that still involves going down the path of trying to kill himself so that we all think it's real, which it fucking is!

Ugh. Tick. Tock.

At about 1 a.m., a nurse comes to see Amir. She has a long conversation with him, nearly all one-way. She examines him, then she goes to see Gabriel. I'm not privy to whatever discussions occur between the managers and nurses, but about

2 a.m. the car they use as a makeshift ambulance drives into our compound. I'm informed that Amir is being removed. He is so dangerously dehydrated that he's at risk of organ failure and death. He's headed straight to Derby Hospital.

About 5 a.m., Gabriel gets a call from administration advising him to strike Amir from our records and to revise our numbers for headcount. Arrangements are being made to fly Amir to Graylands Hospital, formerly known as Claremont Hospital for the Insane.

I'm relieved Amir is gone. Relieved for both of our sakes, so that I don't have to watch over him and he doesn't have to endure more of whatever this place is doing to him.

RESPONSE

It's the following night. I've been allocated to Red Compound again. It's just after the end of dinner service. I'm walking back from the mess when a man calls from behind: "Officer, officer!"

I assume he wants to use my lighter. I turn and walk toward him.

"Come quick," he says, "man is smashing window near mess."

What? I just came from there, and there are still officers inside. There's been no radio chatter, no Code Black called. It doesn't make sense, yet the man's urgency is real. Something must be happening, somewhere.

I walk as fast as I can without running. I get to open ground and look to the mess, fifty yards to my right. There's no broken window, no crowd, no noise. I'm glancing about, trying to figure out the who or what, when a man runs past me and through the Red Compound gates. The detainee who alerted me points after him and says, "Over there."

"Is that the man?"

"Yes. Yes."

My natural reaction is to chase after him, to try and stop him from doing anything worse than breaking windows. My step turns into a skip, but before I begin running I stop myself, calm myself, slow myself back to a walk—fast, but a walk. That's our training. Never run. Detainees are only human, they're bored and curious, they want to see and be part of whatever shit is happening, so you can guarantee a crowd to any incident if you run, and once you have a big crowd you have a potential mob: unstable, unpredictable and liable to be set off without warning. Don't run, rookie. Don't bring the crowd.

I'm just outside the Red Compound gates when the radios arc into life.

"Code Black, Code Black, internet room."

That's the direction the man was running. Then two Sri Lankan men sprint past me. What is happening?

"Response One, Response One," comes the call over the radio.

This shit's serious. They don't call a Response One, summoning every senior officer in the centre, unless it's getting out of control.

"Response Two, Response Two."

Holy fuck. They've now called in about twenty officers. I'm fourth in line — Response Four — so were it not for the fact I'm already following some man who may or may not be involved, I wouldn't be involved. As I near the internet room, I see a crowd, but the initial trouble looks to be over. I push my way to the front. There's a broken window; beneath it a Sri Lankan man is sprawled on the ground, surrounded by a large pool of blood. He must have put his fist through the glass. His upper arm is sliced open and blood is streaming from the wound. He is awake and moaning, but motionless.

Other officers are already trying to help him, so I flank two officers on the north side of the corridor, pushing the growing crowd of detainees back. More officers arrive. I look to the other end of the corridor and see an even bigger crowd with just two officers stopping them — or not stopping them, as it is, for they're watching the bleeding man, gawking at the spectacle, rather than doing their job of keeping the crowd at bay. I quickly walk across and start telling detainees to move back. I try to keep my voice calm, while strong and assertive. I realise the Sri Lankan man is going to have to be stretchered out at some stage, so the area needs to be kept clear.

Detainees keep pouring in. On the other side of the corridor a number of Sri Lankans jostle to the front. They're extremely agitated. I hear the voices, angry and panicked; maybe they don't understand what's happening to their friend, maybe they see the blood and think officers are somehow responsible. Still the crowd grows, maybe seventy detainees now. It's intense, at once exhilarating and intimidating.

I see Benedict, Darren and Paul, three of our most senior officers, sit the man on a chair. They hold his arm high above his head and push gauze padding against the wound. There is a lot of blood. The officers beside me are like the crowd, fixated on the injured man, on all that blood, the spectacle of it. They let the crowd push in on them. I too shoot a glance, then try to refocus.

"Back! Stay back!" I order.

I hear Benedict. He says they can't wait for the nurses or a transport to arrive; the man is losing too much blood, an artery must be cut, they've got to move him now.

"We're walking him out! We're walking him out! Clear a way!"

I know it's a mistake the moment I hear it. It'll only stress his heart, pump more and more blood out of his wound, but it's not for me to decide. They pull the man to his feet and it's then that a fracas breaks out on the other side of the corridor. It's the Sri Lankans. I see glimpses of a melee, of officers restraining men.

It's happening fast. The bleeding man is dragged out amid a bundle of officers. They pass our position, at which point we flank the group, protecting the officers escorting the casualty. Sri Lankan men run back and forth. They're hysterical—yelling, flinging their arms, dashing every which way. The officer on the left of the bleeding man yells, "Protect my back." It's directed at Gabriel, but Gabriel already has hold of a wild-eyed Sri Lankan man trying to push past. I drop in and flank the officer, walking variously sideways and backward, watching the crowd that follows.

About forty metres from the gates to the administration compound, the casualty collapses to the ground. His white shirt is soaked red. His upper arm is dangling meat. An officer reapplies pressure to the wound. Two others hoist his limp form into the air, an arm each under his legs and around his back.

"I'm slipping! I can't hold him!"

I dash in, taking the officer's place before the Sri Lankan man is dropped. We rush for the gates, the man cradled in our arms. With each step a bizarre thought forms: this man smells like a sheep carcass, freshly butchered. He smells like death.

We carry his unconscious body through the gates. His head lolls back.

"Watch his airway! Hold his head!"

We push through the medical centre doors, crash into all manner of tables and equipment, then unload him on a gurney. I don't stop to stare. I'm back out the door the instant he leaves my arms. I hurdle the rail, pass through the gates and re-enter the compound.

A group of managers and first response officers are storming my way. Among them is Gabriel and Darren.

"Darren, do we still need people at the internet room?"

"You get back to your compound, Harris! Stay with Mary," erupts Gabriel, before Darren can respond.

I don't understand the anger behind the instruction, but do as I'm told.

NORMAL

My pulse hasn't yet calmed, but I feel ok. A little woolly, but steady. In the midst of it all I think I was losing clarity, acting on pure impulse, pure instinct, but my wits are with me now.

I find Mary, standing by a broken window in Red Compound, making sure detainees don't nick any of the broken glass. I begin collecting shards and put them in a bin. The glass will have to be securely removed to make sure it stays out of detainees' hands or soon we'll be attending Code Blues where the cuts are jagged, not neat, all the harder to patch up.

Mary asks me what happened. I tell her what I know, working it out in my own mind as I do. The Sri Lankan man must have become enraged over something, so he broke this window in the Red Compound kitchenette. It's not a mess hall, it's just a sink, fridge and microwave in a little room, but it makes sense that the man who raised the alarm would call it that. Then he must have run across to the internet room in Brown Compound where he put his fist through another window, a bigger window with thicker glass, slicing open his arm.

I start to describe the scene at the internet room, when I see Gabriel storming toward us. Two other officers are in the process of putting up tape and cones to cordon off the kitchenette and broken glass. Gabriel ignores them and me, crunching across the broken glass, dozens of pieces shattering into ever smaller shards. He swings the door to the donga open with so much force that pieces of glass still dangling in the frame of the window shudder loose and crash to the ground.

"Hey, Gabriel. Gabriel."

He stomps back out, a single finger stabbing the air. "Don't you speak to me! You caused that whole thing! I saw you run, and I saw the Sri Lankans follow you because of it. When that response was called, you shouldn't have been there! They all followed you over."

"No, that's not ... I didn't run. I was just following a guy I saw running, because a detainee told me he'd broken a window."

"Bullshit. You're responsible for that entire thing. You!"

"The Sri Lankans were running over before me. They didn't follow. You don't know what you're talking about."

"I don't wanna hear your bullshit excuses!"

Gabriel's face is red and his scowl is held so tight that his cheeks dimple. I watch his accusing finger spring back, both of his hands now fists. This is some type of performance for my benefit and I'm meant to cower, I'm meant to yield to his manliness and authority, but I don't. He's wrong, yes, but it's more that I see the man isn't even present in his own body. His glazed eyes are tiny rag-doll beads. Some sort of rage is speaking above whatever shitty mind he normally possesses. He's pumped up on the adrenaline of what just happened and he doesn't want to let it go.

"Ok, Gabriel, whatever you reckon, mate."

"I've already put in a complaint. You're fucking gone!"

Gabriel slams the door a second time, still more glass falling from the broken window, still more glass shards for shitkickers like Mary and I to pick from the dirt.

It's not five minutes before the radio crackles and I'm summoned to find Benedict in Brown Compound. I walk through the gates and see him striding my way, his long legs attacking the dirt like he's found a fresh field of babes to crush.

"Hi, Benedict, you wanted—"

"You don't run to an emergency!"

I try to explain, try to tell him Gabriel is full of shit and that I did not run and that I did not cause any of what just happened—and, by the way, thanks for the concern about my welfare, you old prick—but he just keeps barrelling on and butting in and telling me to shut up and listen and learn.

I let Benedict's inane words wash over me just so the sound of his animal grunting will stop. I tell him I understand, but what I understand is far different to what he's finished telling me. I remember the first piece of advice Benedict gave us as new recruits. "It's all well and good to be friendly to the clients," he told us, "but you never trust them. They'll turn on you in a second." Seems the same goes for your co-workers.

I return to help Mary finish cleaning up the glass. Soheil's room is nearby; he wanders over and asks me what all the commotion was about. I tell him as best I know. He nods his head slowly.

"The Sri Lankans, they have been here twenty, twenty-one, twenty-two month. No good."

Of everything that happened today, probably the only thing that truly surprises me is the reaction of the Sri Lankans after the incident. The very same men who'd been skirmishing with officers, hysterical at the sight of their friend, are perfectly normal an hour later. Cheerful. Relaxed.

The blood is washed away and glass is picked up and we all get on with it.

NAMES

Briefing. Chief swinging-dick Benedict is speaking.

"As of today, there will be delegates from Amnesty International walking around the compounds. One of the things they can get us on is not using client names. So whenever you get on the radio, I want you to please try to also provide the client's name. I know they're hard to pronounce, but these people may hear radio traffic, so be careful. If you can find a name, use it."

Six hours later, I'm in the mess. I've been here nearly four weeks, so I pretty much know how everything works, what my role is, how to get the job done. On occasion I've even been graduated from cordial duty to the "tick and flick", sitting by the door, marking off detainees' names as they enter the building. And I'm pretty good at it, because I've made an effort to learn the names. There's about two hundred men in Brown Compound. I'd say I know forty or so off the top of my head, maybe another twenty with a little thought. Not because I'm good at remembering names, but because I try. I repeat names once I've heard them; I ask when I don't remember; I use little mental tricks to jog my memory. That first day I spent in the medical centre waiting room listening to my colleagues calling humans by a number — that's when I decided to make the effort and learn the names.

Quincy and I were talking about it a few nights back, about how easy it is to fall into the practice of using the detainee's number. I do it sometimes out of sheer frustration, but always feel shitty enough to then ask their name. Quincy mentioned that when he got back from his most recent break he asked one detainee what happened to a friend of his, a chap no longer at the centre. He asked after him using his number. "What is his name?" asked the friend. After six months of conversations with that man, Quincy didn't know.

Most of the other officers don't understand why I bother. They don't. They slide the office window open, ask their number, give the detainee milk. Stop them as they enter the mess, mark off their number, let them eat. Sound off a number, send them through for an appointment.

Yet today, because there are Amnesty International delegates walking the grounds, they have finally asked us to use names. Well, good luck—Scott and I are on the door this evening.

Scott's not a bad man by any stretch, just a simple one. Apart from the occasional bit of light jest, there's little meaningful conversation to be had. I've tried on a bunch of occasions, and it's always painful. Here's what I've found out about Scott since meeting him a month ago.

He grew up in Northam. A few years ago he and a few mates moved to some shitty Perth suburb where they rent a shitty house (which is probably lined with a shit-ton of asbestos that Scott eats in the middle of the night like a rat snacking on radiator hose, though that's just my supposition). He likes to drink bourbon and cola. He likes cars, especially the loud and fast ones. He had a car, a loud and fast one, but doesn't now because he did one too many doughies and instead of a car he has a suspended licence and a really big fine.

He also has no middle tooth. He had some roadwork job out near Dwellingup when an old prostitute showed up at the camp and did the rounds. When Scott's turn came, she started with a little foreplay that involved her jamming a hard vibrator into his mouth, but seeing as he wasn't expecting an acrylic cock to the face, or perhaps anywhere, the correct orifice was not fully open and she knocked that middle tooth right the hell out. He still fucked her. Or she fucked him. I forget.

That's everything I have learned about Scott. My medical opinion is that the enormous bulk of his dwarf-like head is mostly made up of gristle and chicken nuggets. And yet, when it comes to memorising detainees' numbers, there's a bit of the idiot savant about him. While I've been memorising names, he's been memorising alpha-numeric identifiers.

"Hi. Mahdi, right?" I say to a balding Iranian in his thirties who wears the smile of a much younger man.

"Mahdi. Yes. Yes. Thank you."

Mahdi is really chuffed. He seems genuinely happy that I remembered his name.

"And how's it going today, Mahdi."

"I am very good. I am very pleased to meet you. Thank you, officer."

"Nick, that's my name."

"I am very pleased to meet you, Officer Nick."

"Pleased to meet you, too, Mahdi," I say, even though I've met him a few times now.

By this time the queue out the door has backed up, so Scott and I try to get through the names quickly.

"Hey, LAR-12! How are you brother?" says Scott.

"Yousif. How's it going?" I say.

"BAK-92, hey man."

"Mohammed, good to see you."

"WAC-8!"

"Uday!"

"POR-45!"

"Barak!"

"LAR-2!"

"Reza!"

On it goes, till I'm no longer directing my greetings at the detainees so much as at Scott, hoping he will notice that these people have names, and that they're no harder to find on the tick and flick than a number. But he doesn't flinch. Scott probably just thinks I'm weird, if he's thinking at all.

KAREN

Halfway through the dinner service, the queue is pretty much gone. There's no need for two of us on the door. I leave Scott at the desk and take up a position near a bain-marie filled with rice and chicken drumsticks. I'm hungry, but looking at the chicken makes me less hungry.

Karen is standing about ten yards away. She's guarding the cordial machine. Akbar, an Iranian man with a permanent scowl, enters the mess. He's been at Curtin over a year. It is well known that he is an intensely unhappy man. He looks especially miserable and aggravated tonight. It's probably the weather. The heat and humidity seem to have peaked; the air feels heavy, though it could be it's the other way round—the air makes us feel heavy. Slow and blunt. I'm not exactly feeling chipper tonight, myself.

Akbar looks at the chicken, stares at the chicken, scowls at the chicken; after a long while he shakes his head and walks on. He grabs half a loaf of bread and a tub of margarine, then sits at a table just in front of Karen.

I hear him muttering something about the food. Everyone mutters about the food. It's mass-produced hospital-grade slop: rarely appetising, but gets the job done (the job being sustenance, not comfort). Akbar goes on and on, working himself up as he stolidly chews bread and margarine.

"DIAC bullshit!" he exclaims.

I see Karen looking at him, wearing her own version of a

scowl. I know she doesn't like Akbar, because no one likes Akbar. Akbar mutters some more, then exclaims, "Australia bullshit!"

It's too much for Karen. Straight away she shoots back, "Why don't you go home, then?"

Akbar looks at Karen with fresh disgust. He stands up, grabs the loaf of bread and throws it on the ground. He storms out of the mess, slamming the door as he goes.

I see Karen's face. She's shaken. I walk over to her.

"You ok?"

"I shouldn't have said that, I shouldn't have said it."

"Yeah, well, no point worrying about it now."

"I'm going to have to report it. I have to write an incident report."

"I dunno, Karen, I mean, you reckon?"

"I shouldn't have said it ..."

No, she shouldn't have said it, but this place does strange things to even the gentlest, sanest people, officers and detainees alike. I pick up the loaf of bread and throw it in the bin.

At 9.30 p.m., Karen submits an incident report describing her exchange with Akbar.

At 10.30 p.m., a manager comes down from admin and tells Karen she's technically done the right thing reporting it, but that, really, there's no point wasting time on paperwork with such minor incidents.

At 11 p.m., a Code Blue is called over the radio. Gabriel and Bailey rush off, while Karen and I staff the office. A few minutes pass. Control requests an update over the radio. I listen to the exchange.

"Control, this is Red Two. Detainee is J-A-W-0-2-9, Akbar Ghasem. Has a cut to the back of his head. We're trying to stop the bleeding, but it's still bleeding, so we're gonna walk him straight to medical. Please advise nurses that we are on our way."

Karen looks at me—the face of a child waiting for a parent's censure. She's ready to burst into tears.

"It's probably just a coincidence," I say.

Karen nods, a little too readily.

"I wouldn't worry about it," I say.

And it probably is a coincidence. But in a place as volatile as this, we both know it might not be.

Karen is like a zombie the rest of the shift. She barely speaks. Just before changeover, Gabriel gets a call from admin telling him that Akbar won't be back in the compound today. They had to take him to Derby Hospital. Detainees don't normally cut the back of the head, so I guess he either couldn't see what he was doing or didn't know what he was doing. He sliced right through a vein. The nurses couldn't stop the bleeding. He nearly died.

MANI

I'm walking down a corridor when a faint voice calls. I look around but don't see anyone in the corridor.

"Officer," says the weak voice.

I realise it's coming from inside a room where the door is propped open. It's Mani's room. I've never spoken with him, but I know who he is. Everyone knows who he is: the guy who shuffles and winces.

Mani walks in small, pained steps with his back bolt-straight, seemingly in constant agony. The first time I saw him, I queried the other officers. The response was unequivocal.

"He's putting it on."

"Back injury my arse."

"Playing it up."

I didn't find a single officer with an ounce of sympathy. It was universally assumed that he was faking an injury to try to get out of detention. As a new chum, I supposed they knew better than me, even though it really did look like he was in considerable pain. He must be exceptionally crafty, I figured, the sort of person I'd been warned to watch out for before even getting to the centre.

Then one night, unannounced, I quietly entered his room at 2 a.m. to conduct a welfare check. There's no way he could've heard me coming. Yet there he was, sitting on the edge of his bed, staring at the wall, feet squarely planted on the floor, back arrow-straight. His face was puffy, his eyes beady, his expression pained. We exchanged no words. It was at that point I knew Mani was for real. He wasn't putting anything on.

I walk closer. I see Mani. His whole body convulses as he holds onto the doorknob to keep himself upright. I see blood-red filling the corners of his almond-shaped eyes.

"Where Elen?" he stutters.

Elen is a welfare officer. Her job is to take care of those detainees who aren't doing so well; to tend any special needs, check up on their wellbeing, coax them through whatever they're struggling with. I look up the corridor and see her. I tell him she's thirty seconds away. I'm not sure if Mani wants me to stay or go, so I just stand a few metres back. By the time Elen arrives, tears are dribbling down Mani's face. I figure no man wants another man to watch him cry, so I go.

Elen comes by the office after she's seen Mani. I ask her about him. Her understanding is that he has a severely prolapsed disk in his spine from being repeatedly kicked in the back by Iranian police before he fled to Australia. He then took a heavy fall on the boat crossing from Indonesia to Christmas Island. She has been fetching Mani food to eat in his room because his pain medication has to be taken after a meal and he can't make it to the mess hall. That's why Mani was desperate to see Elen—she had his food and painkillers.

"Why isn't he in a hospital?"

"Well, the doctor has seen him and said there's nothing we can do."

"That doesn't sound right."

Elen looks at me and shrugs. "We're not doctors. We just do the best we can with what we've got."

It's my turn to shrug. I don't know why I'm doing so, my shoulders high and hands held wide like an idiot, or what it means to Elen, but she smiles at me as if we've nutted out the problem and everything is resolved to satisfaction. I suppose, in a way, it is, for expressing concern takes us to the very limit of our job responsibilities. Elen leaves. I decide to have a cup of tea.

RELEASE

4 a.m. and I'm hot, annoyed and tired, but mostly annoyed. I don't even know why.

I hear thunder. I look beyond the perimeter fences. Distant clouds quiver with lightning. Surely this is it. This is the night that the spell breaks—when dry becomes wet. It has to be. One more day of this shit ...

I complete the few pointless tasks that need doing and sneak across to no-man's-land. I grab a plastic chair and go around to the back of my favourite unused building where I'm unlikely to be disturbed. I sit and wait. Eventually I start to enjoy the solitude. It's peaceful. I almost feel normal, like I'm not in a prison.

I sniff the air. There's something in it I recognise. The trees and bushes must know. They must be releasing pollen or oils or seeds, something to catch the winds and be the first to stake a claim to the precious water they sense coming.

Of course, it's not quite the same as at home. Nothing smells like karri and jarrah. They're such beautiful trees. It's possible I think that just because I grew up with them, but I know there's some truth to it. Thousands come to see those forests every year, and thousands pay top money to have a piece of furniture made from the timber.

All those farmers who clear-felled their paddocks to make way for pasture or potatoes, they regret it now. It's about the only good Clem ever did, saving our patch of forest. It had never been cleared of the big karri, jarrah and red gum trees because it was so damned rocky and muddy and difficult. On one side, Karlup Creek cuts through a gulley and spreads out in a natural depression; it's prone to flooding in winter, and otherwise forms a swampy glade where one of the last groves of wild boronia in Manji can still be found. That depression rises up into a stand of forest protected on the east and north by the curving path of the creek, on the south by the sides of a precipitous hillock, and on the west by an outcrop of quartz and granite. In agricultural terms, it is almost useless, but it is just about the most beautiful piece of land in the whole region.

I guess I was just the promise of life in Mum's belly when they moved out there. I don't know the exact details; from what Mum has said I think they began life together in a hurry. They were both working in an abattoir in Albany. Clem was on the knives and Mum was a packer. Mum doesn't ever talk specifics, but she had a bad time of it growing up, and she isn't in touch with her family anymore, not except her Uncle Jeremy who lives in Mt Barker.

Mum and Clem hit it off, and knowing Clem he would have promised Mum the world. I guess part of that promised world was a home he would build with his very own hands in a beautiful patch of forest that no one would ever take away from them. They would make a family of their own and live happily ever after.

Some of it was true. They came back to Manji and to Grandad's farm. The old man was smitten with Mum—I reckon it's because she was like the daughter he'd wished for. Esther certainly wasn't, and he'd lost his first, Elsie, back in 1960 at twelve weeks. They buried her on the farm. I'd go look at the little grave sometimes, out in the rose garden. Grandad told me that Grandma made that garden just for Elsie; before that it was lawn or paddock or something. When Grandma died not long after she gave birth to Clem, the responsibility of tending the garden fell to Grandad. He was good at it. I don't like roses, but they bloomed big and red every year and it meant a lot to the old man.

Anyway, he agreed to let Clem build a house on a corner of the farm. When I was born, Mum was only twenty-one and Clem was only twenty-three, and they were living in a shed. Clem built the house bit by bit, learning as he went through trial and error. He was still adding to it when he died.

It's a funny house. Strong and mostly well built, but if you look you can see where Clem changed his mind or picked up a new skill. My favourite bit is the front door. God's eye. He salvaged it from a church, though the line between salvaged and stole was always hazy. Sometimes, when he was in a good mood, he used the God's eye ruse to bluff about knowing we'd done something wrong. "God's eye saw you," he'd say, meaning the big stained glass inset. I don't remember ever being fooled by it, but Oli was. Confessed to all sorts of things, even though I told him to shut up.

I suppose the trouble set in when Grandad started to lose his marbles and couldn't run the farm anymore. They could have helped him run it; it's not as though any of his kids had careers that demanded attention. But Filthy and Esther and Clem all wanted him to sell—to get their share. They didn't want to wait till he croaked.

A family can get a senile old man to do just about anything with enough badgering. They talked him into it. I've always thought that's what did him in. I was twelve when he died. It wasn't cancer or heart disease or any of the normal stuff—he just didn't wake up one day. He had no reason to, not after they moved him away from the land to a fucking townhouse in Manji, away from that connection and purpose, and from Elsie's grave.

The irony is that once they'd convinced him to sell and moved him out, the three siblings couldn't agree on how to divvy things up. It dragged on for years. Clem wanted an equal share of the cash as well as the fifteen acres he'd fenced off and made into our home. Filthy and Esther knew he was desperate to own that piece of the farm, so they held out. They said it was only fair that Clem buy the land at market rates with his share of the proceeds.

He didn't think that was right. The old man had given him that land. Not by legal deed, but by act, by promise. Grandad wanted Mum and Oli and me to always have a home. But Esther and Phil wouldn't budge, and Clem knew that those fifteen acres would cost as much, maybe more, than his share of the property. The timber alone was worth a fortune; Clem called it his superannuation, but I don't think he would have ever touched a single tree. He'd happily go onto someone else's land and cut timber—legally or illegally, it didn't much matter to him. But he loved the giants in his own backyard; wouldn't countenance taking a single one down, even when we were in deep shit with overdue bills and fines.

He eventually caved, agreed to take just the land and no money from the sale, and that was the end of him and Esther. Decided he hated her, too. The following year, Clem was dead. At least Grandad was already gone.

I figure my father didn't do much right, but protecting that piece of dirt is his true legacy.

I look up as the sky flashes with lightning, revealing towers of cloud sweeping toward camp. A sapling beyond the fence suddenly bends horizontal and cool air follows. It's the first real breeze I've felt in a month. It's ridiculously good.

The breeze builds into a gust that tangles twigs and dry spinifex grass into oval balls that tumble down the graded road meant for security vehicles. The air fills with the dim haze of misting rain. I retreat further under cover of the verandah. Black and blue clouds roll overhead and the rain falls harder, peeling sideways.

The sound of the squall—wind shearing from square cornices and gutters—makes me think of crashing waves, like a certain type of wind makes everyone think of crashing waves. There's something else. I twist my head and listen. Piercing the storm, I hear a man on a loud speaker singing the Muslim call to prayer — in the middle of an Australian desert.

INVITATION

I get up at a reasonable hour in an effort to recalibrate myself; I intend to get some sleep tonight in preparation for dayshift.

I make bacon and eggs and a satisfactory cup of coffee. It's gone past noon, and it is my day off, so I fetch my whisky from my room and add a dollop. Some days you just wake up and feel like it.

I sit at a cheap plastic table under an ugly tin porch and eat my food and drink my drink while I look out on the bush butting onto the back of Spinifex City. For all I know, that bush stretches unbroken to the Northern Territory.

Roy walks over and takes a seat. He's got a cup of black tea in one hand, a pie in the other. The pie looks cold. In fact, the pie looks terrible, and I love pies.

"How's the pie, mate?"

"Ah, just gotta fuck'n eat it, don't ya?"

"Did you heat it up?"

"Couldn't be fucked."

"There's a microwave in there," I say, gesturing to the kitchen.

Roy just shrugs.

"Just mad dog it, hey, Mad Dog?"

"Too right," says Roy, hoeing into the pie like a wild animal. When he comes up for air he says, "Eh, I heard you were in that thing with the Sri Lankan bloke. Bit of action, was it?"

"Yeah, it was pretty full-on."

"Need one of them fire hoses, turn it on full blast, 'Back you bastards!'"

"Yeah, might work."

"That your first code?"

"No. I've had a few now. But that's my first Code Black."

"I had me first the other day."

"Really? What was it?"

"Blue, sorta, but I dunno at the time. In the shower blocks in Brown. This little feller I was on watch duty, goes in to brush his teeth or some shit and you're not gonna watch him every second, are ya? Then I poke me head in and he's bleedin' all over the floor—slashed up. Been here goin' on two years. They lose their fuck'n minds, mate. I don't blame 'em. I'd lose me mind too, locked up that long. What are they doin', eh? How long's it take to stamp a fuck'n visa? Nah, it's bullshit."

"Was it ok?"

"I called it in but I couldn't remember the right words. The old prick tells me if I can't use the radio properly I'm out. On the arse."

"Who?"

"Oh, fuck'n ... Benedict, the big bastard. Nah, it's bullshit. You're lookin' at the hole in his head and you're meant to remember some code. I told 'em what it was, a feller had slashed up and where we are, what difference it make, eh? Nah, got it in for me I reckon."

"Yeah, I think I remember hearing the call." And, yes, it was precisely as mumbled, disjointed and tortuous as one would expect Roy's radio communications to be.

"I guess they just want you to advise what code it is first. So they know who to send."

"You know what he said to me? Says, 'These rules are for your protection.' But I reckon it's bullshit, mate. It's for them. Cover their arses. Say they're followin' the rule book while blokes are killin' themselves 'n shit."

"You want a whisky?"

"Eh? Nah. Oh ... fuck it, go on then."

Roy throws the slops of his tea on the ground, and I pour some whisky into his mug.

"Bit of the old Tide's Inn tonight?"

"Oh, I dunno, mate. Not sure I feel like it," I say.

"Nah? What'll I do if I get in another blue, mate? Eh? You're me fuck'n wreckin' ball, Nicko."

"Well shit, Mad Dog, you could always try not getting into a fight."

"Never start 'em, just finish 'em."

"Never start 'em? Fuck off, Roy. I'd guarantee you've started most the fights you've been in."

Roy gives me that look—the sweet, innocent, mildly deranged clown look.

"I'm a choirboy, mate," he says.

"Yeah, some choirboy. You're the choirboy who fucked all the other choirboys."

"Got priests for that. Nah mate, I fucked the priests!"

"So you're the bloke that went around molesting all the priests who molested all the boys?"

"Fuck'n oath!"

Roy jumps to his feet and puts a foot on the table and starts fucking the air, sideways. "Father, forgive me. 'Just stick it in harder, you little bastard!' Father, forgive me. 'Just keep fucking, boy!' Father, you're a dirty old prick. 'Shut up and tickle me balls!' "

On and on Roy goes, till he notices Meg walking toward us, looking at Roy with a disposition I know he recognises. Roy rams one last imaginary cock into one last imaginary priest arsehole, and sits back down, breathless.

"Is that a new dance?" says Meg.

"Oh, it's a dance. The Mad Dog dance," I say.

"Nah, shouldn't pretend, should ya, but gotta have a laugh, don't ya?" says Roy, who then takes a swill of whisky.

"Hey, so what are you up to?" asks Meg.

"This is pretty much it," I say.

"We're going back out to Lennard Gorge. Apparently the waterfalls out there should be really good today from the rain we had last night. Wanna come?"

"You and Gian?" I ask.

"Fuck'n oath," interjects Roy.

Meg gives me a look that only I see, a look that tells me the invitation was not intended for Mad Dog. "Mmhmm," she hums.

"Um, yeah, I think Roy and I could manage that. What do you think, Mad Dog?"

"Bring a fishing rod. Reel in a freshy!"

"Are there freshwater crocodiles out there?" I ask.

"Yep," says Meg. "Sheee-ite loads."

"And you still went swimming?"

"Mmhmm. Just a daredevil kind of girl," Meg says. "So, gonna come?"

FALLS

Gian and his housemate Derrick are in the front. Meg and Roy and I are bouncing around in the back. Somehow I have been sandwiched in the middle seat, when I am clearly the biggest of we three. I don't much like the prospect of Mad Dog the priest rapist touching me up, so I lean toward the other side, my hip, leg, arm and shoulder pushing into the softness of Meg.

People are like fuel for Meg. She's burning off energy by fidgeting and chatting, her hands doing a lot of talking. At one point she knocks my hand and I playfully snatch her fingers, as if she's fallen into a trap. She jerks away and looks at me defiantly. Without saying anything, we start playing a game, my hand palm up, resting on Meg's thigh, opened like the jaws of a crocodile. Meg then tries to poke my palm without getting caught. She's not very good. She gets caught time and time again, until finally I snatch her hand and don't let go. When I do release, Meg doesn't pull away. Our hands rest on one another. Little by little, our fingers thread together.

Meg leans into me with her upper body. Her head and face are close. It reminds me of the position we were in at the pub, about to kiss. There's no chance for that to happen now, but it's still sort of sweet. I say sort of, for truly nothing is sweet in the back seat of a Barina, bouncing and shuddering along a corrugated dirt road in semi-arid but-fuck-nowhere with Roy leaning out the window, yelling at Gian to stop the car so he can get out and go fuck an emu he sees. I'm beyond grateful when we finally tumble out.

The car park sits on a rise that looks over flat terrain, imperceptibly sloping away to the coast. I can see the dark line of the Lennard River cutting a gentle weave through the landscape, before it curves around on itself and disappears. In the middle of a billabong with a long sandbank rising in its centre, I see a dozen or more freshwater crocodiles sunning themselves. The temperature must be in the mid-thirties, perfect weather for a plunge into cool river water, but now I'm not so sure.

We follow a trail in the opposite direction, to the east. Already, just half a day after rain, the bush looks different. It could be that I'm imagining it, it could be that I'm just seeing what I want to see, but there seems to be a tinge of livened green, the hint of new shoots already pressing through the dry husks of flaxen grasses and silvered bushes. There's red, too — not the red of rust and dirt, but the red of life, of nature's blood, a faint smear across scraggly gum tree leaves and in the marrow beneath bark. The aspect of the entire landscape is softened by these subtle changes, and I start to wonder if this place could almost be beautiful.

The walk is long, though not hard. We're fit from the job, anyway, being that it's comprised mostly of either standing around doing nothing or walking the compounds completing chores and patrols. We gain maybe thirty metres in altitude, not much for mountainous country, but a major geological event amid the profound Australian flatness. The dirt solidifies into pure rock. We climb across a series of shelves and come into the gorge, high on the northern flank. We look down into a broad pool that gradually narrows, leading the eye toward three cascades spilling across a single rock parapet. I don't see any crocodiles, freshwater or salt, and understand now how someone might swim here without concern. Crocodiles aren't much known for rock climbing, and that's precisely what is required to access this pool.

Once at water's edge, we strip off; the boys to shorts, Roy to beige underwear, Meg to a bikini that seems at risk of disgorging her breasts. I dive into the water, cutting through a thin layer of warmth to the cool beneath. I pull my submerged body through the resistance, then open my eyes and aim for the surface. It feels like an extravagant luxury to emerge from water so chilled it's actually cold into air buzzing with heat.

I paddle out into the middle of the pool and slowly rotate. Above the waterfall and high where the water doesn't reach, it is an ochrous red borrowed straight from Uluru. The red rock sits on layer after layer of bleached grey slabs that are piled together like a mass Lego structure, receding in a series of steeples. It could be climbed without too much trouble to access the top of the waterfalls.

I paddle round till I'm looking at the south wall, and it's completely different. It's like a giant hand is pushing from beneath the rock, tilting the slabs so far from the horizontal that any second they might slide from their perch and crash into the pool. The wall's overall incline is sheer, the water having worn at it with much greater force than the other side. It's impressive, and a little intimidating.

I swim overarm toward the white water, where the cascades join the pool. I dip into the biggest fall, heedless of the danger till it pushes me under, tumbles me over and pops me out. I emerge chastened, surprised at the water's force and my own relative weakness—but, then, it did carve out this entire gorge. I reach out and dip my hand into the cascade.

The sound hides the approach of Meg. I don't realise she is there till she lunges forward and pushes my head under. I come up sputtering. I roll around and see Meg making her retreat. She's slow, and with a few quick strokes I'm able to reach out and grasp her ankle. Meg gives up almost immediately; she lets herself be pulled backward. She paddles around so that she's facing me, but as I draw her in she pushes her arms out, her palms flat against my chest. I grab her hands and pull her close, and she lets me.

"What are you going to do?" she giggles.

"What do you want me to do?"

"Hmm ..."

"Come on," I say.

Meg follows me under the thin curtain of water of the smallest cascade. Behind, there is a little protected space where I back onto a submerged rock shelf. I slide my hand down Meg's side, around the small of her back and onto the soft flesh of her arse. I pull her waist toward mine. Our eyes are locked. My other hand works up from Meg's hip till I'm gently caressing the side of her breast. I lean in and kiss her.

Meg kisses me back, her hands reaching for my shoulders, drawing our bodies close. I squeeze her arse with one hand and her breast with the other. Meg pulls her mouth away, opens her eyes, smiles and arches her brow. She nods toward my hand.

"You like them?" she says.

"I like all of it, a lot," I say.

I lean into her and we kiss, harder, the passion carrying away other thoughts. I know Meg can feel me, my cock pushing into her crotch. For a second I'm lost in it, then I'm not.

"Hoo-ahh!" comes the cry, just before a splash of water beyond the cascades, followed by two more indistinct cries and two more splashes. It's the boys. The crazy bastards have climbed up and are chucking bombies.

Through a watery curtain I can see one of them swimming toward us. Meg and I push away. Then I hear Roy above the sound of the white water.

"Lost me fuck'n undies! Me fuck'n undies!"

I swim out from behind the falls to see Roy turning circles. I can't believe the old bastard actually climbed the cliff and jumped in.

"What the fuck are you doing, Mad Dog?"

"Lost me undies, mate. Hello!" he calls, when he sees Meg emerge from the cascade. "Seen me undies?"

"Ooh, gross," says Meg.

At that moment Roy flips his body to the surface, floating on his back. Sure enough, he's lost his undies. A little old prick rises above the surface and hangs limp, like a flag planted in terra nullius.

"Ahh! Get it away!" screams Meg.

She swims for the opposite shore. I see Roy's head tip up, that deranged clown I know all too well smiling at me. I know he's gonna try to touch me with that thing. I swim for my life.

DANCE

We head back to Gian's place, where we drink and listen to music. Gian, Derrick and a few others I've just met listen intently as Roy regales us with a pig-hunting story. His dog had cornered a big boar in a gully, but it was a tusker and it gored the dog to death. Roy loved that dog, so he was justifiably upset.

He grabbed a fallen branch and set upon the pig with the sort of lunatic fury that has rightly earned him the "Mad Dog" nickname. No one but Roy could have been surprised when the intended flailing went awry. The branch broke across the boar's back, at which point the old tusker proceeded to gore Roy's leg. When Roy finally got his knife out of his belt, he tried to stab the pig, but—in Roy's words—the pig stabbed him with his own knife. So he had two gashed legs, a dead dog, no pig and was about two kilometres from his ute, which, when he got back, had a flat tyre, and Roy wondered if the fucking pig didn't do that, too.

While the others are laughing, I wink at Meg, then exit to the laundry. A moment later Meg joins me and we spend a few minutes kissing and fondling. I guess we look a bit guilty when we return; Gian gives me a wink that makes me think he has a pretty good idea what's going on, or maybe he just wants a piece of me, too.

The others are keen to go to the pub. I'm not. I don't need a repeat of the last time, and there's something else I'd rather be doing. I tell them I'm going to head back to Spinifex City, get an earlyish night for our start tomorrow. I'm hoping Meg will also suddenly find herself all petered out and in desperate need of a good sleep, and decide to come back with me. Lo and behold, she does, but then Roy decides to call it a night, too. I'd figured him for another big one.

When we get back to Spinifex City, Roy wants one more drink. He's so enthusiastic and so insistent that I can't stand saying no to the old bastard, though Meg has no such compunctions. She gives me a look, says good night and heads off to her room.

I pull up a plastic pew at the outdoor tables and I pour two whiskies. Roy is still thinking about the good old days. He tells me about the time he found a feral goat submerged up to its neck in mud, though in Roy's telling it was quicksand. He put a rope around its neck, attached it to the winch on his ute and pulled the animal out. Roy went down to loosen the noose. The goat wasn't moving, as he'd damn near choked it to death. He got the rope off and the goat eventually sat up, but still didn't try to get away. Roy started patting the goat like it was a dog. The goat realised it was not a dog; the goat realised it was a very scared and confused goat. It jumped up and bolted, knocking the feet from under Roy, who landed hard on his tail bone. The goat swung around and ran straight back into the bog, stuck in pretty much the same spot as before. Such an act of betrayal was too much for Roy. He went to his ute, retrieved his gun and shot the goat about fourteen times. Then, not wanting to contaminate a watering hole, he had to carefully wade into the bog, put the rope back around the goat's neck and winch it out again, except this time it didn't move when he took the noose off and he could pat it to his heart's content.

I haven't stopped laughing when Roy starts telling me about his grand plans once he's done six months at the centre. It's not just Thailand in his sights; Roy wants to do a trip to Mongolia. I ask him how he settled on such a peculiar destination, and he tells me that he's seen it on TV a few times and it's always just sounded interesting to him. He reckons it'd be good to see another culture like the Mongols in their tents or huts or whatever they are, with all that open space and grass and living like it's the Middle Ages, and they've got some horse milk booze that he wouldn't mind trying, too. First, though, is Thailand, where his non-English-speaking whore is waiting. He thinks she might even marry him, if he asks.

I pull the pin after half an hour with Roy. I get back to my room, shower, then lie in bed, thinking about what could have been and what should have been. Not long after, there's a very faint knock on my door. I open it and see Meg. I drag her inside.

"I wasn't sure if you'd be here," says Meg in a whisper. "Thought you were more interested in Roy. Thought I might find you in his room, doing that dance."

"Well, I thought maybe we could do that dance."

"Oh really?"

"Ah-huh. Do you know it?"

"I'm not sure. How does it go?"

"Like this," I say, pushing my body into Meg's, my mouth searching for hers, my tongue parting her lips. We sway side to side. Our hips press into each other. I pull Meg's shirt up and over her head, then with my right hand I flick open the strap on her bra. Meg lets it fall away to reveal luscious milky breasts. I gently bury my face in her cleavage.

I manage to push Meg's little shorts down over the curve of her arse; she lets them drop to the floor. She pulls my own shirt up and over my head; I stand and unbutton my shorts and let them drop. Meg runs her hand along my back and over my shoulders, around onto my chest, then down, reaching for my cock. As we kiss, I slip my hand into Meg's panties and squeeze her arse, firm but not too firm, then follow the curve of her hip till my hand dips into her crotch, my fingers finding the warm wet of her pussy.

I pull her panties off, then step Meg across until she falls onto my bed. She lies back and I straddle her, kissing her mouth, then her breasts, then her belly, till I reach her pussy where I stay, my tongue licking and thrusting and pulsing across the mound of flesh until she gasps and grips the bed sheets, and I feel the orgasm ripple through the thighs pressed tight around my head.

Meg tells me she wants me inside her and so I quickly put on a condom then pull my body on top of hers and we fuck, just how I imagined, deep and passionate and intense. When neither of us have more to give I slide my body from Meg's and whisper into her ear, "And I'm going to fuck you like that all night long."

Meg pulls away and looks at me. "Oh really?"

I smile, hoping my boyish charm mitigates my vulgar mouth. "Well, if you want me to. If you tell me to."

Meg laughs. "And if I don't?"

"Hmm. Then I'll sit in the corner and sulk. While I play with myself."

She laughs again. "And I suppose I'm sleeping while you're watching me?"

"Of course. Be creepy otherwise."

"You are weeeeird, Nick. Naughty and weird."

"Of course ... you could just tell me to fuck you again," I say, looking at her eyes, her gaze darting away then coming back to my own.

I find Meg's hand without looking and hold it, then she leans over and gently kisses me on the neck. She keeps kissing, slowly moving higher until she is at my cheek and then moves across to my ear. She kisses the lobe softly, then whispers, "Fuck me."

I turn and we kiss and Meg's hand finds my cock and soon we're fucking again. After we finish we fall asleep, Meg's head snuggled into my chest. When I wake at 4 a.m., my cock is hard, so I stroke Meg until she wakes, then we kiss and fondle and fuck.

With only twenty minutes till the bus is due, Meg pokes her head out of my door to check the way is clear, then slips away. I shower and dress then I head out to the bus stop with the rest of the crew. I see Meg walk over. She stands away from me, but I catch her gaze and subtly lick my lips, glancing at her crotch. She bites down on a smile. I get on the bus, expecting Meg to sit next to me, but instead I get Roy and we talk about pigs.

GOSSIP

Meg has been given the role of rover today—and not like when I was rover and just sat with Matthew for the night. She's actually roving, frittering through the compounds doing tasks. I'm delivering appointment slips when I spot Meg coming through the Brown Compound gates. I stand clear of the corridor and call out her name, then wave her over. There's no one else around. When Meg is close enough for me to whisper, I say, "I really enjoyed last night."

"Mmhmm. I had an ok time, I guess," Meg says, a sly look on her face.

"Just ok?"

"It was pretty good."

"Wow. I'm gonna have to lift my game. Maybe I need help. One man might not be enough to satisfy your sexual appetite. Hmm, I know, maybe I'll call Gian and ask him to drive over in his Barina to help ..."

"Well, you could, but I know which hole he's interested in—not any of mine."

"Really? So, what, he's definitely gay?"

"Ahh, yeaaah. Obviously. And he said he thinks you're hot. Actually, he said he'd like to Brokeback Mountain you. I told him to back off, that you're taken."

"You warned off another bitch?"

"Mmhmm."

"I'm impressed. Maybe you should help me deliver a slip to

this dark, empty room. You know, make sure it's safe inside."

Meg laughs. "I don't think so."

"No?"

"Nn-nn."

"Why not?"

"I have to see Grace. Got some paperwork for a new PSP."

"Sexy."

"Very."

"So, will I see you tonight?" I say.

"Umm, maybe. But people might notice me going to your room."

"And?"

"You know what they're like. I don't want any of those dicks gossiping about us."

"Well, it's not really gossip if we're doing whatever they say we're doing, which sounds a whole lot better than them gossiping anyway and us not doing what they say we're doing."

"What?"

"I'm just saying that you should do whatever you want, and not worry about those guys."

"Well, I'll try to come by tonight. But Scott is always hanging around outside after our shift, so, I don't know if I'll be able to. I want to …"

"Yeah, that's cool. If I see you I see you. I hope I see you."

Meg gives me a wink then walks off toward the Brown Compound office. I continue distributing appointment slips. Once I finish, I make my way to the office. As I'm walking in, Meg is walking out. I let my hand brush against her side as we pass.

"Ahh, just the man I wanted to see," says Grace.

"Oh shit, here we go."

"Rasa Dasouli," says Grace, handing me a pink file. "He's just been put on constant watch. Said he's thinking about self-harm. Sit on him for a few hours, then I'll get someone to take over for you."

TENSION

Rasa is an Iranian man in his early twenties. He's been in detention about six months. I see him around whenever I'm in Brown Compound, normally joking with officers and other detainees. I had him down as the sort to cop his period of internment with a cool philosophical insouciance; the sort who accepts the various indignities and tribulations of his time inside a desert prison as a necessary precursor to a much broader, richer life. I'm starting to figure out, however, that just about all detainees, no matter their personality or beliefs, have their ups and downs. Tension, the detainees call it.

"Officer, I have tension."

"Nick, I feel tension."

"Oh, don't worry about him, he has tension."

I hear it all day. Sometimes it's a specific event that precipitates it, sometimes it's an accumulation of unknowing and numbing repetitions. I mean, there's times I've felt it myself—just a sort of dread, an empty dread—and I'm the guy who's been here not even two months and gets to go home every day.

According to his case file, Rasa was talking to an officer when he said something about hurting himself. It may be that he was merely joking, but it doesn't matter. The procedure is clear: any self-harm ideation triggers a constant watch that continues till the mental health professionals give the all clear.

Grace comes with me to Rasa's room and explains to him why he's being placed on constant watch. It means having an officer follow him around, and Rasa is not impressed. For a cool kid like him, having an officer hold his hand is humiliating. Besides, Rasa says he has no intention of harming himself; he's not one of those guys. It is what it is, Grace tells him.

Rasa, his roommate and a friend are inside. I say hello then prop the door open, put a chair outside the room and sit myself down. It's a busy corridor. A stream of other detainees come and go. For a man with tension, Rasa remains popular and personable, joking and laughing with friends, though perhaps without the exuberance for which he is known.

We don't say much to each other at first. He's just a name and a number to me, I'm just a nameless blue shirt to him. But, after a while, we begin to chat. At first I ask him about his visa. He tells me he received a positive decision, deemed a legitimate refugee. I congratulate him. But then Rasa tells me it's already been two months since getting his positive, two months of waiting for an ASIO security clearance. It's starting to do his head in; two months is enough time for all the anxiety and confusion and doubt to stream back into a detainee's mind. I know this is true because I've heard it from so many other detainees here who are also waiting on their security clearance. ASIO backlog.

As Rasa tells me about being locked up, about waiting for his release, about the trip from Indonesia to Christmas Island, I realise I am only making him focus on the source of his discontent. If there is one platitude in the world I consider true, it is that for happiness in life a person must have something to do, something to look forward to and someone to love. Clearly Rasa has nothing to do but wait, so I change the subject. We talk about the future—a future, Rasa tells me, that will be filled with beautiful women. He explains that another officer has told him of a certain category of woman in Australia that does not exist in Iran.

"Eepie."

"Eepie?"

"Yes, they have much hair down here," says Rasa, gesturing to the crotch area.

"Ahh, hippie."

"Yes, heepie!"

Apparently they smell and don't wash enough and are very hairy, but like to have lots of sex. I tell Rasa that there are not just hippies, but many beautiful women in Sydney, the city of his dreams where his brother and brother's wife and their children already live.

"Oh, they will like you, Rasa. They will think you are exotic. Long hair, olive skin, dark eyes. They will be falling all over you. Throwing themselves at you."

"Really," says Rasa, "you think they will like me?"

"You will have no worries, my friend. Beautiful women everywhere! You will have many girlfriends, no doubt."

He is pleased with this. But it's not just girls. His whole life will change, I tell him.

"I don't know what it's like in Iran, but there's lots of opportunity in Australia. There are jobs, you can get an education, a degree at university if you want. And the real Australia, the Australia where people live, it's nothing like this. It's green and there are hills and trees and the coast has amazing beaches. You will like it. You'll like all of it."

"Yes, yes I think so. I think I will like it very much. Especially the women. The heepies the most!"

"Especially the hippies."

We don't speak for a moment. Rasa just sits there, nodding his head. He turns to me and says, "Thank you, man. Thank you."

"Of course, Rasa. You're going to make a good Australian. A great Australian."

"Yes, yes, thank you."

Our easy conversation and Rasa's whimsical turn makes

me wonder if other officers have ever spoken to him about his future, or spoken to him like he will soon be part of Australia. Personally, I see these guys as future Australians out of sheer pragmatism. The sods who end up bobbing around in Australia's corner of the Indian Ocean aren't the economic migrants a lot of people assume them to be. That would be the Irish, English, Kiwis, Indians, Chinese, South Africans and plenty of others — people who immigrate to Australia for the better job prospects and nicer beaches. The boat people are the ones fleeing war-torn hellholes, oppressive theocracies, clan or caste pogroms and political persecution. I was curious, so I looked up the figures on the internet. Something like seventy to ninety percent of all these guys will be deemed legitimate refugees and granted asylum by the time everything is said and done. Throw a dart in this joint and you couldn't fail to hit a future Australian. That's why I talk to Rasa and others like they are Aussies-in-waiting.

Rasa and I joke and talk some more, then just before noon he goes to see the psychologist. When he returns, we wait to hear if he must remain under constant supervision. He listens to music. At one point a gaunt fellow with an electric mop of hair walks past, provoking a little flurry of excitement. Rasa tells me that the man I see walking away is a famed Iranian musician, recently arrived. I'm incredulous; what would a famous musician be doing in an Australian detention centre? He was imprisoned, then fled the country when he was released, Rasa tells me. All because he was lead singer in a metal band.

For a moment I think, yeah, sure, maybe the ayatollahs have a point, heavy metal does blow, but then I think about something the comedian Patton Oswalt said, about however much you hate certain music — for instance, the bland rock of Creed or Nickelback — you need to remember that it's just music, it's just a bunch of people making music, perhaps bad music, which you are free to listen to or not listen to, while others are out there hating, killing, raping and torturing. I watch the wraith-like figure walk away, a man forced to flee a country because he makes music.

A little while later word comes over the radio: Rasa has been lifted from constant supervision. He is relieved, and he also seems a little happier from our chats. I wish him well; his security clearance must surely be due soon, and the thought of him in Sydney enjoying our freedoms and lifestyle pleases me. Rasa seems like the perfect refugee.

Later, I'm in the compound office with Bailey. The case of Rasa comes up and I mention that he's down about how long he's been waiting for his security clearance. Bailey says yeah, sure, but there's more to it than that.

A few weeks ago, during a dayshift when I was back in my tin hut, sleeping, there was a disturbance in the centre. I heard about it in that night's briefing but didn't give it too much thought. After a confrontation at the phones, apparently a bunch of Afghanis saw some of the Iranians pointing at them in the Red Compound mess hall. Two got up, went over and attempted to settle the problem; threats may have been made, a scuffle ensued. Bailey's not sure who truly started it, but he is sure of this: Rasa was in the melee, seen clubbing an Afghani man over the back with a chair. I quiz Bailey to see if he's sure of that detail, and he is.

I'm stunned. It's madness. It makes no sense. Had he just continued to wait patiently and peacefully for the security clearance, Rasa would soon be free to settle in Sydney with his brother. But now he is facing an assault charge, possibly assault with a weapon, and his visa is in jeopardy. It's obvious why Rasa has tension: he knows he messed up. He knows he's risked his one chance for a better life. He's a fool. Worse, he's a violent fool.

Yet I still feel sorry for him. Attacking a man with a chair is a low act, but should it disqualify Rasa from becoming an Australian? There must be mitigating factors, a multitude of vexations and stresses that conspired into a single mental breakdown and this—this epic fuck-up. Maybe there was an earlier stoush, or a particularly cutting jibe, threats, the tension of detention, mental health questions, epoch-long racial tensions between Persians and Afghans. A happy-go-lucky man with a visa doesn't just attack another man for no reason.

I leave the office, headed straight for Rasa's room. I intend to tell him I know why he is depressed, and tell him maybe there is still a way out of this. Bailey told me that the Afghani man made a complaint to the federal police, and wants charges to be pressed. But if Rasa apologises and the Afghani man can be convinced to withdraw his complaint, then maybe they'll let the matter drop. Maybe he can still live happily ever after in Australia.

we've never had so much as a passing exchange before today, yet Uday is familiar to me. I've probably heard more commentary from other officers on this individual than any other detainee in the centre. To sum up the overwhelming consensus of officers and managers, this bloke is a complete and utter fuckwit. Officers would love to smash him. There are iterations on that theme, but I think that captures the essence: fuckwit, desperately needs a good corrective beatdown.

Now, I'm not so sure about all that, not because I know the man not to be a fuckwit, but because I simply don't know him well enough. None of us do. I do know the man is in distress. Two nights ago, he lit a fire in a waste-paper basket and burned himself on the leg. He also cut his arm, chest and abdomen with a piece of broken glass, no doubt sourced from the kitchenette window before we sealed off the site last week. Uday was miserable for weeks before he lit the fire; everyone knew he would self-harm or do something stupid, it was only a question of when.

I'm almost rooting for him, so pointless and pathetic is his little protest. He's trying to find agency in a process that treats him like a number. He's clearly losing the battle. He will lose. Yet he's fighting it anyway. Makes me wonder if he might not be the quintessential little Aussie battler. Or maybe he's just a fuckwit.

When I look in the DIAC interview room where Uday is being temporarily housed, I see a whiteboard covered in platitudes. I hate platitudes. With few exceptions, they're narrow statements of the obvious wrapped up in pretentious language or saccharine imagery to create the illusion of profundity. Or they're outright bullshit—pretty lies and magical thinking. They certainly have no place in the real world of suffering and struggle. Yet some well-intentioned moron thought they were doing a good thing by educating dumbshit detainees on the appropriate mental frame for their predicament, via platitude. This is what's on the board:

Peace of mind comes from accepting life as it is, not how you want it to be.

We don't see things as they are, we see them as we are.

Yesterday is history, tomorrow is a mystery, today is a gift to be used wisely.

You cannot live in a world of "if".

Entry to the sanctuary of peace lies within.

Happiness is not a destination, it is how we travel to get there.

Winners never quit. Quitters never win.

I cried because I had no shoes, until I met a man with no feet.

Pain is inevitable—misery is a choice.

As I watch Uday lie on a bare mattress, exhausted, his eyes puffy, countenance drawn, contemplating his lot in life, I wonder to myself if the person who scribbled this combination of falsehoods and banal observations on the human condition ever tried to imagine themselves in Uday's or Matthew's or Soheil's position.

These asylum seekers are doing everything they can to find happiness and better their lives—the core theme of most platitudes—by making their outlandish journeys to Australia. It's only now, here, in this strange prison, that they have lost their sense of self-determination, and so the drip of time pounds into their consciousness like water torture. The sense of failure and shame and the loss of dignity—that is what drives them to act out in the only ways they know how, not lack of purpose or vision, not some failure of will.

Advice that exhorts these people to perk up and cop it on the chin and choose to enjoy their six-month to three-year journey through refugee prison, which comes, as it is, with no guarantee of anything other than a suntan and a mental illness, amounts to the ugliest lack of empathy I've ever seen.

There is one more platitude on the whiteboard. It's so well known it isn't even expressed in words. It's just a picture of a cup, a horizontal line drawn across its middle.

EMPTY

I should have been relieved from duty by now. I could just radio control and remind them, but I think I'd prefer to stay here, given Gabriel is running Red Compound and I'm Red Six.

Over the radio I hear a Code Blue: the third of the day, about the fifteenth of the week. The idea of cutting seems to work like a virus, getting into detainees' heads from hearing of others doing the deed. Half an hour later, the subject of the code has been patched up at medical and is escorted into the room next to mine by Benedict and Darren, plus Meg, who seems to be on a fast track to management. Or maybe just a fast track to Darren's cock. I try to catch Meg's eye, but she's totally focused on the detainee. Benedict sits the man on a plastic chair then kneels next to him.

"Let me tell you something," Benedict says. "You think eight months is a long time. It's not. Some people have been here for three years. You need to understand that our government is very busy. Very busy. All your people keep coming on boats, so it takes time. Everyone has to wait. Don't be selfish, you've got to just wait."

The detainee nods now and again as Benedict talks.

"You know, you're lucky to be here. Right now you are safe. You have food, clothes. There's no one with guns trying to kill you. All you need to be thinking about is your family, not this cutting business. It just slows everything down. Your wife wouldn't want to know you were doing this, would she? Or your son. You've got responsibilities, so no more of this cutting. Yes? You going to be a man?"

The detainee nods. Benedict puts his big hand on the detainee's shoulder and squeezes.

"Ok. We'll get you some dinner later on. We'll talk about getting you back into the compound after the psychologist sees you."

Benedict walks away. Meg sees me looking at her and she flashes a quick smile, then she turns and follows in Benedict's wake.

I'm left looking at this man, a little cherub-faced Afghani, just about the saddest goddamn refugee I think I've ever seen. He's so sad they should call some Save the World charity and take his photo for one of those poverty-porn posters that beseech guilt-laden middle-class people to make a donation that goes straight into the wages of a twenty-year-old Irish chick working the phones to solicit even more donations to pay for the Save the World summer mail-out campaign. Yeah, that motherfucker's cup is definitely half empty.

VIRUS

It's now four Code Blues. The latest cutter has been to medical and Meg is overseeing his constant watch in a room down the corridor. I recognise him as one of Rasa's friends; one of the cool kids. He's also a very big kid, somewhere around six foot three, almost as wide as the donga door frame, chest puffed up like a strongman in a circus. He's fucking enormous, which makes me a little worried for Meg, but then I correct myself for thinking that way because I know most of these guys will only ever harm themselves. Besides, I'm twenty metres away.

I watch Meg watch her client like a hawk. She's one very eager little officer. Very much by the book. She doesn't wave, doesn't exchange eyes with me, doesn't seem to notice I'm right there, close enough to have a loud conversation. Then I hear the man start crying. A high-pitched faltering squeal grows into a lower, more desperate wail, matched by a bashing sound—methodical. I'm not sure what it is. It's loud enough and goes on for long enough that Darren comes around to check what's happening. He speaks to Meg briefly, then she walks away and Darren stays. The noise continues. Meg walks down the corridor, finally recognising my presence.

"Hi," I say.

"Hey."

"So what's going on in there?"

"He's the guy from the last Code Blue."

"Yeah. What's the noise?"

"Oh, the fat idiot is hitting his head against the wall. He's such a crybaby. It's pathetic. Did you see the size of him?" Meg turns and looks in the direction of the noise. "I wish he would shut up."

"Do you know what he's upset about?"

"He just wants attention," Meg says, turning back.

"But he's obviously upset about something."

"He's just a crybaby who wants attention."

"I mean, it sounds like he's in distress."

"Distress? Oh my God, Nick, you sound like Quincy. He's just throwing a tantrum 'cause he's a little brat. I've been at four of these today, it's ridiculous. I know what's going on, I've seen how they play the system. I've been in control about ten times now, and I've been rover; I see what happens at the whole centre. They're not upset. Or if they are it's just because they're not getting their way. You can't be soft or they'll target you."

"Jesus, Meg, I just said the guy is upset. The dude's carrying on and bashing his head against a wall, so I'm pretty sure he's upset. That's all."

"I've gotta get back to the compound. Bye," says Meg, turning and walking away.

I watch Meg go. I squint a "fuck you" at her retreating frame, but my eyes gradually drop down till I'm staring at the abundant curve of her arse. I notice how her black work-pants pinch between her peachy arse cheeks, almost like the very evolution of her form is designed to lead my attention to the crease at the top of her thighs ...

Jesus, Nick. What is wrong with you? She just ripped you a new arsehole, and for no good reason. My cock murmurs at the same time as a flash of hot shame crosses my cheeks, and I feel confused and annoyed and stupid.

OBJECTORS

Thick purple clouds roll overhead, though the sun is still visible on the horizon. It's strange, and strangely beautiful, how the entire landscape seems bathed with warmth and colour in defiance of the strengthening storm. A slick twilight sheen is caught in the water sloughing from leaves and needles and bark.

I sit next to Meg on the bus. I have to move her bag from the spare seat to do so, a sure sign she wants to be alone, but I'm not comfortable with how we left things.

"Good timing," I say, as the bus shudders from a powerful gust of wind. The shower is thickening by the second into a proper downpour.

"Yeah. It'd suck to be out in that."

"Nice to watch, though. I like a good storm. I like to listen to rain on the tin roof when I'm in bed."

"Me too," says Meg, smiling at me with affection for the first time that day.

I spent the afternoon thinking about what I wanted to say to Meg. I've settled on an analogy that sums up my take on the situation.

"Hey, so I was reading this book before I came up here. A science and history book about ... food, I guess. Anyway, there's this story in it—not a story story, a real story—it's about an experiment during World War Two."

"Ok."

"So, these Americans, conscientious objectors, they're people who refused to fight in the war—"

"I know what a conscientious objector is."

"Right. Well, they were put on a semi-starvation diet for a bit less than six months, about twenty weeks, I think. The idea was that researchers could simulate what their troops might have to go through if the war dragged on. So there's about thirty of these guys and they're being fed normal stuff in their diets, just less than they're used to. About fourteen hundred calories I think, which isn't that bad, it's not really starvation, not when you consider that most people normally consume about two thousand calories a day. Though up here it's probably four thousand."

Meg cuts in, a puzzled look on her face. "Are you trying to tell me I should go on a diet or something?"

"What? No, no. Just wait, it's a story. I'll get to the point, I promise. Anyway, these guys are constantly hungry, really screamingly hungry, because their food intake is restricted and there are no cheat days. But they're not in prison or anything, they're not off in the war being shot or killed, they're just hanging around a research institute and getting fed less than what they're used to. Which is sort of shit, but it's just food, just hunger. So, any guesses what happened?"

"Ah, they lost weight?"

"Yeah, no, of course, but otherwise?"

"Like, what, some of them couldn't hack it and were caught scoffing Mars bars?"

"Well, some of them did cheat. But on the diet, which wasn't even as severe as a lot of the diets people follow now—well, follow for a week maybe—but some of these men, hard men, specifically chosen for their character, willing to go to prison for their beliefs ..."

Meg is looking at me, waiting.

"Some of them literally lost their minds. Less than halfway through the experiment one guy was committed to a psychiatric hospital because he was threatening violence and suicide. Because he was so hungry. And two other guys actually self-harmed. They cut themselves up. Because they were so hungry."

I let the point sink in, the silence sitting heavy between us.

"So ..." says Meg, and I realise I haven't communicated my point at all.

"What I'm getting at is how easily people can crack up. Those guys had strong personalities, and they weren't cut off from families and they were still in their homeland, and yet some of them still lost their shit, and just from hunger. And that wasn't even as long as most of the detainees are in the centre."

"Are you kidding? Is that what this is about?"

"Yeah, it is. I mean, some of the detainees are dickheads, for sure, but how do you know that big guy isn't going through some real shit? We don't know what it's like. I'm not on their side or anything, I'm just saying that we don't know, so why not stay neutral? It's stupid looking down on them if we don't even know what we're looking down on."

"Oh my God, Nick, I can't believe you just called me stupid."

"What? No, I didn't—"

"I can't believe you're some bleeding heart. My God. You're so naïve," she says.

"I'm naïve? Are you nuts? I'm the one with open eyes. What, do you think you wouldn't lose your shit if it was you?"

"I wouldn't get on a stupid boat and jump the queue! So, no."

"What queue? There is no queue. There's not some queue in the middle of Afghanistan or Iran. Do you even know anything about those places? Iran is a theocracy. Theo-cracy. A religious dictatorship. They don't give a fuck about Western bullshit like refugee conventions and queues. There is no queue."

"They can send off to our government. It's the same for everyone. There is a queue. Or do you just want a million people to come in all at once and bring their laws and culture?"

"There is no fucking queue. It's not lining up for the dole, just popping down to the Centrelink branch and standing in line. Jesus, come on, a country like Afghanistan is basically a *Highlander* movie with turbaned psychos riding horses and tanks around and chopping random motherfuckers' heads off. Who's lining up in that queue?"

"I don't even know what that is."

"You don't know what Afghanistan is? Seriously?"

Meg looks at me, furious. "I don't know what *Highlander* is. I know Afghanistan. You're such a dick. You think you're so smart, so much better than everyone else. And you're the one responsible for that Response Two. You screwed up worse than anyone has since we got here."

"What? That's bullshit. Did Gabriel tell you that? Because he doesn't know what the fuck he's talking about. It's bullshit."

"Darren told me. You ran."

"I didn't run. I … nah, I'm not even talking about it. It's bullshit. And you still haven't answered my question."

"What question?"

"Do you or do you not think you would crack up if you were in detention?"

"No, Nick. I wouldn't. Because I wouldn't be in detention."

"Because you're a happy little white Australian."

"No, because I wouldn't jump the queue!"

There's no point. No fucking point.

And you know what? Meg's right. I do think I'm smarter than these fucks. I'm certainly smarter than Meg if she believes that shit about a queue.

But I'm not a bleeding heart, not for merely keeping my eyes wide open and thinking critically, as opposed to blindly believing whatever we're told like most of my dear colleagues. Honestly, I'm so sick of the shit I hear all day, every day. Any time a detainee is in distress he is "trying it on", "looking for attention", "just wants an audience". I lost count tallying up how many officers have said to me that the detainees "are like misbehaving kids".

When it comes down to it, Meg's a *doer*. Just doing what she's told to do. Just thinking what she's told to think.

A long silence passes between us.

"Can you move?" Meg says, without looking at me.

I get my bag and find a free seat. I watch the rain punch into the ruddy mud, Mother Nature releasing the pent-up tension built over the long, dreary dry.

TOUCH

I barely sleep. I don't think I was in the wrong—not in principle, maybe in tact—but I still feel like shit about the argument. Maybe it's because I'm sleep deprived and not thinking straight, but, about 3 a.m., I make the snap decision to go to Meg's room.

I sneak across the grounds as quietly as I can. I knock very gently on Meg's door. I wait a while then knock again. There's still no answer. I knock again. The door opens. Meg's eyes are mere slivers.

"Hey, sorry, I know you were probably sleeping ..."

"What are you doing?" Meg whispers back.

"I just wanted to talk to you."

Meg puts her finger to her lips to shoosh me, then shuts the door. I stand there like an idiot wondering if that is that, but then the door opens. Meg pushes past me. I see she has her key in her hand. I get it. She wants to talk in my room where no one will be listening.

We creep across and slip into my room. Meg sits on the edge of my bed and looks at me. I think she looks sad. Like she's disappointed in me. No doubt she's curious to know what I so desperately need to say. So am I, for the truth is I don't have any words rehearsed. I don't know what I want to say, despite all the hours I've stewed on it through the night, variously upset and indignant and righteous. But now, in Meg's presence at 3 a.m., I find myself feeling and thinking none of those things, merely overwhelmed by tiredness. And not just sleep tired.

Tired of being right, tired of being smarter than everyone else, tired of being so pissed off at everything. So tired that I suddenly feel a dumb ache in my gut for something so basic, something so elementary, that I feel ashamed.

I just want Meg to touch me.

SCARECROW

Making my tenth coffee for the shift, or something like that. No matter how many I have, I can't shake the funk. I think it's mind more than body.

Nothing was resolved last night. I'm not even sure what it is that needs resolving. This thing with Meg—I'm just trying to make it something it isn't. What we have, or what we had, was sex. That's all, and that's fine. So why have I been acting all overwrought and excitable like some pitiful damsel in a period film? I just about cried when Meg hugged me, then again when she let go of me and said we'd speak tomorrow and went back to her own room. I mean, truly, cry—it's becoming embarrassing. For some inexplicable reason I'm pursuing something that isn't there and as a result I've become weak and needy, when I'm never weak and never needy.

For the record, I didn't cry when Meg left. I had a cup of concrete washed down with a chaser of whisky. Then I was so awake and yet so tired that I boiled the kettle and made a coffee. I splashed some whisky in and four hours later I got to work buzzed, head askew, not in a great place for the start of a shift. But I'm just a dumb grunt so it doesn't really matter how badly I do my job or how much I slur my words in conversation or how stupid the things I say are. I'm a body. I could be anyone. I am anyone. No one, in fact. Just a number like the detainees. A blue-shirted scarecrow flagging and flapping in humidity and wind, stopping dumb animals from burning the buildings down.

I think scarecrow is a much better description of the job I do than guard. A scarecrow is passive, its presence alone intended to dissuade certain behaviours, whereas a guard is active, seeking to enforce certain behaviours. But if I am a guard, and the blue shirt says I am, then I must admit to being a particularly shit guard. I fail to turn in contraband, I allow food out of the mess, I disappear out the back of no-man's-land during my shift, I wander aimlessly when I could be performing pointless bureaucratic tasks, and I occasionally show up drunk. Oh, and I don't think all the detainees are scum. To be honest, I feel like I have more in common with some of the detainees than some of my colleagues.

Meg is my opposite. Meg is a very good guard. She's Brown Two today and acting the part. I've been watching her strut up and down the mess hall throughout lunch, conscientious and keen like a roo dog in a pine plantation. It's weird watching her, actually: friendly and gregarious with detainees in one instance, then strict and unsympathetic the moment she judges something a transgression of even the pettiest rule or expectation.

It's a pita bread day, and I've already seen three chaps stash packets into pants or tops. I don't care, whereas Meg does. She strides over to the exit and speaks with Roberto, a strapping Italian bloke who actually rolls up the sleeves on his polo shirt so we can see his biceps better. He also insists on the "o" on the end of his name being pronounced. Need I say more?

Roberto is the perfect sidekick for Meg—he's the dumb muscle captivated by the nice set of tits and arse. I've certainly got no claim on the tits and arse; probably never did. Maybe Roberto is in with a chance. No doubt he thinks he is, if he only plays it right and shows Meg sufficient machismo and toughness to convince her of the size of his Italian cock, even bigger than his nuggety biceps.

They stand either side of the exit. A few people leave without incident, then a group of Sri Lankans get up. I know that two of them have pita bread in their pants. They move toward the door as a group, a common tactic where the innocent party engages the officer in conversation while the guilty one slips past. But Meg isn't letting anyone out. She's obviously on to them.

Roberto steps in front of the exit while Meg initiates an exchange. I can see the Sri Lankans gesticulating, professing their innocence. Then Meg points to one of the guys who I know has pita bread in his pants. They still refuse to give it up. Meg says something to Roberto; he steps into the Sri Lankan's personal space. I think surely not, he wouldn't, and then he does—Roberto attempts to pat the man down. The Sri Lankan man slaps Roberto's hands away. Roberto tries to grab him, but then the other Sri Lankans are yelling and pushing the man out the door, and Roberto and Meg have the sense to yield to the greater numbers. Once outside, one of the Sri Lankans really arcs up, abusing the shit out of Meg and Roberto. A Code Black is called. Five more officers arrive. All because of pita bread.

Once the commotion settles, an older Sri Lankan man approaches me. He speaks as if I was one of the officers on the door patting down his compatriot; as if one blue shirt represents all blue shirts.

"Why you do this, officer? Why the rules, officer? Why so many rules? Why?"

It's a fair question, but a question I cannot answer. There are lots of little, seemingly arbitrary rules, rules that may seem innocuous to a new arrival, but which take on great significance once a detainee has been here six months, twelve months, two years. Rules which come to seem oppressive and humiliating, like not being allowed to lock a door, or being allowed to have two apples but not three, or telling someone that as an adult human they are not responsible enough to consume pita bread at their own discretion without putting their life at risk or otherwise jeopardising the security of the detention centre. Imagine telling a group of Australians that—we'd just as soon burn the place to the ground, then celebrate doing so for the next hundred years.

After lunch, I wander the compound. I pass a portico with a line of microwaves on a bench. The Sri Lankans are gathered around, not even trying to hide the fact that they are microwaving the pita they just smuggled out of the mess, creating rough and ready pappadums. Some of them know me well enough to recognise that I'm not one of the officers who gives a shit. We exchange waves and conspiratorial nods.

I really like the spirit of these guys. I like the fact that they are flouting the rules. I like the fact that they do what they need to do so as to feel like they have a modicum of control over their lives. There's a little plant nursery attached to the detention centre, which the detainees have access to. It used to have barramundi growing in an aquarium, until the Sri Lankans snuck in and ate every single one. There was a feral cat that had a litter of kittens under one of the dongas. One day the kittens were gone and the Sri Lankans were sighted having a feast; conclusions were drawn. Whatever it is they need to do to stay sane, they're doing it.

"Hey, fellers, you see the cricket the other night?" I ask, knowing that they would have seen the one day game where Sri Lanka lost to Australia. "Too bad, too bad. Next time."

"No. We happy. We support Australia," says one man.

"Really?"

"Yes. We hate Sri Lanka. Team all Sinhalese. Only one Tamil. We love Australia."

"Oh. Well, good then."

I should have known better. These men are the Sri Lankan minority, underdogs in the civil war raging for a generation. Now, the war lost, our government deems them terrorists simply because they are Tamil, whereas other countries like Canada see them as freedom fighters. Really, they are neither.

Not these men. Not anymore. Now, they are just refugees. They just want a new life without the violence and, for better or worse, we are their chosen country.

Most have been in detention going on two years, yet they remain staunch, willing to endure for the hope of a better future, all the while playing cricket, building gardens and monuments, barracking for the Aussies, drinking secret homebrew, furtively eating the aquarium barramundi, playing cards and waiting to see the real Australia.

I mean, for Christ's sake, I could be describing POWs in Changi.

BOOT

Mid-afternoon, and most of us are back in the office. Conversation keeps coming back to the incident. Meg and Roberto are adamant that the Sri Lankans were let off too easy. Roberto thinks they should get the ERT into gear, bust the offender's door down, suppress any resistance with maximum force and retrieve the contraband—as in, the pita bread. Meg thinks that the Sri Lankans are just troublemakers. She thinks they should have been sent home already, as their applications for visas have been denied, and their reviews have been denied, and they are all now waiting on judicial appeals.

"They're just going to misbehave worse and worse the longer this goes," says Meg.

"We can't forcibly remove them until their appeals are concluded. By law. It's called procedural fairness," I say.

"Then they should hurry up and reject their appeals," says Meg, her tone sharp.

"What they should do is give them bridging visas. Locking guys up for two years is a recipe for disaster. They should set a reasonable time limit, then after that they should be let out to wait in the community. Make those DIAC cocksuckers pull their finger out."

"But then they're out there," snorts Roberto. "Who knows what they'd do out there."

"Such as?"

"You don't know. Anything. They could be criminals. Terrorists. You might never catch them again."

"And they shouldn't be encouraged. Letting them out early is like a reward for the wrong behaviour," says Meg.

"The absence of punishment is not a reward."

"What?"

"Never mind. Hey," I say, adopting my preferred mode of wry derision, "did you end up getting back any of the pita bread?"

"Nup," says Roberto, thinking it an innocent question. "They got at least one out, I think. That's why we should get over and do a random room search now."

"Wouldn't be random, then, would it?"

"What do you mean?" he says.

"Well, it'd just be a room search. It'd be the opposite of random. It'd be a non-random room search."

"I suppose you would have just let them take it," says Meg.

"The pita bread? Yeah, probably. Doesn't strike me as an urgent matter of national security."

"You let one thing go and then it's something else," says Meg.

"Like stockpiling three apples? I guess you're right. We should pat everyone down on the way out."

Meg's face is scrunched up like she's bitten into a sour vagina; Roberto has just worked out that I've been mocking him and looks like he's thinking about taking a shit, or maybe punching me, or maybe crying while he takes a shit; Karen is unnaturally fixated on a cup of tea; Scott doesn't really know what is going on, but he knows enough to say nothing. The atmosphere in the room is so tense I feel prickles of heat on my face, and I'm standing in front of the aircon. Then Roy bursts through the door.

"Wouldn't fuck'n believe it. Just stepped in a puddle, mate. Lost me fuck'n boot. Had to reach in and pull it out. Look at it, mud everywhere. Ahh, shithouse. That's me only pair. Gonna be soggy, in't? Eh?"

"Highly hazardous job, mate," I say, squeezing past and walking outside.

I wander the grounds, performing my job in the style of Roy, though avoiding the various puddles and mud slicks. I drift into Red Compound, where I talk with Ali and Samir and any other detainee who cares to shoot the breeze, helping me waste away the afternoon without having to look at Meg or Roberto.

On the bus home, I sit next to Roy. Sometimes you need the simplicity of a Roy conversation — a conversation with no guile and no filter where you talk straight at a subject and express your mind as it strikes you and then again as it strikes you completely different five minutes later.

Mostly, we talk about Roy's boot. That strikes me just fine.

NORMAL

We're told of an attempted hanging during the briefing before shift. A detainee named Aslan used a bed sheet to fashion a rough hangman's noose that he then attached to the top rung of his bunk bed. He tied his hands together and got them around his feet so that they were behind his back, probably to make it harder to back out and save himself in a moment of panic. Then he got his neck into the noose and started bashing his head into the wall to try to knock himself out—either to make his body dead weight, or to make sure he didn't have second thoughts.

These are lengths you don't see in most hangings, and it is pretty shocking stuff—I know that intellectually. Yet, the truth is, it isn't shocking. Not to me, not to any of us. It's just information; it's background noise to the clamour of business as usual.

We're desensitised. We've seen or heard about too much self-harming, too many attempted suicides. So, when I hear that someone just tried to kill themselves, I think: oh, ok. My heart doesn't race, my stomach doesn't knot. I'm more uneasy with the knowledge that I've become used to this sort of shit than I am knowing a man wants to die and has attempted to bring that wish to fruition.

The best I can do is recognise something sad is happening, even if I can't muster the gut reaction of a normal human. I figure compassion can and should remain an intellectual response, even when it ceases to be an emotional one.

Apparently, though, that makes me a naïve bleeding heart—simply because I refuse to let myself become totally apathetic. Simply because I'm willing to question the bizarre logic that treats being locked up as normal, but distress at being locked up as abnormal and suspicious. The only thing I know for certain is that nothing and nobody in this place is remotely normal.

Later, I'm wandering the compound when I see a group of Iranians in a corridor. They're drinking tea. I say hello and wave. There's nine or ten of them, all dressed in what must pass for their Sunday best. I normally only see the detainees in those sorts of clothes on their day of release. "What's happening, fellers?" I say.

Soheil steps from the group. He gestures for me to come a few steps aside. He says quietly, "Jabal's mother die in Iran. Today is her funeral. Jabal is here, he cannot go. We have this for him, here."

"Oh. Right," I say.

I realise Jabal is the big guy from the other day, and I understand now why he was upset. I think it was Quincy who was explaining to me that Iranians are very effusive in their grief, that it's important to demonstrate it, not just ball it up into a nice Western cancer.

I walk across to Jabal. I'm conscious that all eyes are on me. I'm not sure if I'm doing the wrong thing or not. I say, "I'm very sorry about your mother, Jabal. Very sorry."

He puts his hand out, and I take it. We shake and he says, "Thank you, officer." He is calm, but his eyes are sunken and red.

I hesitate. I want to offer something. To ask if I can help somehow, but I know that I don't have the power to help with anything other than more noodles or sugar or milk, and so maybe that would be insensitive. I leave the group and keep wandering, conscious of not returning to that particular corridor, of not imposing again on Jabal's grief.

I think back to the other day when he was crying and bashing his head against the wall and how angry Meg was with him. Would she have felt different if she knew? Or maybe she did know, and just didn't care.

I should ask her, but that's not going to happen. I don't think we're on speaking terms.

GUYRA PUBLIC LIBRARY

REASON

Aslan tried to kill himself again last night. He was under constant watch at the time, so he covered himself with a bed sheet, as if sleeping. He tied a loose knot with another sheet, put it around his neck and pulled tight.

He failed. This morning Aslan is in one of the admin dongas, isolated from the compounds. I'm sent to sit on his door and watch him. I ask him how he's feeling. He says: "I want to die."

Not the usual nicety one expects, even from a suicidal man. If I didn't want the truth, though, I shouldn't have asked.

"It'll get better," I say.

He looks me in the eyes and says, "I want to die."

"Why? You've come so far. You are almost there. It'll only get better if you can just wait."

"Visa, negative. Review, negative. No more energy. No more energy. I kill myself."

"Well, we won't let you kill yourself," I say.

"You think officer stop me? I want to die. Officer don't stop me. I kill myself, officer or no officer."

"But if you kill yourself, then the Iranian government is winning. Don't let them win. Don't let them beat you."

Somehow I've become a suicide counsellor. I am not qualified for this job. I do not want this job. I do not like this job. More to the point, I suspect that I am not much good at this job. Aslan looks at me and shakes his head.

"You're suffering," I say, "I get that, you're tired of all this, but you don't want to die. You want the pain to end. And it will, once you are gone from here."

"Yes, I go from here," says Aslan.

"No, that's not what I mean. Listen, this is a tiny part of your life. You'll get your visa, nearly all Iranian refugees eventually get a visa, you know that, and then Australia will be good to you once you are in the community. How long have you been here?"

"Eleven months. Eleven months I see friends come and go, but Aslan still here. I see officer come and go, but Aslan still here. I am tired now. No more energy. I kill myself."

"No. Think about it. If you've been here eleven months, a year, and you'll have forty, maybe fifty more years in Australia after this, that's one of fifty. That's what this is, one of fifty. Like, two percent! I know it's bad in here, but you've got to think about after. You can't just let the one determine your life, when it's the other forty-nine that is your future. That's your life."

"You officer. Not understand."

"I don't. I know I don't. But do you see that what I'm saying might be true? You don't want to live. You want to die. I believe you, but it's possible that how you feel right now will change. Once you have a visa you may want to live again. How you feel will change once you get away from here."

"Maybe. I don't care. No more energy. Too much ..." says Aslan, tapping his temple.

ATTENTION

After a few hours, I'm relieved from the constant watch on Aslan. When I'm brought back for another stint in the afternoon, it's to relieve Bailey. He tells me that the Code Black I heard over the radio about an hour ago was his; that it was Aslan trying to asphyxiate himself again. As Bailey tells it, Aslan ripped the rubber seal off the door, tied it around his neck, and tried to induce asphyxiation—all in full view of Bailey. It took Bailey and another officer to wrest the rubber from Aslan. At the conclusion of it all Aslan was physically ok, apart from the fact he is also on hunger and hydration strike and has sore kidneys. But from a strangling or hanging or asphyxiation perspective, he is good to go again, and promises he will.

Bailey doesn't think this last incident was a real attempt at suicide. Given it had no chance of success, I think he's probably right. I think Aslan just wanted to communicate to us that he is *suicidal*—which is different to actually committing suicide.

Bailey describes this as attention-seeking. I suppose it is, but it's a callous way to frame it. Would you ever say to your friend who took an overdose of prescription tablets in an apparent suicide attempt that she is just a silly attention-seeker? That she is just being childish? Just acting up?

If you did, you would be abused and pilloried. You'd be considered heartless, insensitive, basically the worst sort of bastard. No, it wouldn't happen, not these days.

Aslan has been here eleven months; not nearly as long as

some, but he just cannot take it any longer. He's mentally and emotionally tired. "No more energy," as he puts it. Whether he really has lost the will to live, or whether he is pleading for our help, what's the difference? Well-adjusted, contented souls do not try to hang themselves. End of story.

CRUELTY

I knew it was coming. Everybody knew it was coming. Even he must have known it was coming. But I still can't believe it.

It's a puppy running around your feet in excitement till you become so exasperated you scream at the creature, but it keeps swirling and rolling on the ground and licking at your toes, so you kick it, you make it squeal, you hurt it out of dumb frustration and you become guilty of an unkindness verging on a cruelty, so you go to the whimpering puppy and say "bad dog", as if the puppy should have known better, but it didn't because it couldn't because that's just how the dumb animal is.

That's Mad Dog and that's the centre. They kicked him in the guts and made him yelp when he doesn't and never will understand what he did wrong.

I heard it over the radio. Not the sort of call that comes through too often. Maybe not ever.

"Control, this is Green Three. Ahh, I think there's a client outside the Green Compound fence. Umm, I dunno if he's meant to be there. He's sort of just wandering in the safety perimeter. Do you wanna check that he's meant to be there?"

A shitstorm followed, officers frantically pursuing the escapee who was not an escapee in any sense of the word, just a client who casually walked through an open gate and took a wander until asked to rejoin his fellow prisoners. A headcount followed, and then another, and the whole centre was on edge, all because Roy had been manning the internal gate that has to be opened occasionally to incoming vehicle traffic. He simply forgot to shut it. No big deal. The detainee didn't escape; he was still locked between the compound fence and the perimeter fence. A good learning experience for everyone.

But they fired him. They fired the best fucking bloke in the entire godawful centre.

I know it's madness to say such a thing because of all the horrible, bigoted, wretched things Roy says, but I'll swear it up and down till blue in the face that that illiterate, prejudiced, risible vessel of filth and verbiage is the purest, most decent, most unguarded man I've ever known.

When I get back to Spinifex City, I find Roy cooling his heels, beer in hand, sent home early like a naughty school boy. He wears a sad, puzzled look.

"Fuck, Roy. I'm sorry, mate."

"Didn't know, did I? You shut this gate, you shut that gate, how the fuck you meant to keep track of it, eh? Just lookin' for a reason to fire me, I reckon. Didn't like me."

"You're unique, mate. Some people just like bland. Sameness. They didn't know what to do with you. I'm sorry to hear it, Roy, I really am. I've enjoyed working with you."

Roy looks at me hard. The puzzlement lifts into a coy smile and that right there is what I love about the man.

"Did ya? Yer mean that—you enjoyed workin' with me?"

"Fuck'n oath, Roy. Of course I did."

An immodest shit-eating grin sweeps Roy's face. Small things like appreciation matter, especially to a man who screws things up as much as Roy.

Tomorrow is my day off, and Roy is booked on the flight back to Perth, so I go get my bottle and we drink till we're talking shit. It's the night for it. The air is dry and cool. The insects are calling. I can see the moon, three-quarters full, low in the sky, and my mate needs commiseration. Drinking conditions.

I shouldn't be talking freely in earshot of snoops, but at the moment I couldn't care less. I tell Roy about me and Meg, about the one-night stand and the drama to follow. He doesn't dispense any advice—he's got none to give—he just listens and laughs and makes the occasional grunt or wisecrack. Once I finish my lament, we enjoy a silence. I don't know what Roy is thinking, but I'm thinking that I'm sick of being on my own. That I've met some damn fine women over the years and left some damn fine women, mostly because I don't want to buy into that life. Settling down and rusting in. Becoming staid. Turning away from new experience. Yeah, some warped view of relationships I've got.

Then Roy says, "Fuck, I miss her."

"Who?"

"Denise. Me missus. We were engaged and everything. Did I tell you what she looked like? Long brown hair. Wavy-like. Slim little thing. I could pick her up in one arm. Fuck'n beautiful, mate. Didn't think she'd go for me. Look at me. Eh? I'm an ugly bastard. But I just give it a crack, din't I? Nothing to lose. Asked her out and she blew me socks off when she came. That was that. She was me missus then. I had this place out York. Fantastic spot, mate. Little love nest in the trees, I called it. Farmin' about three hundred sheep. I owned it, too. Or bank did. We were goin' a year or so then she moved out with me and we were there a while before I asked her. I din't know if she'd say yes, but I asked her and she did."

"What? Did what?"

"Marry me. I asked her to marry me and she said yes. I thought she'd run, mate. Say nah, not you, I was expectin' somethin' better. But she did. I wasn't sure it was real, you know? Still don't reckon it's real. Bird like that ... best I've ever met. Just sweet and kind and everything. Nah, best life ever was when I was out there with her. Shot me there n' then and I'd 'ave died happy."

"So did you marry her?"

Roy shakes his head. He looks at his beer, shakes the can, drops it onto the table. He stares out at nothing.

"What happened, Mad Dog? Did she do a runner?"

"Nah, nah wouldn't. Too good to me. Woulda stuck with me through anything."

"What happened?"

"She's fuck'n dead, mate. Died, din't she? Never got married. Shoulda killed me with her. Be better off."

"Jesus, sorry mate. What ... did something happen? Or ..."

"You just think someone's havin' off days, don't ya? Eh? You don't know. I still dunno if it was me. If I did it to her, takin' her out there, away from her family. I thought we were good as it got, mate, but what's Roy know? I'm a dumb cunt. Two weeks before we get hitched, I come back in for breakfast and she had it ready for me and she give me a kiss and a hug and all that, said she loved me, I didn't know nothin' about it, all that shit she'd taken. Then I come back in about one and I didn't hear anything, so I thought she might be sleepin', she did that sometimes. I had a look and she was, and I just stood there watching her for a bit. I used to like doin' that. Couldn't help meself. Just look at her, think, 'Fuck, Roy, how? How'd this happen to a bloke like you? Luckiest man in the world.' And I left her there. I seen her breathin'. Coulda saved her, couldn't I? Call an ambulance. Pump her gut, whatever. But I went out and dug fuck'n post holes while she died. May as well killed her meself."

Roy finishes and I feel wrong in the gut.

"That's horrible mate. I'm really sorry."

"Couldn't stay after that. Place was toxic. I killed 'em all and I left. Bank can have it."

"What do you mean, what'd you kill?"

"Me sheep. I shot 'em. I shot all 'em. Left 'em in the paddocks to rot. Never been back. Won't. Won't ever. It's cursed. Maybe it's me. I'm cursed. Stuff keeps followin' me round, don't it? I fucked this up. Best job I ever had. Fucked it up. Nah, I'm done, mate. I'm done."

A long silence passes.

"Can I ask you a question, Roy?"

He nods.

"Do you go back to visit her grave?"

He shakes his head. "Can't. Can't go. Couldn't go to the funeral. I killed her."

Another long silence.

"I haven't been to my dad's. I didn't go to the funeral, either. Said I was too sick. Then just didn't ever go. Mum goes every month. Tends the plot. I've never been."

Roy nods. "No manual on death, mate. No fuck'n manual on death."

OVERDUE

I sleep long, then doze through the daylight hours. The light coming from beneath my door changes from dull orange to warm yellow to a white so bright it's painful.

About 3 p.m. I wake and can't get back to sleep. I go to the main kitchen and put some toast on. Bits of last night's conversation with Roy run through my mind. He's been carrying around some heavy stuff for a long time. He keeps it buried behind bravado and humour and bullshit, but it defines him. I feel sorry for the bastard. He deserves better. He's one of the good ones.

The toaster springs up, launching one of my slices onto the bench. It annoys me. What sort of a dickhead engineer spring-loads a toaster with that much force? It's not like the consumer of the toast is waiting with a mitt.

I retrieve the slice and put it back in the toaster and push the lever down again. For some reason, most of civilisation likes a tepid version of toast where the bread is merely warmed to the point of taking on the texture of staleness. If you're going to toast bread, fucking well toast the bread. I want it browned. Not pale, not golden. I crank the knob to what I hope equates to very dark. If there was a setting for charcoal I'd set it to that just so the motherfuckers who keep turning the toaster down can experience a measure of the annoyance I feel every time I return, expecting to find my toast just how it should be done and it's not.

Jesus. Am I really raving about toast?

I head back to my room. I've been meaning to write something on the postcard I bought weeks ago, the one with a picture of King Sound. I sit down and pen a few words:

Dear Mum, so this is what it looks like up here—mud, mangroves, red dirt. A few more weeks then I get a fortnight off if I want. Thought I could visit home, if that sounds all right?
Not sure if I'll head back up after, to be honest. Not really cut out to be a therapist/security guard. Pays well, so we'll see. Love, Nick.

I put the postcard aside, lie on my bed and watch some TV. It's boring, so I do some push-ups and sit-ups, shower and get ready, stand and wait for the bus, get on the bus which should have a Roy onboard but doesn't, stare out a window for an hour, read that fucked-in-the-head "Welcome" sign and think about smashing it into kindling and burning it, go through security, sit in the briefing, walk into the compound and wonder:

How many more times till I have had enough?

As the steel gate swings shut behind me, I feel the heaviness of the place. I think about all that surrounds me—the animosity of guards who've decided I'm a bleeding heart, the artificial cones of light, the heavy skies, the indistinct scrub and the wire and the weariness and then Ali is strolling toward me and he calls out, "Hiii, Nick!"

"Hi, Ali," I smile. "Let me guess, you need a light?"

"Yeees," drawls Ali.

I reach into my pocket. Ali leans over with a fag hanging from his mouth. He puffs his cigarette alight as I cup the lighter and roll the flint.

"Where you off to?" I ask.

"Nurse. Headaches."

"Still? Jesus. I think you might have a brain tumour, mate."

"I think so, too. That is why I smoke."

"What, it relieves the pain?"

"No. To give my brain tumour cancer!"

I manage a laugh as I remind myself that I'm not the prisoner. It's not fair for me to pout and act pissy and petulant while blokes like Ali are soldiering on with a grin and a joke.

"And how are you, Nick? I have not seen you."

"Good, Ali. Good. Well, a bit hungover, but good."

"Ahh, you drink?"

"Yes, I'm Australian, it's the law, didn't you know?"

"Ahh, yes, like Iran, the opposite, you must drink, we must not drink!"

"Exactly."

"Many detainees drink. I don't drink."

"Ever?"

"No! In here. The jungle juice, this is the ... it is called this. It is bad."

"Oh, yeah, I know, some of the guys make alcohol with the fruit."

"Yeeees. It is bad. Taste is bad, make you feel very bad."

"But you drink outside?"

"Yes. Not too much. Many Iranians drink."

"But it's illegal in Iran, right?"

"Yes, Nick, of course, everything fun is illegal in Iran, but everything is in Iran. You find the person and house and everything is there."

"So you drank alcohol back there?"

"Some. I drink beer."

"Ahh, beer. We've got a lot of beers in Australia. Hundreds of different beers. It's a beer oasis."

"Oasis? Like a lake of beer?"

"Exactly. Well, no, an oasis filled with different cans of beer, different types of beer. More beer than all Iran could drink in a year."

"A lot of beer."

"Yep."

"I knew Australia is right place to come."

"Probably. Yes. It is. Definitely. Hey, I've gotta go inside, relieve the other officer. I'll talk with you later, ok?"

"Yeees, Nick. I am here. I am always here."

TEETH

Soheil skipped tonight's meal. He's been skipping a lot of meals lately. I spoke to him about it last week. He told me he had a toothache. He'd seen a nurse and told her he needed a dentist. The nurse sent him away with two Panadol. A few days later I saw Soheil again. I asked how his toothache was. He told me it still hurt. He was still skipping most meals.

I spot Soheil walking toward his room. I intercept him and ask how he is. He still has a toothache. I know it's just a toothache, a pissy little chunk of exoskeleton that little kids rip out of their own face for fun, but I think about the times I've had a toothache that persists, gets worse, won't go away. It's misery.

I ask Soheil if he is on the dental list. He isn't sure. Ahh, I think, there it is again—the not knowing. The worst part of being in detention: you never know the when, what or why of any of the significant events of life behind the fence. Ok, I figure, easy: I can help just by finding out if he is on the dentist's list, and when he is scheduled to go.

Late that night, when I have no other duties, I go to medical. I speak with the duty nurse at the counter.

"Hi there. I was wondering if you could tell me whether a particular client is on the dentist's waiting list? It's Soheil Hamid, M-I-G-3-7."

Her face contorts. She is giving me a purposeful look of

confusion, perhaps bewilderment. I explain that I am enquiring for a client.

"Why?"

"It's for a client."

"Yes, but why?"

Now I am bemused. "Because he would like to know the answer."

The contempt writ on her handsome face suggests that my behaviour is abnormal, probably unpatriotic, potentially traitorous.

"Very odd," she says.

She tells me that if I really must know I should come back during daytime and ask Margaret, the woman responsible for the list. I go back and tell Soheil I don't know yet, but I will find out.

Later, I hear a call over the radio. An officer is asking if they can bring Mani—he of the fucked back and geriatric shuffle—to medical. He's in terrible pain again, though still is probably more accurate. The response from the nurse comes in a single curt word.

"Negative."

The officer persists. It's Quincy, I think. "He's in a lot of pain. I don't think he can make it on his own."

"Negative. He needs to start walking. To put it nicely, he has to get over it and get on with it."

Just "get over" a prolapsed disk? I'm all for tough love. I was raised on tough love. But this shit isn't tough love—it's dumb. Maybe even outright cruel. That bitch on the radio—I want to go kick her in the back and crush a chunk of intervertebral fibrocartilage, then look at her on the ground, writhing, calling for help, and say, "Get up, you pathetic bitch. Start walking."

Just formulating the thought—absurd, obscene, wrong— makes me feel better.

WATCHING

Meg is Red Two, still technically just a shitkicker like me, but she's taken it upon herself to start giving orders. It's fine. I don't care. An order from Meg is no different to an order from Gabriel. In fact, it's good the way she talks to me like I'm beneath her; it's healing; it helps me forget what it was I liked about Meg in the first place — apart from the tits and arse which she still has and which I still notice, though I do feel strange about looking, but look anyway.

Meg sends me to relieve Karen. She's been on constant watch over Younes. He's just a teenager. A boy who's managed to retain a boyish lightness of manner, boyish enthusiasm, boyish sense of humour. Then yesterday he goes and fucks that up by cutting his left arm to shit just like the other Iranian men.

It's a grim corridor this evening. In the room opposite is a depressing fellow named Akmad. He was on constant watch last week for cutting his head. He reeks sad like a kicked dog.

Down the corridor we've got Milad. I like Milad, he's smart; we've shared a few nice chats over the weeks. At present, Milad is taciturn but restless — less like a kicked dog, more like a beaten bear chained to a steel peg. He got off constant watch yesterday but is still on six welfare checks a shift.

Younes's neighbour on the left is Omid. He lit a small fire in his room about a month ago and has since been on and off constant watch. There's an unwritten rule that anyone who lights a fire is a fuckhead, so I guess Omid is a fuckhead.

Next door on the right side is Farzou, a fat man on hunger strike. I think he's bored and hungry; he'll be all right.

Around 8.30, I go with Younes for his appointment to see the mental health nurse. As we are walking through the compound, he jokes that he is my bodyguard. He pretends to clear the way for me.

"Who are you protecting me from, Younes?"

"Everyone. Maybe officer. Big lady officer. *Zahak.*"

I laugh. Younes often makes me laugh. He seems his normal self tonight, so I expect the mental health meeting will result in the constant watch being relaxed. I wait outside a demountable tin shed while Younes goes inside and speaks to the nurse. After about twenty minutes and what would qualify as a robust conversation, Younes storms out. He punches his fist into a wall. I trail after him, suppressing a skip as I struggle to keep up with his furious striding.

Back at his room, Younes sits and broods. I just sit. We don't speak. I know there's no point. He needs time.

About 10.30, I hear a call outside: "Officer, officer."

It's not uncommon. Lighter duty, I figure. I poke my head out the door. I see detainees in the corridor, gathering in front of Milad's door. A detainee sees me. "Milad," yells the man, pointing. Something bad must be happening inside Milad's room. I'm not sure what protocol would have me do. I'm meant to be watching Younes, but I can hardly ignore this.

Younes solves the quandary by leaving his room to see what's happening. He wanders down and tries to open Milad's door. It's locked. He calls to Milad inside. An angry voice responds, then there is thumping on the wall. I hear the knob rattle. Milad throws the door open. He stands just inside the doorway, yelling. Blood is flowing down the side of his face. The rate of flow makes the blood seem thin and watery, yet at the same time it looks luscious and vibrant. I glance at the floor and see a pool of red that somehow seems darker than the red smeared across his face. Who's going to clean that up?

Milad slaps his hand against the wall. He yells in Persian. He looks at me and screams, "Don't come in, or I cut!"

I call a Code Blue over the radio. I stay back, keeping one eye on Milad and one eye on Younes. It's only a handful of seconds before two other officers arrive and take over. I watch on from the corridor, watching Younes watch Milad. The situation soon calms and Milad is whisked away to be patched up.

I return with Younes to his room. About twenty minutes later, Younes is taken off constant watch, despite the incident earlier with the mental health nurse. He tells me he gave assurances to mental health that he would not self-harm. I'm not sure I believe him, so, thinking that we have a rapport and he might be honest with me, I ask him outright if he is going to cut himself.

"Younes not cut himself. But is hard. Everybody refugee. All my friend—all refugee now. But not me. Only Younes not refugee. Why?"

"I don't know, mate. Honestly, no idea. Listen, I'll check in with you later, ok? And you're not going to cut yourself, right?"

"Yes, yes, go," he says, waving me away.

I get a can of Diet Coke and sit under a tree. I'm halfway through when a call comes over the radio. It's Meg summoning me back whence I came.

I arrive in the corridor to see Milad escorted to his room by a manager. His head has a patch on it. Someone has wiped away the pool of blood that was on the floor, but it's left a stain. I sit and watch Milad while he lies on his bed. We talk every now and again. Just brief exchanges. A bit after midnight, when Milad seems calm and reflective, I ask him a question I've been wanting to ask ever since I got here.

"Milad, why do people cut themselves?"

"You don't understand, do you?"

"I don't."

"I don't either. We have ... no options, no ..."

Milad trails off, unable to find the right words.

"Freedom?"

"Yes, freedom. Very hard. We cut because head doesn't work. It just all ... Head doesn't work."

"Does it make you feel better?"

"No."

"Is it because you want officers to know you are angry?"

"No. Is because head doesn't work. You don't understand?"

"No."

BLUE

I'm slumped against a table in the Red Compound mess hall, conscious of every second ticking by.

Ali strolls over.

"Hiii, Nick."

"Hi, Ali."

Ali is wearing his favourite blue shirt. It looks a lot like the shirt I'm wearing as part of my uniform. We often joke that all he needs is a decent pair of shoes and out the gates he goes. Ali looks me over, smiles and shakes his head.

"You have tension, huh? Why you have tension, Nick?"

"Oh, just ... I dunno. I'm just tired."

"If you get tension, oh, wow, think about what it must be like for clients," says Ali.

Ali is always smiling beneath his moustache, though often there is an ironic bite to his observations, a sardonic acceptance of the madness that is detention.

"I spoke to my case manager today," he tells me. "I said to her, 'Do you know what I do when I get angry?' She said, 'Cut yourself.' 'No, no.' I told her that when I get angry, I just laugh. I just laugh."

And, with that, Ali strolls away, laughter trailing behind.

Ali is strong. He's been here almost six months and has maintained his level. But he'll crack. Everyone does, eventually. It happens at the precise moment that life no longer makes sense as an arc of experiences and events, when all one can think about is the illimitable misery of here, now. That's what is so clever about detention. It comes with all the trappings of hospitality—medical assistance, TV, an allowance, food and cordial, ping pong, English lessons—and for all this hospitality we seek no money in return. We seek nothing at all, in fact, except that they wait like good boys while we do our humanitarian thing. Yet still the clients complain and protest and cut themselves and then we get to say, see, they're just ingrates. Fundamentally bad people.

It's sort of brilliant.

HOPE

In this corridor alone, there are three white men staring at three sad brown men. I'm stationed outside the room of Parviz, an Afghani man who has two negative decisions and little hope that his appeal will yield a different result, who must deal with the sense of betrayal he feels for letting down four children who are depending on him to blaze the way for their own escape to someplace better.

Ali wanders over. "I think I need my own personal officer," he says.

"You are jealous, Ali?"

"Yeees. Where is my visa? Is it at the top of a tree? Is it in my blood?"

Ali shakes his head, lights his cigarette with my proffered lighter, then happily draws fumes into his lungs.

"But being here in Red with my crazy friends is good," exhales Ali. "Now, I always have an officer to light my cigarette."

Samir spots Ali and I, and makes a beeline. Samir has settled in well, made many friends, endeared himself to officers. He always appears in a good mood.

After exchanging pleasantries, I say, "Samir, do you know the Tooth Fairy?"

He laughs, thinking I am talking gibberish.

"No, really, do you know about the Tooth Fairy?"

"Tiffery?"

I have a joke I want to make, but I can see Samir is going to make it hard.

"No, ok, do you know the Easter Bunny?"

"What?" Samir gesticulates. "You crazy!"

"No, the Easter Bunny, really. All right, do you know Father Christmas?"

"Christmas?"

"Father Christmas."

"Ahh, the man ..." and Samir gestures to a beard and belly.

"Yes, yes. Waiting for a visa is like waiting for Father Christmas. When you go to sleep, maybe Father Christmas will come and put the visa under your pillow."

"Ahh, yes!"

It was funnier when it was the Tooth Fairy. Samir has his own joke to tell me.

"Nick. Today I see officer. Officer say, 'How — is — it — hanging, Samir?' I say to him, 'You need to pull your finger out!' All officers laugh. Teach me another."

"All right, Samir. Here is something you say when a person is whingeing — you know the word whingeing?"

"No."

"It means complain, to say they feel sick or tired or something like that."

"Yes yes. Ok."

"So if someone is whingeing, like Ali here with his headaches, you say to him: 'You need to drink a cup of concrete and harden up, princess.' "

"Ok, yes."

I write it out for him. Samir tries.

"Ali! You — need — to — drink — a — cup — of — cunkit ..."

"Concrete."

"Con-krit — and — hard — up ... prenses."

"Princess."

"Prin-cess. Ali! You need to drink ... a cup of ... car — "

"Carpet," offers Ali, with a devious glance.

"Car-pet ... No! Cun —"

"Concrete."

"Con-krit. And hard up. Pren-sis."

"Good. Keep practising. I'll teach you something new once you've mastered it."

During headcount — well past midnight, when most detainees are in bed — we fan out in a cordon then proceed through the compound, quickly opening each room to count the people inside, tallying up the numbers to make sure no one has escaped. I quietly open Ali and Samir's door. Samir sits bolt upright in bed. He's obviously been waiting for me.

"Nick! You need to drink a cup of carpen ... of cor-krit ..."

I shut the door in the middle of Samir's stutter and try to laugh quietly.

Twenty minutes later we are doing a repeat of the headcount. Apparently two men have escaped. That, or we counted wrong. I open the door to Samir and Ali's room. Samir jerks to attention like his back is spring-loaded.

"Nick! You need to drink a cup of cor ... con —"

"Concrete!" yells Ali from the bottom bunk.

"Con — con —"

I swing the door shut and chuckle my way through the rest of headcount. Samir has managed to put me in a much better mood. His appreciation of idiom, and the fact he is trying desperately hard to generate laughter in a language he barely understands, is nothing short of awesome.

The escaped prisoners seem to have returned, no doubt for the square meals and security and all-round luxury. I make a cup of tea in the office and sit down to write a welfare report on Parviz. He's clearly unwell; I suspect he hasn't taken food in the last four days, maybe longer, which is something the welfare officers need to know. I ask Karen and Jo what they think, as they've also done stints watching over him. I'm surprised when they express genuine concern. They agree that he's in bad shape, physically and mentally. It's actually a really good feeling to have a conversation where everybody gives a shit; to not have to defend your concern for a detainee's welfare.

Gabriel, Red One and our resident manager, doesn't say anything during our conversation; it appears he isn't even listening. He collects the various forms and papers from the out-tray bound for admin and stands up.

"Sorry, this one, too," I say, and sign the bottom of the paper. "It's a welfare report on Parviz."

Gabriel takes the paper. He looks at it and grunts. "Hopefully he'll die soon," he says, then opens the door and skips down the stairs.

CHAIR

Rained all day. It was still sprinkling this afternoon when I got on the bus. It stopped about an hour ago as the clouds pushed south-east. The crispness of fresh-washed air reminds me of home.

After dinner mess hall duty, I resume my preferred pastime, aimlessly wandering the compound. I can already feel a wet heat returning. I grab a chair from a corridor and put it under a pathetic little tree on the far side of Red Compound. It's a good spot to waste five or ten minutes. Or an hour. Nobody should see me, not unless they're making a point of looking.

I watch the foot traffic along the centre's main thoroughfare. Most of the officers walk in a similar fashion, like they have somewhere to be and see no point in lingering. The detainee's walk is different. I'm unsure if it's boredom or listlessness, perhaps both—the feet kicking out rather than the legs striding, the chest relaxed rather than pressed into service.

Then there is Mani, the Iranian guy with the wrecked back. About half an hour earlier there was an incident. He'd been on his way to the medical centre for his painkillers. The nurses had issued a dictate stating that they would no longer take the painkillers to him. If he wanted them, he had to walk for them. Mani shuffled toward the medical centre with the help of two friends, one either side, while Elen, his welfare officer, followed behind with a plastic chair so Mani could periodically stop and sit. He should have been given use of a wheelchair, but yesterday an email circulated stating that the use of wheelchairs in the compounds was now forbidden. Mani's name wasn't used, but it's pretty obvious it was about him.

By the time Mani had inched his way to within about one hundred and fifty yards of the medical centre, he was in serious bother. In sight of the building, he collapsed to the ground. A Code Blue medical emergency was called. The whole farcical situation was avoidable, yet inevitable.

Now, despite the new policy, Mani is being pushed in a wheelchair by an officer. He's being taken to Derby Hospital for the night. I get up and walk closer. I see a car waiting. Every little bump and divot in the terrain sheets bolts of agony through Mani's spine; the soft features of his face are almost unrecognisable beneath the puffed eyes and facial contortions. When Mani is helped to a standing position, his body shakes violently; I see the sheen of tears in his eyes as he is lowered into the car. Then he just sits there, staring ahead. His expression is hard to look at, but I look anyway. His eyes are wide, sad and scared, fixed on nothing and nobody like a diseased animal waiting to be put down.

I turn away and go back to my chair. I resolve to sit till someone tells me to move.

CONCRETE

Since Roy left, I've had to double the amount of time I waste in aimless wandering to make up for his missed contribution. Right now, I'm sitting at the brick and concrete water feature the Sri Lankans built in Red Compound. It's probably not the best spot to be wasting time, as everybody can see you. Luckily, I don't give a fuck.

An Iranian man I don't know walks over and asks me if I am ok. I tell the man I'm fine, just eager to get out of this place. He nods. I say that in this place it is just waiting: staff, detainees, everybody waiting to leave. Another man approaches.

"You have light, please?"

I produce my lighter and hold a flame while he singes the tip of his rolled cigarette. He taps me on the hand lightly, as is custom. I say goodnight to both men, and leave. Then I see Samir striding—no, bounding—toward me.

"Nick! You need to drink a cup of concrete and harden up, princess!"

"Yes, Samir, yes! Outstanding."

We stop in the middle of the Red Compound desert.

"Are you ready for another phrase?"

"Yes, Nick. Tell me."

"Ok. If you want to say that someone has no chance, you say that they are dreaming. 'He's dreaming.' 'You're dreaming.' So Ali might ask, 'Samir, do you think I will get a visa?' And you tell him, 'You're dreaming.' And then you turn to me and say,

'He's dreaming.' "

"Yes. And he need to drink a cup of concrete and harden up, princess!"

"Exactly."

Samir bounds away, I'm pretty sure headed for his room where Ali is about to be told that he's dreaming if he thinks he will get a visa. After that news, he may need a cup of concrete. I know I sure as shit do.

Shift is up and I'm walking with the rest of the officers through to admin. I see a large gathering of detainees in front of the big gates, the same gates that proved the end of Roy. Many of them are in their Sunday best, so I know it must be a sending-off party for the people who've been granted visas and are on their way out this morning.

I spot a fellow I know, one of about forty Mohammads. I skip over, shake his hand, congratulate him. I ask him where he's headed.

"Adelaide."

I'm a bit surprised. I don't think there's a huge immigrant population there, certainly not like in Melbourne and Sydney. It would be the rare refugee who came to Australia with the idea of settling in Adelaide. But the city has a good footy team, sometimes two. And there's a band there I like called The Beards. They sing about big bushy beards. Mohammad should love them. Besides, the city's an ok place—a manageable sort of bustle. So why not?

I think it shows some balls on Mohammad's part, taking the road less travelled. I wish him the best of luck, shake his hand again and slap him on the back. Quincy is holding the gate for me, waiting. He looks at me in an unusual way. If I didn't know better, I'd say that he was quietly pleased.

DROWNING

It's a funny thing. Every week I do less and less work, waste more and more time, disappear for longer and longer, and yet nobody cares. Not once has a single person said anything. I don't know what it means. Maybe they don't feel my absence. Or there's little work of importance to be done. Or they're gutless. I'd like to know, merely as a matter of intellectual curiosity. But it's not exactly the sort of thing you can just ask: "Hey, Gabriel, you know how I skive off work and disappear all the time — well, how do you feel about that?"

I'm skiving now. I've just been down to Green Compound to have a chat with Matthew. He's in good spirits. Yesterday he had a meeting with a DIAC officer who said they were recommending a bridging visa while he waits for a decision. Not a perfect outcome, but a good one. Matthew said that when he gets out, he wants to go to Perth. I said, "See you there."

Now I'm walking back to Red Compound. The trick to not being questioned for being out of your area is the officer walk. Chest out, long stride, purposefulness. If you've got a folder in hand, all the better. I'm striding along the main thoroughfare with all the purpose I can muster, partly so no one asks me where I've been or what I've been doing, but also because it's raining, squall followed by shower followed by squall. I have to skip and leap every now and again to avoid the puddles. Most people have the sense to be inside. I'm not, because it would mean sharing an office with Gabriel and Meg.

The thing about Curtin detention centre is that it's situated on a plain. There's not a lot of natural drainage. Not a lot of artificial drainage, either. With all the rain, broad stretches of ground are covered by stagnant water. The areas around the internal fences separating the compounds are the worst, because the buried wire is surrounded by a lip of dirt that stops water draining away. After a storm, the gate between Red Compound and Brown Compound looks like a flooded paddy field, the only land remaining dry being the little ridges of red dirt that form the walls of garden beds.

I relax my stride a little as the rain sputters to a stop. It's as deserted as I've ever seen the centre. For a moment, I see not a single other human. Then someone comes into view. Delicate little steps, the arms in a constant dance to find balance, the legs almost as stiff as the back, not an ounce of synchronicity evident. I'd recognise the walk anywhere: Mani.

It's a pitiful spectacle to watch, this man at war with his own body. There can only be one reason for his being out: he needs his pain meds. Despite his recent collapse and obvious suffering, the nurses have made it clear that Mani must continue to fetch them himself—he must walk through the mud and rain and pain—and so he is. He's already made it from his room and through Red Compound without any assistance, but in front of him looms the Red Sea: the flooded gate.

I'm still about seventy yards away. Under the glare of a spotlight, I see Mani's head swivel a little; he is assessing the pool of water spreading from the gate. Then he looks at the ridge of the garden bed, the uppermost crust the only dry way through.

Oh no, don't you dare, I think. Don't you fucking dare. But he does. Mani awkwardly starts up the ridge, needing all his effort to surmount the bare few inches of elevation. He gains the high ground and shuffles forward. I keep walking, resuming my purposeful stride. That piss-weak soil is going to give way, I think.

He's halfway across when it suddenly goes, the chunk of ridge under Mani's right foot sliding into the water. For a normal person it would be a non-event—bend a knee, pick your foot up, keep walking. With Mani, I watch his world disappear and his body respond with what looks like a seizure of the muscles running up his legs and through his core. He doesn't right himself and he doesn't collapse. He slowly tilts over like a tall jarrah scarfed with a chainsaw, tottering as it waits for gravity to grab hold and drag it to earth.

I feel like I'm watching the scene in slow motion, part my own mind's disbelieving response, part Mani's wretched physics. When his body finally slaps into the puddle in a graceless belly flop, a man-sized wave of muddy water spills over ridges and into the garden.

Just six inches. That's all it is, no more than a miserable plash, but enough to partially submerge Mani's face. From forty yards away I can see the muddy water frothing where he's blowing bubbles in panic and exertion; he pushes with his arms to right himself, to turn his body over, but he can't. He's that weak, that immobile: he is drowning in a fucking puddle.

I race to him, no longer skipping, pounding through water and mud. He's been under for maybe a dozen seconds when I grab Mani's right arm and drag him like a bloated sheep's carcass from a dam. He desperately sucks breath and with that breath he howls; I keep dragging him through water then mud till I find firm ground. I roll him into the first aid recovery position; he yelpers in a low falsetto and sheds muddy tears. I grab my radio and call a Code Blue.

As I wait for others to arrive, I look around. Still not a person in sight. There's no doubt. He would have drowned. Face down in a six-inch-deep pool of muddy brown water, Mani would have drowned.

TAUNT

I help stretcher Mani into medical. For some reason, no manager feels it necessary to stay with him. Kylie asks if I'm fine hanging around till Mani is discharged.

"Sure," I say.

The nurses don't like him. I can see it in their faces. I can see it in the severity of their movements—not a hint of the gentle and soothing presence I know they can be. The nurses think he's full of shit, or maybe just as weak in mind as he is in body. Whatever the case, they've decided he's an attention-seeker looking for an advantage, and unworthy of their compassion.

The head nurse checks him over and gives him some painkillers, then asks another nurse to get the translator. Mani's English is at best limited, and she wants to be very clear in what she says to him.

The translator—Roy's mate—comes in. The nurse grabs him by the arm and leads him around so that he's in front of Mani. Mani is lying on his side, facing a bare wall.

"I want you to tell him that he needs to start dealing with his sore back. If he doesn't start walking and dealing with it, then he won't get better."

The translator conveys the message in Farsi.

"He's not going to the hospital tonight. There's no point. We've given him some painkillers, and that's all there is."

The message is translated.

"Now, this is important. I want you to tell him I think he's a malingerer and we're not playing his game anymore. Do you know that word—malingerer?" the nurse asks the translator.

"Yes, I know it."

"Make sure you use the right word. Malingerer, or whatever your word for that is."

The translator looks at the nurse, then across at me, then says something to Mani in Farsi. Mani says nothing. I can't see his face. The man who almost drowned in a puddle just lies there.

An hour later, I accompany Mani as Elen wheels him back to his room. When I open the door I'm struck by the unmistakable aroma of stale piss. I say nothing.

Elen helps Mani from the chair and he gingerly shuffles into the bathroom, partially closing the door. With what the nurse gave him, he's moving a lot better, almost as well as a geriatric. While Mani is in the bathroom, Elen whispers to me that she doesn't think Mani has washed in six days—not until just before, when the nurses helped shower him.

It's beyond a joke. There's no way this man should be in a detention centre. He can't walk, can't wash, is in constant pain, and now he's gone and just about drowned in a puddle. And he's one of the lucky ones, granted a visa after just three months—I guess that's the advantage of having a Muslim working for a theocracy kick your back in. Soon as ASIO processes his security clearance, Mani will be released. Till then, I just can't believe that this is the best we can do for a man who will probably live the rest of his life in Australia.

Elen helps balance and support Mani as he manoeuvres onto his bed. When his arse and then shoulders press into the mattress, the potent stench of urine-rotted foam wafts toward me.

Elen kneels beside Mani and proceeds to give him a pep talk about trying to walk more. The nurses have obviously been in her ear. She tells him he must try harder, while Mani keeps repeating, "Can't walk."

Elen is frustrated. "The nurses say that—"

"Can't walk can't walk can't walk," spits Mani till he is breathless.

"Well, if you don't start walking, we will cancel your visa. So think about that."

Elen retrieves the empty wheelchair and pushes it out the door.

JOHN

Shift ended, I'm back in my room. It's just gone 7 a.m.

I think about Mani. I'm not one to carry on about the imaginary novelties we call human rights, but there's a point where you just know something is morally wrong. We're well into that territory.

Mani should not be in the centre. He should be in a hospital or someplace where he can be made more comfortable and know his welfare is of paramount concern. I know that's not going to happen. The managers at the centre and the government's immigration officers are going to let him waste away, lying in his own piss, crying himself to sleep. No one gives a fuck.

To an extent, I don't either. Working nights does something to body and mind—you're up all night, sleep deficit building and building across your six shifts, till you're spent, utterly spent, and all you want and all you care about is sleep. That's all I want now: sleep. I think about how annoying this whole thing is. Working a twelve-hour night shift then having to worry about this. I'm tempted to just say screw it. Too hard.

I think about Mum. About what she'd say. Whether she'd be proud of me—and I know she wouldn't. I think about the stupid sign Mum put up on the wall when we were kids: *He who sees wrong and fails to act is no better than he who fails to see wrong.* I suppose even hackneyed platitudes have a point.

But I'm just a blue-shirted shitkicker. The power I wield

in the centre is over the distribution of milk and noodles, not over the treatment or housing of detainees.

There is something, though. An external party. I could contact the Red Cross. They have a detention program which gives them limited access to the centre. They have respect and a little influence. It's risky. I could lose my job, or worse; there were all kinds of threats in the paperwork I signed before starting.

Fuck it. Sooner I get this done, sooner I can put this shit from my mind and go to sleep. I turn on my laptop, fire up my dongle and google the Red Cross. I find a few numbers that I jot down. Their office is over east, so they should be open. I call.

A woman answers. I tell her I need to urgently speak with the head of their refugee detention program. She says the relevant person is in a meeting, but she takes my number so he can call me back. I want to stay anonymous, just to be safe, so when she asks for a name I say: "It's John."

"John …"

"Just John."

I shower then go to bed, expecting John to be woken by a phone call in the next few hours. I sleep fitfully. Every now and again I check the time.

2 p.m.: still no phone call. For Christ's sake.

I decide to call them back. I get up, dial the number. There's no answer. I look in my notepad for another number to try. That's when I realise what I've done.

I have two SIM cards and two phone numbers. I gave them my normal number, the one with Virgin that doesn't work up here, the one that goes straight to voice mail.

So the Red Cross have been calling anonymous John, only to be greeted thus: "This is the phone Nazi. You want to speak to Nick Harris? You? If Nick Harris want to speak, Nick Harris answer phone. No message for you! Call back: one year."

I did the accent and all. Thought I was so funny when I made it. Been my greeting forever. What a fuckhead.

I call the Red Cross. Someone answers.

"Oh yes," they say, "John ... we've been trying to contact you."

"Mmm, I might have given you the wrong number," I explain.

I'm put through to the boss man, who graciously continues to call me John. I feel stupid and embarrassed. Maybe Mum's sign should have read: *No good deed goes unpunished.* I should have just gone to sleep.

The man tells me they have some people scheduled for a visit to Curtin in the next fortnight; he promises they will see Mani.

Awesome. Now it's someone else's problem. I've done my bit. I go to sleep.

DEVIANT

That afternoon and evening, I slink around Spinifex City like a
guilty man, expecting someone to pull me aside and whisper, "I
know what you did." It's ridiculous. Nobody knows about the
phone call. The sum of my conversation with fellow Spinifex
citizens amounts to, "Hi," and, "How are you?"

I barely exist.

I'm on my own and into the whisky. I guess it stings a bit
to be excluded and ignored—there's no shame in admitting
that—but I'm not one to try to drink away sadness or anger or
whatever it is so many fools think they're doing when they hit
the piss. I drink when I want to relax; it's my day off; of course
I'm going to have a drink.

I know what did it, what made everyone start to look at
me funny and give me a wide berth. It's the arguments I had
with Meg. Now they think I'm a bleeding heart. And it's not
even that they so very much despise bleeding hearts. It's that
it marks me as different. Tells them that I don't see things the
way they do. That I don't think the way they do. It's a simple
equation: anything different is deviant. That Nick, haven't you
heard? Not to be trusted.

I've come close some places, but have never completely fit in
anywhere. My parts just don't add up to a recognisable whole.
I'm a mongrel. Bits of bumpkin and bits of philosopher and bits
of thug and bits of pacifist, and all these other irregular chunks
of personality and culture and psyche that seem to come from

different places that aren't meant to mix. It means I can walk among all sorts, but sooner or later they notice the other stuff, and that makes them suspicious.

I mean, blokes familiar with qualia and Quine don't shotgun tinnies of Emu Export for fun. Atheist sceptics don't take religious communion with the Quechua just to see how it feels. Prolific readers don't light bonfires with books. Non-voting rednecks don't care about the welfare of refugees. Refugee sympathisers don't agree that an influx of refugees would be a disaster.

A mongrel.

SHAME

I feel ok about going to work today. I get to talk to Ali and Samir and Soheil, to Matthew when I'm in Green Compound, and to dozens of others who greet me with warmth. It's what Roy loved about it, and he was right. There are some really good blokes in there.

First thing I do the moment I have a free chunk of time is go to the medical centre. I ask the nurse behind the desk if she is Margaret. She is not Margaret. Margaret emerges from the room behind the desk.

I recognise her. She's the one who told Mani he is a malingerer.

"Yes?"

"Hi. I was told you'd be able to check the dental waiting list for me to confirm if a client is on it."

"What do you mean?"

"Can you check the list and see if Soheil Hamid, M-I-G-3-7, is on it? He's not sure if he is. He's had a toothache for weeks."

"I don't know why you would want to know that," she says, her eyes narrowing.

"Because he doesn't know and he wants to know."

"Well, that's his problem."

"Is that the list?" I say, pointing to a folder that says "Dental Surgeon".

She looks at it and raises her head—half a nod as good an acknowledgement as I'm going to get.

"Maybe you could take a moment and open the folder and tell me if he is on the waiting list so I can tell him if he is on the waiting list. Or you could tell him, if you like."

Her face creases with the familiarity of origami. Her lip quivers and I think she's going to say something, but she doesn't. Instead, she opens the folder.

"What number?"

"M-I-G-3-7, Soheil—"

"I don't need the name."

"Soheil Hamid."

She runs her finger down, then stops. She looks at me, oh-so-cross. It reminds me of how Miss Della used to look at me in seventh grade. Back then it was enough to intimidate me into something like good behaviour. Now, I just think: you dumb bitch.

"He's on the list."

"And do you know how long the wait is? Does he have an appointment?"

"No. They'll get to him when they get to him."

End of conversation.

I go back to the compound, find Soheil, tell him. He reacts like I've just agreed to donate a kidney. As I think about it, an ache builds in my gut. I've done nothing more than extend a courtesy requiring minimal personal effort. Soheil insists I drink a cup of tea with him as thanks. The warm drink drains toward the sick feeling. I try to ignore it.

SMASH

Benedict informs us at briefing that four Iranian detainees are scheduled to receive negative decisions today. He tells us that they are known troublemakers and asks us to be extra vigilant.

The morning is no different to any morning, but something changes about 11 a.m.; I realise that the detainees Benedict mentioned have now seen their DIAC case managers and have been told their applications for visas have been rejected. Walking through the centre, I feel a tension, some sort of charge. It's not a thing you can define; it's something subtle that senses of sight and hearing detect, analyse, then layer with meaning, all below consciousness, but it's no less real because of that. I only know the conclusion: for the first time since I got here, this place feels genuinely dangerous. I sort of like it; it's exciting. There is newfound pep in my step, and not just because I'm imitating the purposefulness of the good officer's walk.

The first provocation comes at lunch. A couple of officers manning the Brown Compound mess hall exit attempt to stop some guys taking pita bread out. Normally when this stuff happens, it's good-natured. But the detainees are unwilling to heed. They brush past in defiance. The officers have the sense not to escalate the situation. Still, it's proof enough that something ill is brewing.

As I walk around the compounds after lunch, speaking to

the detainees in their rooms and around communal benches, I notice that the usual "hellos" and "how are yous" are largely absent. People aren't looking me in the eye — they're looking me up and down.

About 3.30 p.m., I escort a detainee to medical. In Brown Compound, under the big shed, I see a large gathering of men.

"It's no problem, officer, just talking," assures an Iranian man when I enquire what is afoot. I call it in.

It's about 4 p.m. when I start walking around the compound, handing out appointment slips. The group of men in the distance have finished talking, presumably agreeing upon a protest. They set off, fairly quiet, a procession of around sixty walking first through Brown Compound, then through Red Compound, and then back over to Brown Compound, encouraging others to join them, and they do.

There are relatively few officers in the compounds so, seeing the mass of numbers and nobody to stop them, my adrenaline spikes. I've no idea what's going to happen, but I want to make sure I don't miss it. I follow at a safe distance. The group make their way back to Brown. A call comes over the radio, not entirely unexpected: "Things are no longer peaceful, they're smashing everything as they go through." A Code Black is called. Officers are advised not to approach, to just observe. We can't afford for the situation to turn hostile. The group makes its way back to Red Compound.

Chanting "Iran, Iran," they methodically work their way up each corridor of dongas. I can't see what's being broken, but I can certainly hear it. The bangs, crashes, shattering and yelling make an incredible sound. It's transitioned from protest to riot. My very first riot. Not particularly fearsome compared to the sorts of riots that make the news, but remarkable all the same.

The ERT is called to assemble. The crowd of over a hundred detainees wander back and forth between compounds, chanting, breaking fixtures, then suddenly, like a storm blowing out, the mob dissipates till there's just five or six diehards yelling and moving like they are angry, then even they lose enthusiasm and stop at a bench and sit down and sulk. It's all over in fifteen minutes.

I ponder how these Iranian men must have rationalised their impulses. They can't be so naïve as to think a little riot will make a difference. Maybe they consider it a moral riot. The riot they had to have. Or maybe they weren't thinking, just acting. Doing something so they could feel like they were doing something, even though they don't fully understand why.

When it's clear the action is over, I accompany a superior to survey the damage. Maybe ten fridges have been upended and broken; a few light fixtures ripped off or smashed, a few power points destroyed, a few benches broken. Superficial, noisy damage. It seems cleverly considered. They haven't broken anything that will significantly affect their quality of life, and they haven't damaged any individuals' rooms. The officers' quarters were spared (after all, we're the keepers of milk, noodles, razors and forms), and they haven't ventured anywhere near the Afghani compounds—the Afghanis easily outnumber Iranians in the camp, and are certainly capable of outfighting them.

The ERT arrive, all suited up, carrying shields and batons and sporting massive hard-ons for a rumble, but there's nothing left for them to do. I hold a gate open for the head of security, the second most senior officer in the entire centre.

"I hope they fire up again and we get to smash the cunts tonight, hey?" he says.

"Yeah," I say, chuckling, not really thinking, our exchange just a form of pleasantries. Then I do think and my mind reels. What's wrong with him? More to the point, what's wrong with me? Some of those people are my friends. Do I really want another riot just so that the Iranians who are upset about being denied visas can be bashed—because I'm an officer and they're scum?

My own hard-on shrivels and I taste the saliva in my dumb white-trash Harris mouth.

When I get back to Spinifex City, I see a missed call from Oli from a few minutes ago. I didn't give him my number up here, but I guess he has it from when I called him. The phone's in my hand when it starts vibrating, then starts ringing. It's Oli again. I should answer it. I should talk to my brother. But after today I just don't want to. I just want to sleep it away. I hit the red decline button then switch my phone off. I go to sleep without showering.

RADIO

The tension and sense of danger I felt yesterday has completely evaporated, but the riot remains all anyone can talk about.
I'm in the office with everyone else. I should leave before I
say something that makes my position worse, but I will not be
denied the cup of tea I've been thinking about for the last half
hour.

"I tell you one thing, how many bearded fellers were in
it?" says Darren. "It's 'cause it's the Muslims. They're the
troublemakers. That's how you know it's a put-on when they
say they converted to Christianity. If they've still got their
beard, they're a Muslim."

"Jihad," giggles Scott in a funny voice, though nobody knows
why he's giggling.

"That's what they think. Their bible says they've got to fight
the white man and then they go to heaven. The faggots from
yesterday are probably counting how many virgins each one of
'em gets," says Darren.

I open the bar fridge and reach for the milk. There's not
enough room for this many people, especially with Karen
among us. The corner of the fridge door stabs into my waist.
The radio hitched to my belt falls to the ground for the second
time in as many minutes. I pick the prick of a thing up and
dump it on the table, then get the milk and finish making my
tea.

"I reckon the ringleader was that one who lit a fire the other week," says Gabriel.

"The one with the scars on his face?" says Darren.

"No no, not him, the light-skinned one. In Brown Compound."

"Oh, yeah, I think I know who you mean."

"Isn't he the guy who lost his entire family in that capsizing a while back?" I ask.

"Yeah, I think so," says Darren.

"I say we get an extraction squad together and take him down. Put him in isolation. Worked in prison. You get rid of the ringleader and the problem's solved," says Gabriel.

"It's their culture, though. That's what they do in those places. Riot and guerrilla war. You can't stop it. It's how they are," says Darren.

"I still reckon you put that prick down and the rest pull their head in. Fuck it, put him down anyway. I'll do it."

"No no, please officer, me good refugee," says Scott, again giggling.

Can't Scott see that Darren and Gabriel are trying to have a serious conversation?

"The moment you riot, that's it, no visa. Break a law, you're gone. First plane back to Iran. Solve the problem straight away," says Darren.

"I'll cut your beard off, cocksucker!" yells Scott, who, I realise, must still be drunk from the night before. I laugh heartily at the Roy-like irreverence. Gabriel stares at me with contempt. Maybe he thinks I'm laughing at him. Maybe I am.

There's a knock at the window. No one motions to move, so I go. It's Ali.

"Hiii, Nick. Can you ...?" he says, tilting his head.

"Yeah, hold on," I say.

I grab my cup of tea and head out. I follow Ali to his room. He's been writing a letter detailing the errors contained in the initial negative decision he received. He's finally finished and

I've agreed to check it over for spelling and whatnot. I take a seat while Ali sits on his bed. He passes me a wad of papers.

"Wow, this looks like a long letter. You must have spent a lot of time on this."

"Yeees. But it's ok. I have a lot of time," Ali says.

I read the letter, making notations as I go to correct grammar and clarify expression. The incompetence and indifference Ali details is stunning. It gels with snippets other detainees have told me, and I have no reason to think any of it untrue. From the outside, you'd think the whole refugee visa application process is performed with the utmost care and professionalism. But it appears to be the same shitshow of incompetence, muddling and petty power trips that characterises the rest of life.

I'm almost through the letter when I hear the hurried footfall of an officer in the corridor outside. Then I hear the distorted crackle of a radio and what sounds like my name. Strange. I reach for my own radio—and that's when I realise it's not on my belt.

I remember now: I left it sitting on the table in the officers' donga. Shit-o-shit-o-shit. I spring from my seat and rush outside.

"Hey," I call to the back of Scott's head. He turns around. "What's happening?"

"Oh, fuck, man. Gabriel couldn't get you on the radio, so called a Code Black. I'll let him know."

Scott grabs his handset and hails control.

"This is Red Four. Ahh, Red Six has been located in Red Compound. It's all good. Over," says Scott, then he giggles.

I don't giggle. I know I'm in deep shit.

I quickly walk back to the office. I open the door as Gabriel is putting the phone down. He reclines in his swivel chair. There's a smug grin on his face.

I look around. My radio is on the table exactly where I left it. I pick it up and put it on my belt.

"Tried to reach you on the radio," says Gabriel. "Hailed you three times. You should remember to take your radio. Anyway, that was the big man. Benedict. You're wanted at admin at your earliest convenience."

Gabriel smiles at me and I know he did it on purpose. He knew exactly where my radio was. That's why he hailed me—to trigger a Code Black. To trip me up so I'd receive a formal warning for breaking the cardinal rule: your radio must always be on, and on hand. It's your lifeline, and you are your workmate's lifeline.

"Now that I'm here, what was it you needed me for?"

"Like I said, you're wanted in admin," says Gabriel.

"Yeah, I am now because a Code Black has just been called for me. But why were you hailing me before?"

"You don't listen too well, do you? Admin wanted to see you. I can say it all day."

"Right. Well you look pretty pleased with yourself."

"Just doin' my job," he says.

I stare at him a second, weighing up what I want to say.

"You're pathetic, cunt."

Gabriel springs from his chair like he's been waiting for it. I barely flinch as he rushes forward and closes in till there's just centimetres separating us. I know he won't jeopardise his position as a manager; it's all bluster.

"What'd you fuck'n say, faggot?" he says.

He eyeballs me with his best prison guard gaze, but he's shorter than me and has to arch his neck, so that he's looking up like a petulant child scowling at a parent. I smile and deploy my most polite voice as I slowly repeat the words—"You are a pathetic fucking cunt"—then stare him down long enough so he knows.

I am not some anaemic Iranian refugee. I am not his prisoner.

I turn and walk away.

BISCUIT

If one didn't know better, one might think I had adopted an overly strident version of the officer's gait. The fact is, I'm just pissed off. If Benedict thinks he's going to give me one of his wise-old-man lectures and that I'm going to stand there and nod and say, "Thank you, O great leader," he is sorely mistaken. I may have fucked up, but this whole place is fucked-up, and that's precisely what I intend to tell him.

I see Meg in the distance. I think maybe she hasn't seen me, but then she veers toward my line. I look at her out of the corner of my eye; I see what I take to be her very best officious expression. If she's coming over to tell me that I've pulled a Roy and that I'm a naughty boy, I'm not sure what, only that there will be ill-considered and unpleasant words.

I don't slow. Maybe we can just walk past each other in mutual ignorance—and in peace. We get within speaking range.

"Nick. Hey, Nick," says Meg.

I keep walking till I'm past her.

"Nick. Nick!" she shouts.

I stop and turn. "What?"

"Jesus Christ. I just wanted to see if you were ok. I heard the Code Black. I was worried, you dick."

I close my eyes for a second. I open them and Meg is still standing there. I look at her face. Maybe it's not contempt I see. Maybe it's concern. Wouldn't that be nice? Someone who actually gives a shit about me. I want it to be true.

I mutter my least favourite word: "Sorry." I shake my head. "Fuck. Sorry. Yeah, ok." I turn to go.

"Hey," Meg says, walking toward me.

I turn back.

"What happened? Are you ok?" she says, and then she is close, looking at my face, seeing something that clearly worries her.

"I'm just ... sick of it, Meg. Ok?"

"Nick, listen, I know that—"

"Nah, don't. I'm just pissed off. It's no big deal."

"You look like you're about to say or do something stupid."

"What? What have I said?"

"Not with me, you idiot. Christ, Nick, why are you always stomping around so angry?"

"That's not ..." I say, trailing off as I shake my head, denying the very possibility from entering my thoughts.

"Do you have to speak to a manager?"

"Yeah. Benedict."

"Well, don't go angry."

"I told you, I'm not angry. I'm just ... This whole fucking place. Everything's bullshit. The way they—"

Meg grabs my wrist and interrupts me. "Wait. Shut up and come with me."

"What for?" I say, as I'm dragged behind. "Where?"

"Just come."

Meg doesn't say anything else. I let her lead me through Brown Compound, weaving behind dongas, steering clear of the main thoroughfares, till we're among the disused buildings of no-man's-land. Meg glances around, so I glance around, too. Neither of us sees anyone. Meg gets her keys out and unlocks the door to one of the buildings.

"Come on," she says, so I follow her in.

She shuts the door. "This is my chill-out room."

"Ok ..."

"No one else comes here. Sometimes I get away for fifteen minutes. When I need to be alone."

"You skive off work?"

"No. It's just where I take a break. On my own."

"Without telling anyone."

"Yeah," she says, smiling at me, "just like you sit for hours on the verandah of building five."

"You know about that?"

"Ahh, yeah, of course I do."

"You never said anything."

"If I said anything then you wouldn't think it was your own private spot anymore."

"I guess so, yeah. Thanks, I suppose."

I survey the room. There's almost nothing inside. A desk. Three chairs. A box. There is no rag and bucket prepped for waterboarding.

"Why did you bring me here?"

Meg walks over to the cardboard box and pulls a flap open. She reaches inside and grabs something crinkly.

"You're shitting me," I say, as I see the packet. "You have your own private room so you can come and eat Tim Tams?"

"Umm, yeah, pretty much. You want one?" says Meg, holding out the packet.

"I don't really eat that stuff. But thanks anyway."

"Seriously? I don't think I've ever seen someone who needs a Tim Tam more than you, Nick."

"What—a Tim Tam will solve all my problems?"

"Yes. A Tim Tam will solve all your problems."

Meg is standing close. I look at her face. She's still smiling at me. Her eyes are warm. If I didn't know better, I'd say she was trying to cheer me up.

I don't get it. Five minutes ago we were mortal enemies. Now—I don't even know what this is. With the adrenaline still in my body, with the anger still bubbling away at the back of my mind, with the lust I always feel when I'm near

Meg—I'm confused. "Screw it. Go on, then, give me one."

Meg hands me a Tim Tam and takes one for herself. We sit side by side on the desk and bite into the chocolate biscuits. It's been seven years since I've had one of these, back before I found out what sugar does to the human body and resolved to cut it from my diet, excepting the occasional hangover curative in the form of a carton of flavoured milk. The Tim Tam is pretty bloody good.

I enjoy the taste and the quiet, and the sensation of brushing arms with an attractive woman. I finish the biscuit and look at Meg.

"Meg, why are you being nice to me?"

"You're such a dick, Nick. I've always been nice to you. You're the one who's been a jerk to me."

It's not what I was expecting. I look Meg in the eyes and I know she is sincere.

"I'm sorry," I say, knowing without needing to really think about it that there is an element of truth to what she says. Neither one of us is without fault.

"Thank you," says Meg.

I feel a tremendous sense of déjà vu. It's like that first day Meg knocked on my door and sat on my bed and our bodies ended up accidentally brushing against one another, the desire palpable, yet neither one of us acted on it.

Meg's hand dangles beside her. I reach across and thread my fingers through hers.

"I really am sorry. I—"

But I say no more because Meg's body is leaning toward mine. I shut my gob and let her lips find my lips and then my tongue find her tongue, tasting the chocolate. It's gentle because we're both tentative after all that's happened between us, but that only lasts a second. I slide off the desk and pull Meg to her feet. My hands move across her curves, digging into the soft flesh of hips and arse. Her hands wrap around my head and sift through my hair.

We kiss for a while, but my lust overwhelms any sort of tender romantic feelings. I pull Meg's blue shirt out where it's tucked in at the waist and drag it over her head. I shower her neck and chest with little kisses as I unclip her bra, then I bury my face in her breasts, licking and sucking greedily. My hands work at the buckle of her belt; I pull and tug gently, then less gently, unable to work the pin from its snug hole. Meg's hands push mine away to finish the job. I rip my own clothes off, but my pants get stuck around my ankles. I wedge my left shoe off, then my right, and kick them away. One shoe hits the wall with an unexpected boom. Meg and I both pause, holding breath. We hear nothing.

Our bodies slap together. We kiss passionately, still standing. Meg's hand wraps around my cock. Her grip is almost too eager as she begins to stroke up and down. I drag my hand up the inside of her leg, over her pussy, finding her clit with my finger. She makes a whimpering sound as I trace little circles, then my hand slips down and Meg almost buckles as two of my fingers push into her pussy. I steady her with one arm then swing her around by the shoulders so she's facing the desk. I don't use words, I just push her forward and Meg responds by leaning over the desk and opening her legs.

I step back and Meg's round arse fills my vision. My eyes drop to the voluptuous double crescent of pink lips between her thighs. I move closer and push my cock against Meg's pussy. It slips down along her crotch. Meg reaches behind and grabs me by the shaft. She guides me inside her then pushes back till my pelvis is pressing against her arse and we fuck, we fuck like prison guards.

WAR

It takes Meg longer to put her uniform on than me, so I sit on the floor where it's coolest and lean back on the wall while I get my breath back. I wipe big beads of sweat from my forehead and lip.

"Thanks for the Tim Tam," I say.

"Anytime."

"Really? Wasn't just a one-time offer? You don't want me to erase your secret chill-out room from my mind?"

Right then our radios crackle to life.

"Red Six, Red Six, this is Red One, come in, over."

Meg and I share a look.

"You going to answer that?" asks Meg.

I glare at my radio, heaped next to me on the floor. I sigh. "Yeah. Two Code Blacks in one day might be a bit much."

I grab the handset and press the transmit button. "Red One, come in Red One, this is Red Six. What can I do for you?"

"Red Six, can you give us a heads-up on your location? Benedict is looking for you."

I pause a moment. "Red One, Red Six be taking a shit. Over."

Meg suppresses a giggle as she shakes her head. There's a lull in the transmission. I assume Benedict is in the office with Gabriel, talking through their options.

"Ahh, roger that Red Six. When you're ready, please report to Benedict at admin. Over."

"Soon as I've snapped it off. Over and out."

Fuck 'em.

"I can't believe you said that," says Meg, chortling. It's a magnificent sound, a girl laughing.

"Could hardly tell them the truth."

Meg fixes her radio onto her belt. "So, do you know what Benedict wants?"

"Well, yeah, it's pretty obvious. He's gonna give me a formal warning for triggering that Code Black. He wants me gone."

"I don't think he wants you gone."

"Ahh, yeah, he wants me gone. I'm about as popular as Roy around this joint. That's why that piece of shit Gabriel hung me out to dry."

"What do you mean?"

"The Code Black. It was an accident when I left my radio in the office, but it wasn't an accident when Gabriel saw it sitting there and decided it'd be a good time to hail me."

"Well, just don't go in there angry. If you have to get a warning, get a warning. It's no big deal. If you go in there and argue with Benedict then you might give him an actual reason to fire you. And that'd be stupid."

I stand up and walk across to Meg. "Are you trying to say you want me to stick around?"

Meg leans forward. I move toward her mouth, but she ignores my overture and kisses me on the cheek.

"Yes. I want you to stick around. Please don't say anything stupid. You don't have to be at war with everyone all the time."

I pull back and stare at Meg. I don't know if it's perverse or uncanny or what it is.

"Why are you looking at me that way?" she says.

"No reason. It's nothing. You just reminded me of something someone said to me once. Anyway, I'd better go. Wouldn't want 'em to think I'm constipated."

CONSEQUENCE

I walk into the admin office. It's not like our officer dongas; it's a proper office with partitions and desks and glass cubicles. Soon as the old giant and his swinging dick see me, I'm directed into an empty room. Benedict shuts the door.

"Take a seat, Nick," says Benedict.

"No thanks. I'll stand."

"If you prefer," he says, resting half his arse on the office desk.

I look him square in the face. I don't see the purple fury I was expecting. Perhaps he likes to gradually work his way into a lather. Just hurry up and get it done with, I think.

"Nick, this is a tough job. Confronting. I've seen all sorts come through, and everyone reacts differently," says Benedict, his big hands held in front of him as he rubs the arthritis away. "Some people leave after a week, some last a month, some of our workers out there have been at it five years, ten years, made a career of it."

"Benedict, no offence, but why does it sound like you're firing me?"

"No no, no, I'm not firing you. Look, I just wanted to say that if you want to come back here, you're welcome. I know you've had your difficulties, but you are welcome back. The reason—"

"Back here after what? What, you're suspending me? Are you kidding? For forgetting my radio?"

Blood rushes to my face and the wave of anger is dizzying. I have to look away. We've got nurses and welfare officers who taunt the seriously injured, we've got managers who threaten mentally unbalanced detainees, we've got officers who tell detainees to fuck off and to go back where they came from, and they're all fine—but I forget my radio, once, and I'm the problem?

"Nick, that's not it. Look, I've already taken care of everything. We're booking you on the next flight back to Perth, day after tomorrow. The thing is—"

"Nup, nup, this is bullshit. This is a fucking joke."

"Just listen, son."

"Nah, fuck that. You haven't even issued me one formal warning yet. Uh-uh. I'm not one of these dickless wonders you can just push around. And where's my union rep?"

"You don't need a union rep, Nick. Just listen, son."

"Bullshit. I've read the bargaining agreement, mate, front to back, every word. You literally cannot fire me without three warnings, and I've got none and you can't issue more than a single warning at once. And I'm entitled to have a union rep in any disciplinary hearing."

"You done?"

"Till my union rep gets here."

"For Christ's sake, you're not being fired, or suspended."

I take short breaths and try to calm.

"The fact of the matter is, you would have been issued a formal warning for not keeping your radio with you, same as anyone, but ... that's not why you're here," says Benedict, and I realise how uneasy he is, how the rubbing of his hands isn't for the arthritis but for him to focus on something other than what he's saying.

"You need to go home, Nick. Oliver Harris, your brother I believe, he called us a short while ago. He said he tried to reach you yesterday and this morning, but he couldn't get through. Nick, I'm sorry. I don't know what happened, I don't have any more information than what he told us." Benedict pauses, searching for words.

It's like I've grabbed hold of an electric fence. A current of knowing—a physical thing—arcs through my body. My eyes lose focus and I'm not looking at anything, just seeing colour.

"Say it," I mutter, barely audible.

"What's that?"

"Say it!" I yell, because I know.

I knew it when she asked me to come home and I said I would but I didn't because I have all the time in the world but only now to make a few more bucks. Five years gone, what's another month or two?

Five years gone. Fuck. Fuck. Five years. What have I done?

Benedict holds out his gnarled hands, gesturing to the people outside, telling them everything is fine. I know it's not.

"I'm so sorry to be giving you this news. Your mother, she passed away yesterday."

My eyes blink closed and don't open. Breath fills my lungs, but it doesn't leave. Mum, Mum...and that's as far as the thought goes, just this concept of a person, that's all that's in my mind and the rest is my body, awareness of my body, it suddenly feels so strange, different bits coming into focus. The heat forcing its way through my veins. Then my forearms, they feel odd, tingly, heavy, I never notice them, I realise. Why am I noticing them? The top of my head is pulling at the rest of my scalp. Is someone trying to lift me like a kitten? My sternum, that's not anything, a dumb bone, only now it's digging into my chest, my own body's spear digging into my chest.

It's not right, any of it. I should be feeling ... something, I don't know what, something else. I become aware of my balance and the moment I do it's gone. I open my eyes and take a step to steady. They must have been shut a while. I thought just a few seconds but it must have been longer because Benedict is coming back through the door with a set of keys in his hand.

"Come on, son, I'll drive you back to Spinifex City."

I don't really think anything, I just move my strange body through space, then I remember that I should say something. "Thanks," I say, and Benedict drives me to my tin shed.

MESSAGE

I lie on my bed till there are thoughts in my head, but not the right thoughts, not grief or love or emotion, just curiosity. It suddenly seems important that I know what it was. She was sick, I could tell that when I spoke to her, what, five weeks ago? She wasn't that sick. Not this sick. Not dying.

She said she had a rash. No, an itch. Something like that. The bees, she tried to use bees to cure it. So she had something for a while, a few months at least.

An itch—that's all I know. I will my brain to remember everything I learned in three years of medicine. Diseases that itch. Diseases that itch that kill. It's hopeless. It could be dozens of things. Maybe if I was a doctor I would know. Maybe if I hadn't dropped out and run away I would know. Maybe if I was there when it started I would have known, and done something, and Mum would be fine. I would have seen her itching and said Mum, I know exactly what's wrong, it's serious but it's ok, we're going to fix it and I would have fixed it. If I'd been there that's what would have happened, rather than ... than Kylie having to do what I should have been there to do.

Oli must have known she was sick. That's why he told me to call her. Did he know she was dying? He couldn't have. He would have said. He'd never keep that from me. Why would Mum keep that from Oli? She didn't know. But she had to. She knew something or she wouldn't have asked me to come home. But she couldn't have known she had mere weeks. She would have asked me to come back.

But she did—she did ask.

Last night, the phone calls, Oli. I turned it off. I was too tired. What if she was still alive? That's why he was calling. She was dying and I turned it off because I wanted to sleep and Mum was still alive. I could have said goodbye and told her I'm sorry for not being everything she deserved and that I love her even though I left and I think about her all the time and she would have forgiven me for leaving, and if I could just have those few minutes, those few seconds so she knew I loved her ...

I grab my phone but my hands are shaking. I find it hard to press the button down that turns it on. Eventually the phone makes a sound then I watch a little blue wave appear on the screen, an ethereal wave that ripples in a void, then it turns to white and the phone starts vibrating. For every missed call it vibrates and I wonder if it will ever stop.

I press a button and scroll through the list of missed calls throughout last night, then this morning. After a lull my phone vibrates a final time and a symbol pops up telling me I have voice mail. A single message. I dial the number and listen.

There's silence for a long time. I wonder if it's worked but I listen intently and I can hear something, a whistle, I think, but then something takes me back to childhood and I recognise it, not a whistle, the plaintive whimper of my little brother.

"Mum ..." says the voice, and that's all he says.

"Here, let me take it," says another voice. "Nick, it's Jen." I can hear the waver, but she's so strong, Jen. "This is really hard, we didn't want to leave a message, but you need to know. Your mum was sick. It was really fast. It was cancer. And she didn't tell anyone because she's ..."

Jen swallows and takes a deep breath. "Umm, I think she didn't want anyone to pity her or ... She's gone, Nick. She wasn't alone. She was at home, with friends. She called Oli and ... she asked us not to come and she didn't want you to worry. She said to tell you she loves you more than anything, and it's ok, none of it matters anymore, to ... to forgive him ... and ..."

I hear Jen crying then an electronic beep.

BURDEN

After a few hours I manage to pull my shit together. I call Oli. I don't particularly want to talk, but he does. I know him, his mind, the way he was always more like Mum when I was always more like Clem.

Mum would be thinking the exact same thing as I know Oli is—that there's a set of magic words that might somehow make this better. Make it bearable.

There aren't.

I feel a weight that is somewhere between my gut and chest. It is black and heavy and has its own gravity, and it is meant to be there. I want to let it be and I can, just as soon as I find the answers to my questions, but Oli can't give them to me. His words fall into incoherence and I suddenly see a face staring at me through time—puffy cheeks, eyes red and glistening, lip trembling—and I want to turn away because it hurts to look.

I ask him to put Jen on and he does. I tell her I need the name and number of the doctor, but she doesn't know. She finds Kylie's number instead and tells me that she should know. I say thanks and Jen lingers and I say bye and hang up.

I dial the number. A woman answers, but it's not the woman I spoke to a few weeks ago. I think it might be Belle. I hesitate a second then end the call, having said nothing. I wait ten minutes and call back.

A tired voice answers. A different voice, but familiar.

"Kylie?" I say.

"Yes."

"It's Nick."

"Oh. Oh. Nick." I hear her heavy breath and then silence. I guess she's holding the phone away from her face. I wait. I hear the heavy breath come back. I can tell she's upset, there's no way she couldn't be. I suppose it's hard talking to a son whose mother has just died.

"Nick. I'm glad you called. I'm so sorry. So sorry. This is ... she ..."

"I know, Kylie, thank you. And for being with her and helping her through it. I just ... I need something. The name and number of Mum's doctor. Her GP, or specialist, or whoever was taking care of her."

Kylie tells me it was Dr Henshaw. I'm relieved it's someone I know, someone who's not a dickhead. Henshaw must be in his seventies now. He's always been straightforward, knows what he needs to know to be effective, and he's said enough things over the years to suggest he's in on the big secret—that half of medicine is just guesswork and bullshit.

I dial his number and the lady at the front desk of his surgery puts me on hold. I'm sitting there staring at the dent in the white wall of my tin shed when a memory comes, a memory from a very long time ago. I'd trod barefoot on the broken base of a glass jar. It was a big cut; I've still got the scar. I was holding the tears back the whole ride in to Dr Henshaw's surgery, because that was what you did, especially for Clem. I don't remember where Mum was, only she wasn't there and I wished she was. I knew that if I cried Clem would say, "Don't cry," like a boy can turn it off, when in truth it only makes you want to cry more. But I was proud and tough. I held it back.

Dr Henshaw had a look at the cut and said it would need sewing shut after he'd washed it out. Said that he could give me some anaesthetic but he'd have to inject right into the cut because the nerves in the foot can be tricky. It'd hurt pretty bad, and might not even work.

He said to Clem, "It's up to you. We can suture it up quick without the local, or try some anaesthetic and give it a few minutes, then try a bit more if it doesn't take."

"No, it's up to him," Clem said. He looked at me, and so did Dr Henshaw.

I wanted that anaesthetic, because it hurt about as bad as I could remember anything hurting and I was scared of the needle I saw sitting in a clear plastic sheath on the steel tray. I couldn't stop imagining it cutting through the flesh in my foot, dragging a thread through my body no different to how Mum did when she was sewing up the arse of my shorts. But I knew the right answer.

"No anaesthetic," I said, and smiled at Clem with my cheeks dimpled from effort. I knew if I tried to say more the tears would come, so I didn't. Dr Henshaw washed out the wound and sewed me up, and maybe there was a little wet that squeezed out of my eyes but they weren't tears. They were just something my body did. Maybe from the strain, from the eyes sweating from being held shut so tight.

When he was done, Dr Henshaw went to organise some crutches and Clem waited so it was just us and I remember he said, "Good boy," and gave me a pat on the leg. And it was worth it, not crying, just for that.

I don't remember crying again, though I suppose I must have. I was only ten and ten-year-old boys can't help but cry, sometimes.

The phone has been ringing and ringing, when Dr Henshaw finally answers. He remembers me; I can tell from the tone in his voice, though I suppose he was expecting the call.

He says he's sorry, but thankfully he doesn't linger with sentimental crap. There's enough people for that. He just does what I need him to. He tells me about Mum's illness.

She had T4 pancreatic cancer. Dr Henshaw knows I went to uni to study medicine, so he asks if I need to know more about it. I tell him no. I remember what happens, because it's simple, really. People with T4 pancreatic cancer die. All of them. It doesn't let them go easy. It is a bad cancer, an evil cancer ... then I remind myself that a cancer can't be evil. It's just cells.

Mum found out so late — not even two months ago. By Dr Henshaw's reckoning, she'd been having the symptoms since the middle of last year and had been treating them with bullshit home remedies. It occurs to me that all that time she didn't hear from me once, not when it mattered, when I might have recognised something amiss, something that could have given her more time.

By January, when she found out, it was too far gone, and Mum knew. For all her herbal teas and gastric detoxes and reiki voodoo, she wasn't the sort to delude herself, to hold onto a lie even if it was comforting. People don't come back from end-stage cancer, and she understood.

Dr Henshaw tells me about Mum's swift decline over the last few weeks. He helped her with morphine at the end. I thank him for that. I don't ask how much. Whatever it was, I know it was the right amount. Whatever let her sleep.

We end the call and I just sit there, staring at the wall. I always thought there'd be time to fix everything, or at least make it good enough. To show her I loved her, if nothing else. Show her that she could count on me when it mattered.

But I didn't. And she couldn't.

VISA

I don't want to be here, I don't have to be here, but I need to tell them I'm leaving, say goodbye, or it would mean that none of it was real, that the friendships were just a client service officer performing a duty to clients, and I can't let that be true.

I walk through the gate. This is my final shift. I know I won't return. Maybe I've confused emotions from the other thing, but I feel guilt. It's wretched and more than being wretched it's exasperating because it's a stupid cliché, yet I can't help but feel like I'm abandoning them.

I'm off to whatever life I have, while they mark off one more person to leave, one more reminder of everything they don't have as they wait and wait in their own version of Groundhog Day—only their Punxsutawney is called Curtin and it is hot not cold and it is red and silver not green and white, and Phil the groundhog is a fat Australian man named Deano who always sees his shadow and always predicts another six weeks of detention.

As soon as the morning's duties are complete I start working through the compounds, finding and telling the people I've met, my friends, that this is the last time they will see me at the centre, that I'm going home, but that I wish them well and hope someday I will see them on the outside. People like Younes, Rasa, Soheil, Matthew and a dozen more who have filled my days with goodwill and levity.

I find Mani lying in his room. The room still smells of piss and Mani stinks of sweat. I apologise; I explain I'm leaving, but tell him the Red Cross have promised they will come and they will do something. I don't know if that's true, but it's the only little bit of hope I can offer. Mani tries to get up, but the effort and pain it brings is too much. I tell him to stay as he is. That's how I shake his proffered hand — standing over his broken body. The truth is, I'm glad I won't have to see Mani suffer anymore. There's nothing I can do; it's easier just to look away. It's easier to feel guilty than to feel useless and angry.

After Mani, I find Meg in Blue Compound, the only officer who really cares that I'm leaving. She heard what happened — everyone has heard what happened — and so she wants to comfort me, but I don't want to be comforted. I don't want to talk about how I feel because I don't know how I feel.

At Meg's urging, we disappear to her secret hideaway. As I enter the room and see the desk, I can't help but think about yesterday, about fucking Meg against that desk while my brother mourned for our mother. I shouldn't be here.

"Sorry Meg, I think I'd better go."

"Already? Umm, yeah, of course, ok. You'll call me if you want to talk. Anytime, ok?"

"Yeah."

Meg hugs me. "I really am so sorry, Nick," she says, a gleam in her eyes. I think she's going to cry — cry for me — and I can't deal with that.

"No, it's fine. I'm fine. Really, I'm fine. Don't worry about me. Ok?"

"Will I ... see you again?"

"Yeah, of course, I mean ..." I nod my head, but I'm not sure either of us believes it. Meg kisses me on the cheek and I go.

I leave till last the two Iranian friends I know I'll miss the most: Ali and Samir. I knock on their door. I'm invited in.

"So, Nick, you have your visa, yes?" says Ali.

News travels fast in this place.

"Yes, I have my visa. I leave tomorrow." I don't tell them about my mother.

"This makes me sad, Nick," says Samir, and it is not a joke.

"I need to see my family, Samir. But I will see you guys again, ok? You'll get your visas soon and I'll see you in Australia, the real Australia."

"Yes, Perth!" says Samir.

"Perth."

For the better part of half an hour we joke and cajole and it's exactly what I need — to not think about the other stuff. Samir has been getting good laughs with the sayings I've taught him, so at his urging I teach him a final Australian saying: "Couldn't organise a root in a brothel." Once he understands all the words, Samir likes the saying very much.

I ask which one of them will be the first to get a girlfriend when they leave. Samir certainly thinks it will be himself. But not just one. He must have ten. I tell him no way. In Australia it is one at a time.

"Five."

"No! One."

"No, four!"

Ali cracks up at Samir's attempt to barter me down.

I give the boys my contact details. Ali is writing his email address down for me, except he forgets what it is and crosses it out and starts again.

"Ali," says Samir, "you couldn't organise a root in a brothel!"

Samir is going to fit in just fine in Australia. They both are.

"Nick. What percent English do you think Samir speaks?" asks Ali.

I think about it for a moment.

"Thirty. Maybe forty."

"That is what I said!" says Ali.

"Nick, do you remember, first day I am here I ask, 'How much English I speak?' Remember?" says Samir.

I don't, so I shake my head.

"You say to me, 'Twenty percent.' So I improve," Samir says with pride.

"By the time you leave here, Samir, you will be up to fifty percent. You will have reached your full potential!"

I don't know if Samir gets the joke, but Ali does so we both laugh and Samir laughs too because he's the sort of guy who does.

It is good to hear so much laughter in this room as we talk shit like friends do. When I tell them I must go it's not with the sense of melancholy I felt earlier. I'm hopeful these guys will keep it together until they get out of here. I will see them again.

Across the rest of the afternoon it seems fitting that I'm tasked to a constant watch. A man who has been threatening suicide for over a month is curled up, sleeping. I sit outside his door, a numb nothingness occupying the body and mind of both prisoner and guard. I swat mosquitoes and wipe away beads of sweat. I won't miss this.

Counting hours and minutes and seconds, I'm aware of the chaos in the rest of the centre. An attempted hanging, two different incidents with men cutting their heads with razors or glass, a Code Black after an officer fails to respond to being hailed—I hear all of it over the radio, and I feel only relief, because I'm the guy with the visa.

At exactly 6 p.m. my replacement strides down the corridor. I pick up my bag and pull the tucked blue shirt out of my pants. I stroll away lighter and happier than a man just told his mother is dead should.

When I round the corner just before the steel gates, I see them—Ali and Samir. It's unexpected and touching. They have come to pay me my due, to execute the ritual played out every week for the lucky few detainees who have their visa and are being released: their friends meet them at the big gates, celebrating good fortune and wishing them well. The seeing off is the last and perhaps only joyous part of the detention process. It makes all the bullshit of the last few months seem worthwhile.

"Shit, guys, you didn't have to come out just for me."

"We want to," says Samir.

"You will not forget us, Nick?" says Ali.

"I will not forget you."

"I want you to take me with you," says Samir.

"Should I put you in my backpack?"

"Yes." Then Samir adds in seriousness: "I am sad you are leaving."

"Samir," I say, "you need to drink a cup of concrete and harden up, princess."

While there are still smiles on our faces, I leave. As I walk through the last gate, I hear my name called. I turn.

I see Ali, just a shape now behind the steel and wire that has always separated us, offering a last wave goodbye.

ALSO AVAILABLE

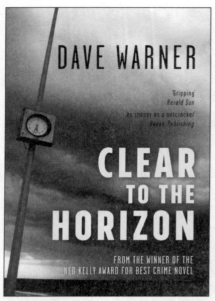

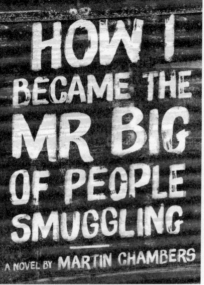

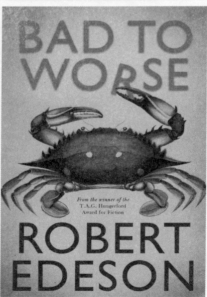

FROM WWW.FREMANTLEPRESS.COM.AU

FROM FREMANTLE PRESS

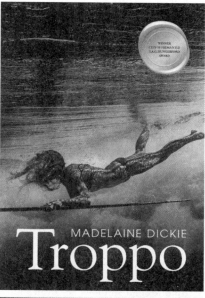

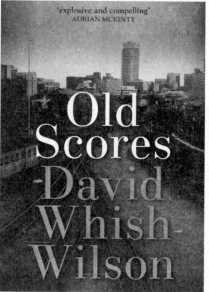

AS EBOOKS AND AT ALL GOOD BOOKSTORES

First published 2018 by
FREMANTLE PRESS
25 Quarry Street, Fremantle WA 6160
(PO Box 158, North Fremantle WA 6159)
www.fremantlepress.com.au

Copyright © Avan Judd Stallard, 2018

The moral rights of the author have been asserted.

This book is copyright. Apart from any fair dealing for the purpose of private
study, research, criticism or review, as permitted under the Copyright Act, no
part may be reproduced by any process without written permission. Enquiries
should be made to the publisher.

Cover image: Danita Delimont / Alamy Stock Photo
Guy on bench: samael334/Istockphoto
Foreground: Shutterstock

Printed by Everbest Printing Company, China

National Library of Australia
Cataloguing-in-Publication entry:
Stallard, Avan Judd, author
Spinifex and Sunflowers / Avan Judd Stallard
Alien detention centres—Australia—Fiction.
Detention of persons—Australia—Fiction.
Inmate guards—Fiction.
Refugees—Fiction.
ISBN 9781925164992 (paperback)

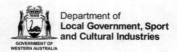

Fremantle Press is supported by the State Government through the Department
of Local Government, Sport and Cultural Industries.

Publication of this title was assisted by the Commonwealth Government
through the Australia Council, its arts funding and advisory body.